Hannah Dennison was born in Britain and originally moved to Los Angeles to pursue screenwriting. She has been an obituary reporter, antiques dealer, private-jet flight attendant and Hollywood story analyst. After twenty-five years living on the West Coast, Hannah returned to the UK, where she shares her life with two high-spirited Hungarian Vizslas in the West Country.

Hannah writes the *Honeychurch Hall Mysteries* and the *Vicky Hill Mysteries*, both set in Devon, as well as the *Island Sisters Mysteries*, set on the fictional island of Tregarrick in the Isles of Scilly.

www.hannahdennison.com
www.facebook.com/hannahdennisonbooks
www.instagram.com/hannahdennisonbooks
www.twitter.com/hannahldennison

Dagger of Death at Honeychurch Hall

Hannah Dennison

CONSTABLE

CONSTABLE

First published in Great Britain in 2023 by Constable

A CIP catalogue record for this book is available from the British Library.

ISBN: 978-1-40871-592-5

Typeset in Janson MT Std by SX Composing DTP, Rayleigh, Essex
Printed and bound in Great Britain by Clays Ltd, Elcograf S.p.A.

Papers used by Constable are from well-managed forests
and other responsible sources.

Constable
An imprint of
Little, Brown Book Group
Carmelite House
50 Victoria Embankment
London EC4Y 0DZ

An Hachette UK Company
www.hachette.co.uk

www.littlebrown.co.uk

For Brenda Dennison, who epitomises the war-time generation with her grace, sense of humour and good old British phlegm. I love you, Mum.

To Little Dipperton

The Honeychurch Estate

Eric's scrapyard
Caravan
Tradesmen's entrance
Iris's carriage house
Main gate
Gatehouse
Kat's Collectibles Showroom
N E S W
Shepherd's hut
Walled garden
Ice house
Service drive
Honeychurch cottages
Stableyard
Alfred's flat
Main drive
Equine cemetery
Servant's entrance
Honeychurch Hall
Ballroom
Formal gardens
Summer house
Ornamental Lake
River Dart
Jane's cottage
Grotto
Sunken garden
Stumpery
Haunted chestnut walk
Ivy cottage
Ha ha
Abandoned chapel

Cast of Characters

The Honeychurch Hall Estate
Kat Stanford (40) antique dealer and our heroine
Iris Stanford (70) widow and novelist aka Krystalle Storm
Earl of Grenville, Lord Rupert Honeychurch (early 50s)
Lady Lavinia (early 30s) Rupert's second wife
The Dowager Countess, Edith Honeychurch (late 80s)
Master Harry Honeychurch, future Earl of Grenville
   (around 10)
Alfred Bushman (70s) stable manager and Iris's stepbrother

Tenants
Eric Pugsley (40s) handyman, operates a scrapyard on the
   estate
Delia Evans (60s) Head of House
Olive Banks (90s) widow of recently deceased war hero,
   George Banks
Trevor Banks (50s) unemployed cemetery groundskeeper
Paula Banks (50s) Trevor's wife and owner of Paula's Field
   Pantry

Little Dipperton

Gladys Knight (late 60s) retired matron and newcomer

Danny Pritchard (60s) the new vicar

Ruby Pritchard (mid 80s) the vicar's widowed mother

Bethany Jarvis and Simon Payne (20-something) run the Post Office and Community Shop

Doreen and Stan Mutters (60s) landlords of the Hare and Hounds

Peggy Cropper (70s) former cook at Honeychurch Hall, Shawn Cropper's grandmother

The Police

Detective Inspector Shawn Cropper (40s) past village police officer

Detective Inspector Greg Mallory (40s) current village police officer

Detective Sergeant Clive Banks (30s) married to Janet, nephew to Trevor Banks and grandson to Olive Banks

Chief Superintendent Stella Barlow (late 40s) Mallory's former boss

Luxton's Auction House

Michael Luxton (70s) owner

Johnny (60s) auction house manager

Arlo (20s) porter

Honorary Mentions

David Wynne (40s) International Art and Antique investigator – Kat's former fiancé

Piers Carew (40s) Earl of Denby and Lavinia's brother

Guy Evans (40s) Delia's son

Di Wilkins (late 30s) Kat's friend

Chapter One

'But I don't understand.' The young woman standing next to me at the collection counter was distraught. 'I bought that lot. Those bears are mine.' Her voice grew shrill. 'I waved my paddle. You said going, going, gone, and you looked straight at me!'

'Sorry, Ms Trotter,' said Johnny, the veteran floor manager of Luxton's. 'Ms Stanford was sitting directly behind you.'

'But that's not fair. I know you were looking at me,' she fumed. 'You've got something wrong with your eyesight, you have.'

Johnny ignored the insult. Having started working at the auction house when he was sixteen – he was now in his sixties – Johnny was the consummate professional and nothing ever seemed to ruffle him.

The woman turned to me and glared.

'Don't worry, it's easily done.' I tried to hide my annoyance. Ms Trotter had pushed the price up for an assortment of stuffed bears of very little value that were worthless to anyone but me. A couple had damaged paws or were missing an eye – granted the stuffed French bulldog with the jaunty straw hat was cute – but that was about it.

I had rescued them all, not to sell on, but to repair those that needed repairing and give to the retired nurse in the village who then donated them to the children's ward in the local hospital.

The saleroom was bustling with the usual chaos that follows an intense day of bidding and tempers were getting frayed. Everything was running late, thanks to someone who set off the smoke alarm. Everyone was ushered outside into the car park and promptly got drenched in a sudden downpour.

'Now, if you wouldn't mind stepping aside,' said Johnny. 'Kat? Was there something else?'

I heard the ping of an incoming text. Ms Trotter turned away to read it.

'Yes. I'm picking up a box of military memorabilia for Olive Banks,' I said. 'Lot 49. It was withdrawn at the last minute.' I pulled out my mobile and showed Johnny the email from Olive's grandson, Detective Sergeant Clive Banks, authorising me to collect the box on his grandmother's behalf.

Clive had called me in a panic after lunch, saying that his ninety-something widowed grandmother had just found out that his Uncle Trevor had put the items in the sale without her knowledge.

I suspected it was the usual misunderstanding that followed a death in the family. Many a time Kat's Collectibles and Mobile Valuation Services, i.e. me, had been asked to value items that were being divvied out to relatives. Many a time I had had to act as referee to the inevitable arguments that resulted in what was fair and what was not.

Johnny nodded. 'Pity they decided to withdraw it. We'd already got a few online bids.'

'I'm not surprised,' I said. 'Apparently, Olive's husband had been a local legend in the Second World War.'

'Wait here and I'll be right back.' Johnny hurried away.

I remembered taking a peek inside the wooden crate of Home Guard equipment when I was viewing the sale a couple of days ago, but there hadn't been anything of interest for me. I didn't have any military memorabilia collectors and if I was ever asked to value a piece, most of the time I would recommend a specialist.

Ms Trotter materialised by my elbow. 'Okay, I'll give you fifty quid.'

I looked at her properly for the first time. She was in her early thirties with a small pale face. Her hair was pulled up into a crisp, tight knot on top of her head and smelled of hairspray. Other than mascara on obvious lash extensions, she wore no make-up. What I hadn't noticed before was that under her open burgundy puffer coat were dark-blue hospital scrubs.

I hesitated. She was a nurse! Had she wanted the bears for the same reason as me?

'I'm sorry,' I said. 'They've already been promised.'

Ms Trotter gave a sheepish smile. 'I didn't realise it was the famous Kat Stanford I was bidding against. I feel a bit of an idiot now. I'm Staci Trotter, by the way. That's Staci with an i.'

She'd certainly changed her tune. Staci had been positively hostile towards Johnny but now she seemed quite friendly.

I found myself soften a little. 'I'm Kat with a K.'

'I've never bid in an auction before,' Staci went on. 'I wasn't sure what to expect but my partner told me to get over myself and get in there with my paddle.' She flashed a smile. It was hard not to smile back.

'It can be intimidating. But no one bites.' I remembered the mortification of my first auction when I'd got caught up in the adrenaline rush of bidding on a doll that in the end turned out to be a cheap copy. It had been an expensive and hard lesson.

Johnny returned with a rectangular wooden crate marked LOT 49 where a card noted RTO – return to owner – in black Sharpie was taped to the side. An old leather luggage strap with a tarnished buckle kept the lid in place. Even though there were rope handles on either end, it would be a two-man job trying to get this into my car.

'I'll find a porter. Ah, there's Arlo.' Johnny said as he scanned the packed saleroom and called over a young man in the Luxton uniform of hunter-green overalls. 'Where's your car, Kat?'

'I snagged a space in the loading-only bay,' I said. 'I bought a green wicker garden table as well. Lot 304.' My mother had wanted it for her Moroccan-themed patio.

'Arlo will bring it to you, too.' Johnny relayed the instructions and turned to the next customer.

'I'll take the box of bears,' Staci said and swooped in before I could protest.

I grasped one end of the wooden crate and Arlo took the other. We led the way out to my car with Staci following.

Arlo helped me put the crate onto the back seat and went off in search of the garden table. I took the box from Staci. The bears and French bulldog were jammed in tightly along with random doll dresses and knitted garments that had been tucked into any available crack and crevice. The wooden crate took up most of the back seat but I managed to set the box of bears on the top although it wasn't very stable.

Arlo returned with the garden table. I opened the hatch-back. Staci helped me remove the parcel shelf so we could fit the table in.

'Thank you,' I said to both but Staci was back on her phone feverishly texting. I slipped Arlo five pounds and he headed back to the saleroom.

'Excuse me.' I gestured to Staci, who was leaning against my car door.

'Okay,' she said. 'I'll give you eighty pounds. Cash.'

I regarded her with amusement. 'You really want those bears, don't you?'

'You won't be selling them anyway.' She sounded more confident now. 'You only deal in rare bears and dolls.'

'Yes. That's true,' I admitted. 'But as I mentioned, these have already been promised – to another nurse, as a matter of fact.' Gesturing to her scrubs I added, 'Which hospital do you work in? Maybe you might have met her. Gladys Knight.'

A shadow of annoyance crossed her pale features. 'I'm not a nurse. I'm a masseuse. I've got my own business.'

'Sorry,' I apologised. 'It was your uniform.'

'The bears are for my sister,' said Staci suddenly. 'She's
. . . she's got cancer. She collects injured bears. It helps her
not feel so alone.'

'I'm so sorry to hear that.' I was uncomfortable and
suspicious at the same time. Of course, the bears weren't
worth eighty pounds unless I was losing my grip. I faltered.
Would Gladys be *that* disappointed if I reneged on my
promise? At the same time, I didn't like being guilted into
something, sick sister or not.

'Why don't you give me your contact number,' I said. 'I'll
find the perfect bear for your sister and once I've repaired it
you can come and get it.'

I heard the ping of an incoming text. Staci glanced down
at her phone but didn't reply. 'A hundred and that's my final
offer.'

A *hundred*! 'Was that your sister?'

She nodded.

I gave a heavy sigh. 'Okay. I give in.' I opened the passenger door. 'Just pick a bear and take it. I don't want your money.'

I stood there waiting, holding the door open. Staci looked
at something over my shoulder but when I followed her gaze,
I only saw a man in motorcycle leathers standing by a Fiat
500 in a startling shade of hot pink. He was swinging a
helmet with a distinctive purple zig-zag decal. The moment
he saw me looking, he turned away.

'All right, I'll pick a bear for your sister,' I said and was
about to reach in when Staci gave a cry of pain and doubled
over, clutching her stomach.

'Good heavens!' I exclaimed. 'Are you okay?'

Staci waved me away, shaking her head. 'Just a twinge. Perhaps I shouldn't have carried the box.' She gave another sheepish smile. 'I'm pregnant.'

'Why on earth didn't you say in the first place!' I exclaimed. 'I would never have allowed you to lift anything!' Even though it was hard to judge just how pregnant Staci was in her puffer coat, I knew that it was in the early days of pregnancy that mothers-to-be could miscarry. 'Do you want to sit down? Where is your car?'

Staci pointed to the hot pink Fiat 500 that was parked on double yellow lines on the main road. 'You should be careful,' I said. 'Traffic wardens are very quick to give out parking tickets around here.'

'It's okay,' said Staci. 'I've got a disabled badge.'

I locked my car and walked her back to hers. Sure enough, there was a Blue Badge on her dashboard. Since when did pregnancy qualify for a Blue Badge?

I noticed that the Fiat was new. It still had the thin plastic covering from the factory on the pristine cream passenger and rear seats, not exactly practical for carrying baby paraphernalia, let alone a folding massage table.

I helped her into the front seat.

'Perhaps you shouldn't drive for a moment,' I suggested. 'Would you like me to find you some water?'

I heard the ping of yet another incoming text. She glanced down. 'No. I'm fine now, thanks. My partner is coming.'

'Do you want me to wait with you until he comes?'

'It's okay,' she said quickly. 'You can go now. Bye.'

'Wait a minute.' I pulled a business card out of my coat

pocket. 'Here's my phone number. Talk to your sister and let me know. My offer still stands.'

Staci didn't answer. She was reading my business card. 'You live in Little Dipperton.'

'Honeychurch Hall,' I said. 'My showroom is in one of the gatehouses. You know it?'

'Okay. Bye then.' And, to my astonishment, Staci pulled the driver's door shut with such speed that it nearly caught my fingers. She was back on her phone again.

Exasperated, I left her to it and returned to my car.

As I exited the car park, stopping to ease into the passing traffic, Staci's Fiat was still parked on the double yellow lines. She was talking to the man I'd noticed earlier in motorcycle leathers through the passenger side window. He had his back to me so I couldn't see his face. It looked like they were having a heated conversation, judging by the way he was waving his helmet around.

Not your problem, Kat, I reminded myself. Relationships could be so tricky and, as the old saying goes, no one knows what really goes on behind closed doors.

I thought of my own relationship.

What was I going to do about Shawn?

took the risk of sneaking into the Channel Islands to withdraw large sums of cash from Mum's bank account and smuggling it back into the UK.

As I had told Shawn on many occasions, hers was not my secret to tell.

To be honest, I was growing weary of Shawn's attitude in our relationship. He repeatedly told me he loved me and yet his actions certainly didn't feel like he did. We didn't see each other as much any more because his promotion meant that he worked longer hours, not helped by the fact that he was based in Exeter, thirty miles away.

And then there were the twins. I adored them and loved being part of the boys' lives but over the last couple of months, I'd hardly seen them. They would be either staying with their grandmother or having a sleepover with their friends. I knew that the boys must be a constant reminder of Helen. I didn't want to replace her but, at the same time, I always felt in her shadow. How can anyone compete with a dead woman?

Also, when Shawn and I had been intimate, it was as if something had shifted between us. The spark had gone but then, didn't the spark go in most relationships and in its place, something deeper developed? Only in our case, it hadn't.

I thought back to my decade with David Wynne. The spark hadn't gone there, had it? I had forgotten. Now I only looked back through rose-tinted spectacles on that heady glamorous life when I was a well-known TV host of the antique roadshow *Fakes and Treasures*, and David was a legend in the international art investigation world. Our only problem had been the constant grief we got from his estranged wife, tabloid journalist, Trudi. Ironically, the pair divorced after David and I split up.

I couldn't even confide in Di, who had to be my closest friend, because then I would have to betray my mother's secret. I had hinted that things were different between Shawn and me, but Di put it down to the presence of Shawn's replacement, Detective Inspector Greg Mallory.

I'd been irritated by that implication, but she had just laughed and said the fact I was defensive was enough to prove that she'd hit a nerve. It had nothing to do with Mallory! I'd be blind if I said he wasn't attractive in a Desperate Dan/Don Draper kind of way with his 'lantern jaw' as Mum liked to call it.

I knew that there had been someone important in Mallory's life at one time, which was why he had asked for a transfer from the bright lights of Plymouth to the rural South Hams. He never spoke about that to me but then, why would he? We didn't have that sort of relationship. Ours wasn't even a friendship. But even as that thought popped into my head, what happened on New Year's Eve hit me afresh.

It had been in the Hare and Hounds. Shawn had asked for the temporary break and wasn't there. I was feeling depressed. I was talking to Mallory by the archway that led to the snug, and Di appeared holding a sprig of mistletoe. She dangled it between us and when I pointed out that the mistletoe rule only applied in December, Mallory reminded me that the clock wouldn't ring in the new year for seven more minutes and, according to ancient tradition, it was bad luck to refuse a man a kiss.

I'd expected a chaste peck but as our lips touched, we both felt the chemistry and sprang apart. I dashed to the loo and missed the countdown, even missed singing 'Auld Lang Syne', and when I finally came out, Mallory had gone.

The incident had unsettled me but when I bumped into Mallory again a few days later, neither of us talked about it. It was as if that kiss had never happened. The problem was that it *had*, and the more distant Shawn became, the more Mallory frequented my dreams.

And then, one night after sharing a bottle of wine with Di, I did something really stupid. I wrote to the 'Dear Amanda' agony column in the weekly newspaper, the *Dipperton Deal*, and for the past few weeks I'd been terrified that the mysterious Amanda would select my cry for help and, if she did, my mother would guess the author was me.

Dissecting the 'Dear Amanda' problem page was our Saturday guilty pleasure. Identifying the anonymous letter writer was always such fun. And, of course, trying to guess Amanda's identity was an ongoing challenge. Apparently, the agony column had been running since the 1980s, so as the older residents of Little Dipperton died out, the pool of possible suspects was becoming smaller.

I pushed 'Dear Amanda' to the back of my mind as the signpost to Little Dipperton drew closer and I needed to concentrate on the traffic, which seemed busier than usual. I slowed down to make the right-hand turn off the main road but had to hit the brakes when a motorbike suddenly cut in front to make the same turn. I fishtailed on the wet road, hearing a clunk as the box of bears tumbled from the back seat and into the footwell. My tote bag flew off the front passenger seat and all the contents fell out onto the floor. I hit the horn in frustration and the disappearing rider flipped the bird. Rude as well as dangerous!

A steady stream of traffic kept me stationary for a few minutes and when it started to rain again, I had the uncharitable thought that I hoped the rude rider would come to grief. The narrow lane to Little Dipperton was full of hazards and not one to be taken at speed. Due to the steepness of the terrain, the hairpin twists and the gloomy darkness of the overarching trees, that stretch of road was a well-known accident blackspot.

I made the turn. Rain hammered hard on my windshield forcing me to switch the windscreen wipers to double speed. Visibility was almost non-existent and then just as quickly as it had begun, the rain stopped and gave way to a watery grey sky.

I descended another steep hill where the burned-out shell of Bridge Cottage sat at the bottom in the dell next to a raging torrent of water – a trickling stream in the summer but in the winter, more like force-ten rapids. The derelict house and surrounding forecourt bounded by a low stone wall used to be a hot spot for fly-tippers but the installation of a CCTV camera had been remarkably successful. Hefty fines and a few arrests with shaming on social media seemed to have done the trick.

And that's when I saw the motorbike. It was lying on its side in the middle of the road across from the entrance. I guessed at once it was the same rider – no one else had overtaken me. I had wished this on him and felt a pang of guilt.

I stopped my car and got out but couldn't see him anywhere.

'Hello?' I shouted. 'Hello? Is everything okay?'

There was no answering reply. In fact, it was eerily quiet.

Gingerly, I stepped closer to the motorbike. It was a Kawasaki and, by the looks of things, well-cared for so why hadn't he left it on the kickstand? I saw the keys. They were still in the ignition. Something didn't feel right.

Perplexed, I stood there staring at the charred skeleton of the old cottage. I scanned the empty forecourt and the bank of trees beyond. If he'd answered the proverbial call of nature, surely he wouldn't have left his motorbike in the middle of the road?

I scanned the area again, looking for skid marks but there were none.

I heard a car shifting gears and a Skoda Scala in a jarring shade of race blue came into view. At the wheel was a man in his seventies. He pulled up alongside and opened his window. 'Are you all right?'

'I'm not sure.' I gestured to the abandoned motorbike. 'I can't find the rider. I don't know if he fell off or . . .' I shrugged.

The man got out. He was dressed in an olive-green tweed shooting jacket and tan Birkenstock boots. With a shock of silver white hair and the bluest eyes I'd ever seen, he oozed sophistication. I saw the rental sticker on his car and guessed he was a tourist. The South Hams was deemed an AONB

– an area of outstanding natural beauty – and attracted tourists from all over the world year-round.

'We should at least move it off the road. Agreed?' He raised an eyebrow. His voice was polished and crisp.

'Agreed,' I said.

The man righted the Kawasaki and wheeled it through the entrance and behind the low wall. He set it on the kick-stand before removing the keys from the ignition. 'Well, he can't have gone far,' he said, surveying the area. 'And if I'm not mistaken, that's a latch key.'

I felt a shiver of apprehension sweep over me like it always did at Bridge Cottage. 'Perhaps he ran out of petrol and decided to walk to the village?' Although I thought that highly unlikely.

'Possibly. But why would he leave his keys?' The man thought for a moment. 'How far is Little Dipperton from here?'

'A couple of miles,' I said. 'I'm going that way. I'll take the keys to the community shop. I don't think we should leave them here, do you?'

The man turned to the cottage. 'Did you look inside the house?'

'No, but I don't think he's there,' I said. 'I called out several times. I think he must have gone to the village on foot.'

'It looks like there was a fire,' he said.

I nodded. I wasn't going to go into details. I'd only recently managed to pass it without the horror of that night triggering a nightmare. Mum and I had been locked in the cellar. The house had been set on fire and we'd only just managed to escape with our lives.

'Is it part of the Honeychurch Hall estate?' he asked.

The question surprised me. 'You know the area?'

'Theoretically, yes.' He smiled and withdrew a pale green business card from his pocket and passed it to me. I detected the delicate scent of Extract of Limes. I recognised it straight away because David used to wear it. It was expensive.

'Peter Becker,' he said. 'I'm with the Chapel Restoration Trust of Great Britain.'

'Oh!' I was impressed and introduced myself.

'Not *the* Kat Stanford from *Fakes and Treasures*?' Now Peter sounded impressed. 'One of my favourite shows.'

'Thank you. Although I've officially retired from that.' I smiled. 'I am assuming you've come to see the church clock.' Our new vicar, the Reverend just-call-me-Danny Pritchard, had only moved to the area three weeks ago and had already launched an appeal to repair the church clock that had stopped in 1944 and never worked again.

Peter nodded. 'I'll be staying in the village for a few days.'

'At the Hare and Hounds?' I said. 'The food is really good there.' I immediately relaxed. The man was a stranger but knowing he was connected to the church and our new vicar allayed my initial misgivings.

'I hope so.' Peter grinned. I looked into kind eyes. 'The Church of England is conducting a census on places of worship, specifically chapels that have fallen into disuse or been turned into residential dwellings. I believe there is such a chapel in the grounds at Honeychurch Hall.'

'What's left of one,' I said. 'The bell tower is still standing but not much else.'

'Yes, that's what I heard, but no matter,' he said. 'I'd very much like to see it. I assume there is a graveyard?'

'I honestly don't know about that. I've never seen it,' I said and went on to tell him that the chapel was in dense woodland near the north-western boundary of the vast estate. 'I don't even think there is a proper road to it. You should talk to my mother. The sixteenth Earl of Grenville, that's Lord Rupert Honeychurch, has appointed her as the family historian. She knows everything about the house and grounds; the families above and below stairs.'

'Thank you,' said Peter. 'Perhaps you can give me her phone number? Do you have a business card?'

I dived into my pocket but came up empty-handed. I'd given my last card to Staci Trotter. 'There's one in my car.'

Peter followed me back to my Golf. When I opened the passenger side, I saw the contents of my tote bag were scattered in the footwell.

'I had to hit the brakes,' I explained. 'In fact, I had to brake because of him!' I pointed to the motorbike. 'He cut in front of me at the junction.'

'It sounds like he was in a hurry.' Peter frowned. 'Unless the motorbike was stolen and he changed his mind and abandoned it. That's a very expensive bike.'

'It does sound more likely,' I agreed.

I grabbed a pen, retrieved one of my business cards from the central console and scribbled my mother's phone number on the back. 'Her name is Iris Stanford.'

'I suggest we leave a note on the windshield to tell the motorcyclist where the keys will be,' said Peter. 'In case he comes back and we are wrong and it isn't stolen.'

I ripped a page out of a notepad I always kept in my car and jotted down the information.

'I'll stick it on his windshield or perhaps put it in the pannier,' said Peter. 'You go on with the keys. Perhaps we should take down the number plate and report it to the police.'

'I can do that.' I turned to my notepad and jotted it down.

Peter said he'd be in the village for a few days and that perhaps we'd see each other in the pub – or, in church. I drove away, leaving Peter striding towards Bridge Cottage.

As I drove to Little Dipperton, I didn't see anyone on foot or otherwise and soon I forgot all about him. Now it was time to do my good deed for the day: Deliver Lot 49 to Olive Banks.

Chapter Three

Little Dipperton was a typical chocolate-box Devonshire village consisting of whitewashed, thatched and slate-roofed cottages with a handful of shops and a seventeenth-century pub. There was just one narrow road that snaked around the village green past the Norman church of St Mary's which, if the new vicar had anything to do with it, would soon have the old clock working again.

The cottages painted in a distinctive blue trim belonged to the Honeychurch estate and were tenant-occupied. They had no front gardens and there was no pavement. The low front doors opened directly onto the road, with cottage gardens stretching in feudal rows at the rear that overlooked open countryside.

The cottages formed a crescent around a graveyard that was encompassed by a low stone wall. Ancient yew trees and hedges flourished among the dozens of gravestones that commemorated the names of the families who had been born, died and still lived in a village that was mentioned in the Domesday Book.

It wasn't just the Honeychurch clan who had a huge family plot; the five main families of Stark, Pugsley, Banks, Cropper and Jones – families who had worked on the Honeychurch Hall estate for decades – had their own plots there, too.

I thought of George Banks's lavish funeral only a week ago. The church had been packed to honour this heroic man of ninety-six who had lived through so much but had died so tragically having fallen asleep in the bath.

The new vicar might be modern in his casual use of insisting everyone call him by his Christian name, but put him in the pulpit and it was like stepping back into the dark ages.

Danny had given a rousing eulogy on the bravery of the war generation who were stoic to the last, and then went on to reprimand the lack of morals in today's younger generations – specifically condemning sex out of wedlock – and ending in a stern reminder of the Ten Commandments and the importance of the sanctity of marriage, which made a few people uncomfortable and didn't seem exactly appropriate for a funeral.

I turned into Church Lane, a tiny offshoot from the main street that hugged the eastern boundary of the graveyard and dead-ended in what was optimistically known as the church car park. It was just a patch of hardened mud with room for no more than four cars. Behind a thick laurel hedge stood the vicarage that hadn't been lived in for twenty years and was being redecorated at enormous expense – if village gossip was to be believed.

I parked behind a yellow Peugeot 109 and an immaculate vintage Harley-Davidson, complete with a sidecar. They were painted in pillar-box red and had a personalised number plate – PRZ HM. I'd heard a rumour that Danny rode a motorbike but hadn't believed it.

I retraced my steps to a pair of semi-detached stone cottages – Blackberry Cottage, painted in estate blue trim, and Vergers Cottage that belonged to the church for obvious reasons. Clive had mentioned that since his grandfather had died, Olive had moved temporarily into Vergers Cottage with his Aunt Paula and Uncle Trevor – the culprit who had put the Home Guard paraphernalia into Luxton's when he shouldn't have done.

Trevor had been tending the graveyard ever since the former postmistress Muriel Jarvis's husband Fred ('whose ancestors had mown the cemetery since the Gunpowder Plot') had died the year before. Apparently Paula was a Jarvis and so, by default, Trevor was able to continue the tradition.

The first thing I heard was the buzz of a lawnmower coming from the graveyard and a tall, rangy figure came into view.

I had to look twice. It wasn't Trevor. It was our new vicar who, despite the weather and his age – he had to be in his mid-sixties – was stripped to the waist with his grey hair tied back in a man bun. I watched him for a couple of moments deftly navigating the dozens of gravestones and avoiding clumps of wild daffodils, and wondered how long it would be before my mother volunteered to do the church flowers.

I wasn't the only one watching him either.

Retired nurse Gladys Knight emerged from Blackberry Cottage in a raincoat and bright red lipstick. She was clutching a Thermos and carried a small towel. She slipped through a narrow gap in the wall, calling out Danny's name. A futile exercise given the sound of the mower, but Gladys didn't seem to care.

I attempted to pick up Lot 49 by myself but it was just too long and too heavy. I would have to recruit call-me-Danny or, hopefully, Trevor would be home to help.

I rang the bell of Vergers Cottage but there was no reply.

'She won't answer.' Gladys suddenly appeared and stood so close to me I had to take a step back. She regarded me with small beady eyes and a sense of self-righteous determination.

Gladys elbowed me aside and rang the bell long and hard. 'Come along, Ruby. We know you're in there.'

'Ruby?' I was confused. The only Ruby I had heard of was the vicar's mother. 'Doesn't Olive Banks live here?' Clive had given me this address only this morning. What could have possibly changed?

But Gladys was on a mission to get an answer. 'Ruby!' She walked to the front window and peered through the glass, rapping on it smartly. 'Stop this nonsense! I can see you! Don't be silly. Answer the door!' She knocked on the window even harder. 'Ruby! Ruby! You are a very naughty girl!'

Gladys returned to my side. Our arms touched. I took a

step back again. I had a flash of Gladys in uniform, manning the wards and all the nurses being terrified of her.

Gladys crouched down and opened the letterbox. 'Ruby!' she said again. 'Five thirty sharp tonight. I'm driving. Don't be late.'

She turned to me with a look of exasperation but I swiftly said, 'I don't need to see Ruby. I'm looking for Olive—'

'Oh, they moved out this morning,' Gladys declared. 'Vergers Cottage belongs to the church.'

'Do you know where they—'

'Danny and Ruby have moved in while the new kitchen and bathroom are installed at the vicarage,' Gladys rushed on. 'You should have seen it! Wallpaper peeling off the walls, damp, burst pipes. It was a mess but of course, the vicarage hasn't been lived in for donkey's years and when the old vicar was there, he lived in virtual squalor.'

For someone relatively new to the village, Gladys seemed to be well informed. She cocked her head. 'Weren't you bringing me some bears for the children's ward?'

'That's right,' I said. 'They're in my car. I just need to sort—'

'Bring them tomorrow after church,' Gladys interrupted. She laid a hand on my arm and moved in even closer, so close that I could smell coffee on her breath. 'Now, if you'll excuse me, I must check Danny's pulse.'

And with that, she turned away and slipped back into the graveyard. I felt exhausted. No wonder Ruby had refused to open the door.

But suddenly, Ruby did.

A tiny woman who only came up to my shoulders looked out through red-framed glasses. 'Has she gone?'

'Yes.' I smiled. 'We haven't met. I'm Kat Stanford.'

The vicar's mother was a frail little thing, almost birdlike. She wore her grey hair in a chin-length bob with a low side parting that caused a lock to fall over half of her face. But when Ruby looked up, I could see why. Her left cheek was badly scarred.

Ruby caught me staring and hastily pulled her hair forward.

'I'm looking for Olive Banks?' I said.

'Oh! Goodbye.' And Ruby slammed the door!

Gladys was back again, which explained Ruby's abrupt reaction.

'Olive and Paula have moved into number two on the Honeychurch Hall estate,' Gladys said. 'I just asked Danny. He's looking a little pink. I told him he must watch his heart. We don't want another casualty in the village.'

I didn't have a chance to ask what casualty she was referring to but I needn't have worried. Gladys soon filled me in.

'Dickie Banks!' Gladys said and stepped closer to me *again*! 'Older brother to Trevor. Didn't you know he's in hospital? All the Bankses have a weak heart. Hereditary. And – oh no!' Gladys caught sight of Danny, his head coming into view as he was putting his all into navigating a steep bank.

Muttering 'blood pressure' she darted back to her patient.

Ruby didn't come to the door again.

I left my car where it was and cut through the graveyard

to the community shop to pick up Mum's fan mail and grab a copy of the *Dipperton Deal*.

Like many post offices and village shops that were forced to close throughout the UK, some had turned into profitable community-run enterprises and Little Dipperton was one.

Twenty-something Bethany Jarvis and her partner Simon Payne had done a great job of keeping the spirit of the traditional shop alive, hanging onto the old-fashioned cash register and brass bell, and keeping the rows of large glass jars filled with sweets along the back wall – more for nostalgic reasons than anything else. The contents never seemed to drop, and I dreaded to think what creatures lived within the wrappings.

Volunteers from the village gave up an hour or two of their time to help at the counter or stock the shelves. In return the shop carried a vast array of homemade wares from honey to jewellery and knitted scarves. Bethany was proud to support local vendors and sold Sharpham wine from the local vineyard, my mother's homemade Honeychurch Gin and, more recently, artisan fare from Paula's Field Pantry.

I entered the gloom of the little shop-cum-post office and the first thing I noticed was that all the Krystalle Storm titles – Bethany was a huge fan – had been removed from the spinners by the door, leaving just the usual current bestsellers.

'I know,' came a familiar voice. I turned to see Bethany, a dead-ringer for the 1980s pop icon Debbie Harry with heavily kohled eyes and a mass of messy blond hair. 'Can you believe it! Krystalle Storm has been banished until after Lent.'

I was shocked. 'That's a bit extreme, isn't it? And Lent doesn't begin for another week!'

'Gladys took them away,' Bethany went on. 'She claimed that the vicar felt it gave the wrong message at this time of year and wanted to focus on the Bible.' She scowled. 'He's making himself very unpopular. Did you know that he not only fired Trevor, but he and Paula have been evicted from Vergers Cottage. They're homeless!'

'Evicted? That wasn't what I heard,' I said. 'Haven't they moved into one of the cottages on the estate?'

Bethany shrugged. 'Paula and Olive have, but Trevor's gone AWOL.'

'Oh,' I said.

'But he'll have to show up for the plaque-laying ceremony tomorrow,' Bethany went on. 'You're coming, aren't you?'

I hadn't planned on it but it looked like I was now.

'The vicar fired Trevor, you know,' Bethany ran on. 'And do you know why?'

'Wasn't it because the vicarage was being redecorated?' I said gingerly.

'Oh well, yes, that's true but,' she scanned the shop and lowered her voice, 'it's because Trevor is having an affair and the vicar says marriage vows are until death do us part and he needs to stick it out. As it is, call-me-Danny gave me a lecture on living in sin with Simon.'

I knew nothing of Trevor's adultery, but I did know of Bethany's views on marriage, namely that she didn't believe in it. 'It's Paula I feel sorry for,' Bethany went on. 'Not only has her husband cleared off, her mother-in-law has moved in – although Olive's bark is worse than her bite.'

'Olive being . . . ?' I frowned. 'Oh, you mean Olive Banks, Trevor's mother. Clive's grandmother. Sorry. Just trying to keep up here.'

'That's right,' said Bethany. 'After poor George died in the bath – with the taps still running I may add – there was so much water that it brought the ceiling down. Ivy Cottage was an estate cottage. Olive and George had lived there for seventy years. Apparently it was in a disgusting condition. The earl should have been doing regular maintenance but you know what that lot are like.'

I also knew that Bethany was anti-establishment and did not hold the ancient Honeychurch family in high esteem unlike ninety-nine per cent of the village. 'At least Olive has somewhere to live now.'

'Yeah, but it's not her own home, is it?' said Bethany. 'And Paula *and* Trevor must work at the Hall. A quid pro quo arrangement.'

'Would Olive not be better off in a nursing home?' I said then wished I hadn't.

'Are you kidding? Olive! In a home?' Bethany shot back. 'She's still as sharp as a tack. She's a little slow but she's still able to use her walker and navigate the stairs. She didn't want to live with anyone but,' Bethany shrugged, 'beggars can't be choosers.'

I thought of the middle cottage in the terrace of three that was next to the walled garden. It was charming but a bit cramped for three adults – presuming that Trevor returned home – and, from memory, the staircase was narrow and steep. It seemed highly impractical but I wasn't about to add fuel to the fire.

'Sorry to bang on,' Bethany said. 'You've got some post. I'll go and get it.' She disappeared behind the post office counter and through the door to the sorting room.

I headed for the newspaper and magazine shelf. There were no copies of the *Dipperton Deal*, which was annoying. Above the shelf was a notice board that encapsulated village life. Among the usual calls for a babysitter or gardener were three typewritten notices on yellow paper bearing the St Mary's Church letterhead: Verger Wanted. Free Cottage (Bethany was right about Trevor no longer having that job); Monday Movie Night and Raffle at the Hare and Hounds – proceeds to restoration of the church clock – only the letter 'l' in clock had been handwritten in black ink; and the third, The Vicar is In: Tuesday–Thursday afternoons between 1 and 3 p.m. in the vestry. Appointment necessary.

'Yep, that's right.' Bethany appeared and pointed to the notice board. 'The vicar is free to listen to all your problems and I can tell you, it's a very popular service – especially with those ladies of a certain age.'

She handed me a small cylindrical-shaped parcel and a large brown envelope addressed to me which contained my mother's fan mail from the publisher.

'Thanks. Oh, I almost forgot.' I put the post in my tote bag and retrieved the key fob for the Kawasaki motorbike. I told her what had happened at Bridge Cottage.

'He'll have to bring ID and proof that the motorbike is

his,' said Bethany. 'But if you ask me, it sounds as if it's been stolen. I would report it if I were you. I'll put these keys in the safe.'

'Good idea.' I said. 'You don't have any copies of the *Dipperton Deal* left, do you?'

'Sold out,' she said. 'The paper did a four-page special on George in honour of the plaque-laying ceremony tomorrow. It's going to be quite a big deal, you know. They've even got "Devon Live" covering it. Oh,' she lowered her voice again, 'don't look now but here comes call-me-Danny.'

The vicar prowled into the shop, closely followed by Gladys still holding the Thermos and towel. He reminded me of a panther. Sleek and predatory. There was no denying it, Danny was a very good-looking man.

'Bethany, good afternoon,' he smiled. 'You should wear that colour more often. Teal matches your eyes.'

To my surprise, Bethany blushed and managed a quiet thank you.

Danny turned his attention to me. 'And you're Iris's daughter, Kat. I saw you at last Sunday's funeral, but we didn't have a chance to talk.' The vicar took my hands in his and clasped them tightly. I was relieved to find that they were cool and dry despite his physical exertions in the graveyard.

'Iris is such a special woman,' Danny enthused. 'Such an asset to the church. It's very kind of her to offer to help with the church circular.'

My mother? Helping with the church circular? This was news to me but no surprise.

'How are the raffle tickets selling, Bethany?' Danny pointed to another colourful poster with an angel wing and halo print border that had been stuck close to the cash register. Although this announcement was also on the St Mary's Church letterhead, it was handwritten in spidery black felt pen. 'Restore Our Clock Village Fete and Raffle! Proceeds go directly to the Church Clock restoration fund. Prizes: a weekend in the Shepherd's Hut (kindly donated by Lady Edith Honeychurch), a free valuation of an antique of your choice (kindly donated by Kat Stanford), a week of Bible study with Danny (pick your favourite apostle), a bottle of Honeychurch Gin (kindly donated by Iris Stanford) and a hamper featuring delicious baked goods (kindly donated by Paula's Field Pantry).'

'Like hotcakes,' Bethany admitted. 'Paula's worried about Monday night's film. She asked if you managed to get the cassette out of the machine?'

'Not yet.' Danny turned to me again. 'It was George's last request – a screening of his favourite war film. Unfortunately, it's on a VHS cassette that's stuck in the video player.'

'She told me that Trevor tried to get it out but only made it worse,' Bethany said, adding slyly. 'Paula told me she hasn't seen Trevor since the funeral. Have you?'

'Let us pray that he is reflecting on his choices,' Danny said smoothly. 'He and Paula made their marriage vows and in the eyes of God, they are married until death do us part. In sickness and in health, for richer, for poorer—'

'And that's why I'm not making any vows.' Bethany gave a mischievous grin. 'I might want to trade Simon in for a younger model.'

I laughed along with Bethany, but the vicar didn't. He was deadly serious. Danny just stared at Bethany until she had to look away.

There was an uncomfortable silence which I felt compelled to fill. 'I met someone from the Chapel Restoration Trust of Great Britain today.'

'Ah! You see! My prayers have been answered!' Danny beamed and his smile grew broader as I told him all about my chance meeting with Peter Becker.

Danny rubbed his hands with glee. 'A clock man after my own heart!'

'I'm not sure if he mentioned clocks.' I tried to remember my brief conversation with Peter. 'But he definitely mentioned chapels.'

'Churches! Chapels! Clocks. It's all connected, Kat.' Danny beamed again. 'Staying at the Hare and Hounds, you say? Then I must away! What perfect timing.'

Danny hastened for the door, trailed by Gladys and two other elderly ladies clutching what looked like their Bibles, who must have heard that the vicar was in the vicinity.

Happily, I made my escape too and hurried back to my car only to find that Gladys – for some inexplicable reason – had moved her yellow Peugeot and blocked me in.

On one side was the graveyard wall and on the other side was her car, parked so close to mine that I had to squeeze through a twelve-inch gap, coating my clothes with mud. And, during that infuriating manoeuvre, there was a sudden cloudburst and I got utterly drenched for the second time that day.

I set off for home. I had to pass Honeychurch Cottages on my way but, first, I wanted to drop off Mum's garden table and her post. I needed to talk to her too, not just to break the bad news that her books had been removed from the community shop but to find out if she really was helping with the church circular.

Chapter Four

'I've decided to give up drinking for Lent,' Mum declared as she set aside the *Dipperton Deal* newspaper.

'Lent?' I was amused. 'Since when have you ever done Lent and besides, it doesn't start for another week.'

'I know,' Mum said. 'That's why we've got to make the most of pre-Lent tipples.'

'You mean, you will,' I said. 'I'm not giving anything up.' I handed her the package and brown envelope, surprised that my mother showed no interest in opening either. 'By the way, I left your garden table in the carriageway. It looks like it could do with a good clean. I'll pour the drinks.'

I regarded the oak dresser that usually had a bottle of Mum's Honeychurch Gin and cut-glass tumblers ready to go. They weren't there. Although her Coronation china was still on display, she'd rearranged the pieces and now a framed, embroidered sampler with the proverb, 'Cleanliness is Next to Godliness' was front and centre.

'Where are the glasses?' I asked.

'Left cupboard with the mugs,' said Mum. 'What on earth happened to your hair?'

I touched my mane of glory – as my mother loved to call it; a mane that garnered me the nickname Rapunzel because there was so much of it. 'I got caught in the rain. Twice. Does it look that bad?'

Mum raised an eyebrow. 'I suppose you could wear a bag over your head.'

'Very funny.' I pulled a face. 'Nice sampler. Where did you get that?'

'eBay,' said Mum. 'I bought three. The ABCs of Faith – quite lovely and a reminder that we should all strive to be cheerful, take joy in the journey and overflow with kindness. That's in the sitting room.'

'Lovely in theory but difficult in practice.'

'And one above my bed about love,' Mum said. 'Just in case.'

I gave a snort of derision. 'In case of what? A sleepover? You can't fool me. I saw the new vicar mowing the grass and I'm afraid that you aren't alone in your admiration of his physique. You've got rivals. Gladys for one.'

'Oh, Miss Pips,' Mum said.

'Miss Pips?'

'That's what Delia and I call her after Gladys Knight and the Pips,' said Mum. 'Poor thing. Her husband died and left her in terrible debt. That's why she moved to the village. She had a lovely house just outside Plymouth that she had to sell and now she's renting from his lordship. She wanted a fresh start. A bit like I did after your father died.'

'So you must have a lot in common,' I said.

'No,' Mum said. 'We don't.'

I mixed the drinks – gin, tonic, ice and lemon – on the countertop where I spied a tea tray laid with a white cloth and a teapot with three bone-china cups and saucers, a matching milk jug, tea strainer and sugar bowl. A small vase held a posy of primroses.

I regarded my mother's appearance. She was dressed in a simple pale-blue sweater and neat blue and grey tweed skirt. A string of pearls completed her ensemble. She wore just a smudge of rose-pink lipstick, but I could tell that she had taken time to make up her eyes. My mother looked very attractive for seventy.

I handed Mum a glass. 'Are you expecting anyone?'

'We're having a meeting.'

'Has this got anything to do with the vicar?' I asked.

She shrugged but I saw a twinkle in her eye.

I laughed. 'You're so transparent!'

After Dad died and after I had made that promise to him that I would always take care of my mother, even though it meant uprooting my familiar life in London and moving two hundred miles away to Devon, my mother had soon morphed into the merry widow. It wasn't that she hadn't been happy with my father, it was that her newfound freedom – and financial freedom at that – seemed to have unleashed a side of her that I could only describe as reckless.

Apart from Mum's lucrative writing career that she was now able to focus on one hundred per cent, she seemed to be having many *The Roman Spring of Mrs Stone* moments. A few unfortunate love affairs had not left her bruised and battered like most women of her age – or even mine – but seemed to have given her more of a determination to enjoy herself. There had been the doctor, then the odious Monty – God forbid – and now Danny, along with other past flames that occasionally reared their ugly heads. Perhaps that's why she wrote romance.

I gave an exaggerated sigh. 'Don't try to deny it. You're in love with the new vicar.'

Mum blushed.

'He's very striking, I agree,' I went on. 'But he's far too young for you.'

'He's not that much younger than me!' Mum retorted. 'Look at the Italians! They love older women.'

'But you're not Italian and neither is he,' I said. 'Is he looking for a wife?'

'I have no idea,' Mum said. 'I'm certainly not looking for a husband. He's a widower.'

'Good luck with that,' I said, hearing a tinge of bitterness in my tone which caught me by surprise.

'Gladys warned me never to mention her name – it's Caroline – especially in front of Danny,' Mum continued. 'Apparently, Vergers Cottage is like a shrine to her memory. Photographs of Caroline everywhere. What about Shawn? Does he have photographs of Helen?'

'Yes,' I said grimly. It was another thing that bothered me. It hadn't worried me to begin with but now, with how things were going in our relationship, it did.

'And what's the story with Danny's mother?' I asked,

anxious to steer any conversation away from Shawn. 'She wouldn't answer the door.'

'You mean Ruby,' Mum said. 'Gladys thinks she suffers from agoraphobia and irritable bowel syndrome.'

'What?' I exclaimed. 'How does she know?'

'She was a nurse, sorry – *a matron* – and won't let anyone forget it,' Mum said. 'Anyway, I'm working on Ruby. The way to a man's heart is through his mother.'

'If you're Italian,' I reminded her. 'Usually, it's the stomach. But now I know why you volunteered to type the church circulars. You're scheming!'

In the past, a comment like that would have aroused a sharp retort but instead Mum smiled. 'When you were a little girl, I used to help with the church jumble sales all the time. Such happy days.' She gave another smile that I could only describe as beatific but then she started to grin.

'What's so funny?'

'Ruby's typewriter has a sticky key and since we're trying to raise money for the restoration of the clock ... um ...' She started to snigger.

'And that's funny?'

'Um.' She started giggling. 'It's the letter L, dear.' Mum made a strangled cry of mirth. 'That means there would be no L in clock!'

'Oh I *see*!' I grinned too and we both burst into laughter.

'I told Danny we should use my typewriter – none of us are computer savvy,' Mum said. 'They're coming over any minute for a cup of tea. I didn't think I should offer them something stronger. Would you like to stay?'

'Thank you, but no,' I said. 'I bought a box of old bears at Luxton's today and need to sort them out. Your friend Miss Pips is going to take them to the hospital. Speaking of Gladys . . .' I took a deep breath and braced myself for my mother's fury. 'Did you know that all your Krystalle Storm books have been removed from the community shop until after Lent? Gladys said the vicar thought they gave the wrong message for this time of year.'

I waited for a burst of indignation, shock, horror and wailing followed by my mother reaching for the gin bottle.

'I know,' she said simply.

I was stunned. 'You know and you don't mind?'

'I've given up writing.'

I felt my jaw drop. My mother lived to write. That was what she did. 'But . . .' I stammered. 'What about your contracts? Your publisher? Your agent?' I gestured to the unopened post. 'Your fans!'

A caught a tiny flicker of what I hoped was guilt, but Mum just shrugged. 'I can't keep up the pretence any more. I want to lead an honest life. I think it was getting too much for Alfred.'

My head was spinning. 'Well. That's one good thing, I suppose. I was always so worried every time he crossed the Channel.'

'Me too,' Mum admitted. 'I realised that lying doesn't come easily to me and it's time to live true to my conscience.' She took a dainty sip of gin.

'Lying doesn't come easily?' I sputtered and almost lost half of mine when it shot up my nose. My mother had proven to be the most perfect liar. It was her lies that had put such a strain on my relationship with Shawn.

'I won't need to lie to your Shawn because there is nothing to lie about,' Mum said as if reading my mind. 'I would have thought you would be happy.'

'Happy?' I said. 'Oh Mum. I only want you to be happy and you won't be if you give up writing.'

'Although I don't think you can blame me completely for the deterioration of your relationship.' She reached for the *Dipperton Deal*. The front page was filled with George Banks's heroics, grainy black and white photographs of his exploits dressed in his Home Guard paraphernalia and gushing praise that his disability had never let it stop him serving his country on the Home Front.

'Ah, now where is it?' Mum muttered, leafing through the newspaper. 'Where is our lovely Amanda?'

My heart sank.

My mother paused and looked me straight in the eye. 'I really do wish you had come to me first.'

Chapter Five

'Ah, here she is.' Mum pointed to the featured problem letter of the week that even had a heavy black border.

I prayed that it wasn't mine and feigned innocence. 'Anything interesting?'

'Let me read this one aloud. It's hilarious.' Mum cleared her throat. 'Dear Amanda, I am confused. I can't talk to anyone so I am hoping you can advise me. I have a boyfriend, but we've been going through a sticky patch. He's always working and seems to have lost interest in me physically.' Mum lowered the paper and looked me straight in the eye again. I looked away. 'The thing is, something happened with his colleague under the mistletoe which brought up an unexpected feeling. Should I break up with the man – who is a good man, a widower with children – just because I am attracted to someone else who I don't even know is attracted to me? Signed: Confused.'

Hearing my problem read aloud was excruciating. I knew I'd written to Amanda under the influence of a bottle of wine, and it showed. My face burned with embarrassment.

'Why didn't you ask for my advice?' Mum said gently. 'Now everyone in Little Dipperton will know that you've fallen in love with Mallory.'

'I didn't write that letter,' I said quickly, flailing about for someone else to blame. 'It must be from Trevor Banks.'

Mum blinked. 'Trevor Banks? Olive Banks's son? But this is from a woman.'

'He might have pretended to be a woman to hide his identity.' I said desperately. 'Trevor is having an affair. Isn't that shocking?'

'Yes.' Mum rolled her eyes. 'I think everyone in the county is aware of Trevor's midlife crisis with a woman half his age.'

'I wasn't aware,' I pointed out.

'I don't believe in gossip,' Mum declared. 'But since you are forcing me . . . rumour has it that Trevor has run off with the carer who used to deliver meals on wheels to his parents – or something like that. It was the same carer who found George dead in the bath.'

'Good heavens,' I exclaimed, relieved to change the subject. 'I had no idea! Where was Olive?'

'God knows – oh,' Mum frowned then brightened. 'I suppose He does. She was out.'

I thought for a moment. 'George Banks was taking a bath at lunchtime. Don't you think that a little strange?'

'I thought that was a bit odd as well, but according to Gladys, it took that long for the water to heat up. And of course he did have a touch of dementia. That cottage should have been pulled down years ago.'

'I heard it was in bad shape,' I said.

'It's an estate cottage,' Mum said. 'According to my below-stairs Honeychurch family tree, the Banks clan were gardeners on the estate for decades until well into the nineteen-eighties.'

'Oh,' I nodded. 'Is that why Edith is giving number two to Trevor and Paula – and of course Olive since it sounds like she's homeless, too.'

'In exchange for Paula working in the house and Trevor in the grounds,' Mum said. 'That is, according to Gladys.'

'Gladys seems to know a lot,' I said.

'Between you and me—' Mum paused to take a sip of gin. 'You've heard that the vicar has a consultation service—'

'Yes,' I said. 'I saw the notice in the community shop. You have to make an appointment.'

'Gladys likes to eavesdrop,' Mum said. 'I see her pretending to clean the brass in the church and dust the pews, but I've also seen a chair behind a red velvet curtain next to the vestry wall – it's just a plywood partition – I know she hides there and listens in.'

I was appalled. 'You should call her out on that. It's a private conversation!'

'God is all-seeing and all-knowing. She'll get her just deserts.' Mum turned her attention back to the newspaper. 'But speaking of confidences, don't you want to know what Amanda advises?'

I shrugged. 'Maybe.'

My mother smoothed out the newspaper and settled back in her chair. 'Amanda says, "Man A is not interested anymore. Have a crack at Man B. All is fair in love and war. Good luck."'

My stomach turned over. It was a knee-jerk reaction that, over the years, I'd come to regard as a sixth sense when my heart knew the answer before my mind. Amanda had confirmed my worst fears. My relationship with Shawn was as good as over.

Mum reached across the table, took my hand and gave it a squeeze. 'So, what are you going to do about it, dear?'

I hesitated. I didn't want to discuss it – especially with my mother. She had never really warmed towards Shawn in the first place so if anything, she'd be relieved.

I removed my hand. 'There's nothing *to* do.'

'If you decide to crack on with Man B, just be careful,' Mum said. 'I don't want to see you hurt again. We all know the unwritten rule that mates don't sleep with other mates' birds.'

I rolled my eyes. 'Where on earth did you hear that expression?'

'Television. *Emmerdale* or some other daytime drama.' She smiled. 'That's why duels were invented.'

'You don't say,' I said drily.

'And, if Man B is interested, perhaps he feels he can't step on Man A's toes,' Mum declared. 'Speaking of toes, did you know that George Banks only had two on his left foot, which was why he couldn't enlist in the regular army. Lawnmower accident at the Hall years ago.'

'Ugh. That sounds horrible.' I was about to ask which toes were missing but the phone rang and I didn't have a chance.

I heard Mum say, 'Yes. That's me.' I couldn't hear what was said on the other end, but my mother's face lit up as she kept saying, yes, yes, and ended the conversation with a cheerful, 'Yes! Tomorrow!'

'I suppose that was your Danny.'

'No, it wasn't,' Mum smirked. 'Someone has heard of my historian skills – someone who doesn't even live here! Someone important, way up in the church who works for an important restoration trust for all the churches in the British Isles! Someone who—'

'Peter Becker,' I said. 'I know, I told him about you.'

Mum's face fell. 'Oh,' she said crossly. 'Why didn't you say?'

'He's staying at the Hare and Hounds,' I said. 'In fact, it's perfect timing for your circular because he knows all about clocks or, perhaps I should say . . .'

'There's no need to be smutty,' Mum scolded, although she grinned. 'We're going to meet up after the unveiling of George's plaque in the church.'

There was a long, piercing buzz from a doorbell, which made me jump. I clamped my hands over my ears. 'Good grief, Mother!'

'It's open!' Mum yelled.

'You nearly gave me a heart attack.'

'You told me to get a bell.' Mum primped up her hair and licked her lips in obvious expectation. 'Quick, move those glasses!'

I only just had time to do so before Gladys strode into the kitchen dressed in a bright yellow sou'wester. Judging by my mother's expression of ill-disguised disappointment, her appearance was unexpected. 'Oh. It's you.'

Ruby brought up the rear. She was using a cane and was bundled up in a red raincoat that was far too big for her. She set a plastic shopping bag on the kitchen table and pulled out a chair.

'Tea, anyone?' said Mum. 'Do you think Danny would prefer China or Indian tea? Or perhaps herbal or green? Whole milk or skimmed? Soya or almond milk?'

'Danny's not coming,' Gladys declared. 'He doesn't get involved in the parish circulars.'

I stifled a snigger.

'Besides, he's got an appointment in Newton Abbot.' Gladys took off her sou'wester and attempted to hang it behind the kitchen door but gave up and left it in a heap. 'We will have PG Tips. And no sugar for Ruby.'

'Perhaps a little tipple, Iris?' Ruby pointed to the gin bottle on the countertop, clearly ignoring Gladys's order.

'Tipple?' Gladys boomed. 'It'll be Lent soon. What would your son say?'

Ruby ignored her again.

'Yes, let's have a small one.' Mum winked at Ruby, obviously feeling she had the edge on befriending the mother of her intended. 'Kat will do the honours.'

'Now, stand up, Ruby, so we can get that coat off,' Gladys commanded.

Ruby remained seated. The tension between the pair was almost comical.

'What a lovely raincoat,' Mum said.

'Thank you,' said Ruby. 'It used to belong to Mrs Riddle at our former parish in Wandsworth. She'd asked to be buried in it but when she knew I liked it, she gave it to me just before she died.'

Gladys looked startled. Whether it was because Ruby was wearing a dead woman's raincoat or because Ruby had spoken an entire sentence was anyone's guess.

'Wandsworth!' Mum jumped in. 'But . . . I used to live in Tooting!'

'No!' Ruby cried. 'You don't say! Well I'll be blowed. What a small world. Good lord. I thought I caught an accent. You can take a Londoner out of London but not London out of a Londoner.'

'Personally, I don't like London,' Gladys said.

'Don't you miss it, Ruby?' said Mum. 'I know Kat does.'

'Do I?' I didn't. But it never occurred to me that perhaps my mother did.

'How can anyone miss all that dirt and noise?' Gladys said, determined to have her say.

'How did you end up in the back of beyond, Ruby?' Mum asked.

'If you'll excuse me,' I said and gestured vaguely to the door. 'Gladys, I'll bring over the bears tomorrow. It's very kind of you to offer to take them. Saves me a trip to Plymouth.'

'Kat's donating some teddy bears to the children's ward,' Mum explained to Ruby. 'If there are any that need serious operations, Kat gives them to me. I'm very handy with the needle.'

'Are you?' Ruby exclaimed. 'Would you mind helping with the curtains at the vicarage?'

'I thought I was helping with the curtains,' Gladys's voice was getting louder. 'I've already been in the vicarage and taken the measurements.'

'Okay!' I shouted. 'I think I'd better get going.'

As I looked at Mum, she mouthed the word 'Help!' I had no sympathy. *Welcome to the parish council*, I thought to myself and made a hasty exit.

I left by the carriageway and couldn't believe it. Gladys's wretched yellow Peugeot was right next to mine again. I had parked close to the wall and couldn't open either door. What was wrong with her? She could have parked anywhere in the carriageway. Back in the day there had been room for four horse-drawn carriages. It was plenty big enough. But no, Gladys had parked right next to my Golf. I would have to get into my car through the rear hatchback.

My eye caught the Grenville coat of arms embedded in the wall bearing the motto *ad perseverate est ad triumphum* – to endure is to triumph. Today, I felt as if I had had a lot to endure. It seemed most apt.

I stopped for a moment to take a breath. There was something about this part of Mum's eighteenth-century carriage house that I found so restful. Apart from the cobbled floors being swept clean, it had been left as it was during the halcyon days of the country house. Even the stalls bearing the metal name plaques of the equine residents of another age – now buried in the equine cemetery just off the main drive – remained in place. I liked to think I could still make out the faint smell of horses. I thought of my busy life in the city, and I knew I could never live in a town again.

I got into my car through the rear hatchback and clambered over Olive's wooden crate, making sure not to squash the bears, which I had scooped back into the box. I reversed out of the carriageway into a very grey and rainy evening.

As I joined the service drive, I had to look twice. Parked in front of the ugly corrugated iron gates to Eric Pugsley's scrapyard was a hot pink Fiat.

Hot pink was such an unusual colour. Surely there couldn't be two hot pink Fiats in Devon and if there weren't, what on earth was Staci Trotter doing at Eric's scrapyard?

Chapter Six

The Fiat was empty but as I crawled by, I noticed that the gate stood ajar, which was unusual.

Eric was obsessed about security and always kept the gate padlocked. Razor wire stretched along the top, accompanied by a warning: TRESPASSERS WILL BE PROSECUTED, POACHERS WILL BE SHOT. Perhaps Eric was having a massage in the old caravan that he used as an office. *Kat!* I caught myself. Was this what happened when you lived in a small community; thinking that everyone's business was your own?

I carried up the service road and stopped outside the terrace of three stone cottages behind a dirty Ford Escort and a small U-Haul with the rear doors open. The cottages backed onto the Victorian walled garden – another nod to the past since they'd originally been built for the gardeners. Window boxes bloomed with daffodils and grape hyacinths.

Two chairs and a large standard lamp stood on the gravel along with a few cardboard boxes. Eric Pugsley jumped out of the rear of the U-Haul. He had his jacket off and sleeves rolled up, revealing a forest of hair on his forearms. He was obviously helping with the move. But if he was helping Olive here, what was Staci doing at his scrapyard?

We made the usual greetings, politeness on my side and just a series of eyebrow wiggles from his. Mum nicknamed him beetle-brows and it was easy to see why.

'Your masseuse is waiting for you at the scrapyard,' I couldn't help but say.

Eric looked blank.

'Staci Trotter,' I said. 'And the gate is open, so if you're not expecting her, perhaps she's there to steal a few tyres.'

'Right.' He gave a hasty glance over his shoulder – my joke clearly having fallen flat – before saying in a loud voice, 'Where do you want this box, Paula?'

Paula Banks emerged from the cottage. She was late fifties but looked a lot older. Donned in unattractive leggings that did little to disguise the cellulite that covered her ample thighs and rear and an over-sized sweatshirt, her shoulder-length grey hair was unwashed and had come partially loose from an elastic band. Misery seeped from every pore.

'Hi, Paula,' I said. 'We haven't been formally introduced. I saw you at the funeral.' Gesturing to my car I added, 'I've brought the crate back from Luxton's. Can someone give me a hand?'

Paula glared. 'God knows where you're going to put it,' she said, and stalked back inside.

Eric came over and picked the crate up with ease. 'Olive is in the kitchen. Go on in.'

I stepped into the front room. There was no hallway. The

staircase to the two bedrooms above was accessed through a latch door in the corner. Beyond this sitting-cum-dining room was a kitchen with the bathroom tacked on under a catslide roof.

The cottage was in disarray. Unpacked boxes sat in every available space.

I felt that overwhelming stress that accompanies moving house, but I had relocated to Devon in stages and kept a storage unit in London with a lot of my boxes and some artwork that just wouldn't fit into Jane's Cottage. I made a mental note that I really needed to sort that out. There was plenty of room in the east gatehouse. Edith's generosity hit me afresh. She'd leased me Jane's Cottage and the pair of gatehouses for peanuts and here she was finding a new home for Trevor, Paula and Olive, too.

I found Olive sitting on the seat of her walker surrounded by a sea of kitchenware. She seemed bewildered. Like Paula, I'd noticed her at her husband's funeral.

Olive's choice of clothing was a little eccentric – a handknitted jumper from ball-ends of wool in a variety of mismatched colours. She wore a grey Crimplene skirt, thick tights and sensible shoes with Velcro fastenings. Her hair was pure white and held back from her face by a barrette. Heavy tortoiseshell glasses gave her a bookish appearance.

Paula shouted the introductions ending with a loud, 'She was on the telly. *Fakes and Treasures*!'

'Oh, thank you, dear, so kind,' said Olive. 'I'm so sorry to have been a problem. It's just that,' she swallowed hard, wiping a stray tear from under her glasses, 'I'm just not ready to let go of my George's possessions yet. I'm very cross with Trevor for assuming that I did.'

Paula stood, arms akimbo, and scowled. 'It wasn't Trevor's idea, Ma. It was Dickie's idea and because he's not here to take the blame, you put it on Trevor. You always blame Trevor and, besides, we had to find the money to pay for the funeral and the plaque from somewhere.'

I remembered that Dickie was Clive's father. Sometimes it was hard to keep all the interconnecting relationships straight.

'How is Dickie?' I asked politely. 'Will he be out of hospital for the plaque-laying ceremony tomorrow?'

Olive shook her head. 'They've fitted him with a pace-maker. He's got to stay in for a few more days under observation. Heart. It runs in both sides of the family. I told Trevor he should watch it. All this stress you're putting him under, Paula. It's not good for him.'

Paula opened her mouth to say something – probably unsavoury, judging by her expression.

I realised that Eric was still holding the crate and scanning the kitchen for a place to put it down.

'Paula!' Olive said sharply. 'Move all those baking tins and let's put the crate on the table.' Paula did as she was told, and Eric set the crate down.

'I'll have to leave the U-Haul outside tonight,' said Eric. 'We'll be able to return it tomorrow.'

'Who is we?' Paula demanded. 'You've seen Trevor, haven't you? Where is he?'

Eric reddened. 'No.'

'Then why did you say we?' Paula demanded.

'I didn't,' Eric stammered. 'I said me. Me is going to return the U-Haul.'

Paula's eyes narrowed with accusation. 'So, you haven't seen Trevor?'

Eric's beetle-brows went into overdrive. 'No, Paula. I haven't. And keep me out of it.'

Paula bit her lip. 'Just tell me where he is.'

'Let it go, Paula,' Olive chimed in. 'You won't get him back like that.'

'Right,' I said quickly, sensing a family feud brewing. 'I'll be—'

'Hello, hello!' Delia Evans breezed in holding a plastic dry-cleaning bag. Eric seized the distraction to scuttle away.

Dressed in a black dress with white collar and with a new chic mahogany brown wig – poor Delia suffered from alopecia – she exuded confidence and power.

Following the departure of the Cartwrights last Christmas, Delia had had a promotion and was now the official head of house at Honeychurch Hall. Her dream to live in the end cottage, the largest, had come true. Much as I hated to admit it, Delia excelled at household management and had a team of 'dailies' at her disposal from the neighbouring villages as well as two part-time gardeners. And now she had Paula and Trevor to add to her staff.

Usually, my presence was greeted with a sneer but, for some reason, her nod of acknowledgement held no disapproval today, probably because her attention was focused on Paula.

'Oh dear,' Delia cried. 'We'll have to do something about you, won't we?' she tut-tutted. 'I've brought your uniform. Hair off the shoulders please. No jewellery.'

'I'm not taking off my wedding ring,' Paula whined. 'It's unlucky.'

I could see now that the arrangement for Paula to work at the Hall was not something Paula relished but, to my surprise, Delia's face softened. 'Of course not. And let's hope Trevor comes to his senses. It's just a mid-life crisis, luv.'

Delia had also been betrayed by her husband – who was currently serving a prison sentence – and always felt an affinity for anyone in the same position.

'But he's never done it before,' Paula said with a whimper. 'I don't know where I went wrong.'

'You should have paid him more attention,' Olive said. 'In my day, a woman's place was in the home.'

'This isn't the nineteen-fifties, Ma,' Paula retorted.

Delia rolled her eyes. 'I'll call for you tomorrow at seven-fifty sharp since it will be your first day, but I thought we could go to the pub tonight – although you'll have to drive.'

'You don't drive?' Olive seemed shocked. 'Goodness. Even I know how to drive.'

Delia stiffened. I knew that she could drive but there had been an incident years ago that she didn't like to talk about. Mum and I still didn't know the details.

Delia ignored Olive. 'Supper will be on me, Paula,' she said. 'And you can tell me everything.'

'But tonight I've got some baking to do for tomorrow's reception,' Paula whined again. 'And I've got orders to fill.'

'You'll just have to do that when you get back,' said Delia, all business. 'We may as well go now. Get your car keys.'

I was trying to edge my way to the door, anxious to leave.

'Oh Kat,' Delia said, taking my arm and pulling me aside. She lowered her voice to a whisper. 'I just wanted to warn you that Danny will be reading the banns in church tomorrow for Guy's nuptials. I didn't want you to be caught off-guard.'

And there it was. Even after all this time, she couldn't stop thinking that I cared about her wretched son, Guy. He wasn't a bad person. We just hadn't seen eye-to-eye on so many levels and Delia had taken my rejection of him personally.

'Especially now with things as they are with Shawn,' she continued. 'I always knew that would never last.'

'I don't know where you got that idea from,' I said quickly then wondered if she too had recognised my anguished letter to 'Dear Amanda' in the *Dipperton Deal*.

'And if you don't mind me saying so,' Delia went on. 'You really need to do something with your hair.'

I made my escape and was never happier to be going home with my box of comforting bears.

As I climbed the hill to Jane's Cottage my heart lifted. There, parked outside the former summer house and my beautiful home, was a familiar car. It was Shawn.

I pulled up alongside, surprised at how fast my heart was beating. This was unexpected. Oh God! What if he had read my letter to 'Dear Amanda'!

I took a deep breath and smiled as he gallantly got out of his car and strode towards me. He looked unusually smart and had even discarded his usual battered trench coat for a navy blazer and flannel trousers. I noticed he was wearing the tie I'd bought him for his birthday. It was pillar-box red and covered in old-fashioned railway signals, a nod to his passion for steam trains.

Shawn opened my driver's door. 'What a lovely surprise,' I said as I took his helping hand.

'You didn't get my message?'

All too late I realised that I'd turned off my ringer when I was in the saleroom and, with all the hoop-la there and at Bridge Cottage, then seeing my mother and finally, stopping at Olive's cottage, I had just forgotten to turn it back on.

'Dinner at the Royal Castle Hotel?' He seemed annoyed. 'I was just about to give up on you. The reservation is for seven p.m.'

'I'm so sorry!'

'I suppose I can try to push it back but they're busy tonight,' Shawn said. 'It's a Saturday.'

'I'll just rush in and freshen up—'

'We don't have time for that,' he cut in. 'We'll have to go straight away.'

'But I can't go looking like this,' I exclaimed. 'My hair – and I need to change.' I was wearing jeans and a white shirt under my favourite old cashmere with the frayed cuffs. 'At least let me grab a better coat.'

'I'll wait in the car.'

I grabbed the box of bears from the back seat and dashed inside. Shawn kept the engine running, which made me stress even more, but I managed to be back in five minutes having switched my tatty Barbour raincoat with a black tailored coat over my jeans and jumper, and hastily changed my tote bag for a black leather clutch. I intended to tie my hair back in the car but then I realised that I had forgotten a hair band.

Shawn glanced over and smiled. 'You look fine. Really.'

We sped down the drive. As we passed Eric's scrapyard, I noticed that the pink Fiat was still outside and the gate was still ajar.

I filled Shawn in about my day at Luxton's and the odd encounter with Staci and the bears.

'And suddenly, she is here on the estate,' I said. 'That is, if it is her parked outside Eric's scrapyard. Can you call him and find out?'

'Whatever for?' Shawn sounded amused.

'I don't know,' I hesitated. 'She was determined to buy those bears from me.'

'Does she know where you live?'

My stomach tightened. 'Only the showroom. It's on my business card. Why? Do you think she might break in?'

'The showroom is alarmed,' Shawn reminded me.

'But the bears are at Jane's Cottage, which isn't,' I said.

Shawn gave my knee a quick squeeze. 'Don't worry. I'm sure everything will be fine. And maybe Eric is having a massage. He's allowed to, isn't he?'

'I told him that someone was waiting for him,' I said. 'But he didn't seem bothered. The gate was unlocked, too. Don't you think that unusual?'

Shawn gave a heavy sigh. 'Do you want to go back?'

I gave a sideways glance. His hands were clenched on the steering wheel. I knew he had a thing about punctuality.

'Of course not,' I said.

'We can,' he said. 'And cancel the meal. It's up to you.'

'No, it's fine,' I said.

'I don't want you to be worried all evening.'

'I'm not,' I retorted and thought I sounded more defensive than I actually felt. 'Ignore me. I'm just hungry.'

It was only when we parked, luckily in a parking spot right outside the hotel, that he visibly relaxed. We were ten minutes early, which I found irritating. I would have had time to change after all.

Getting out of the driver's side, Shawn came around to mine and opened the door. 'Ready?' he said and when I took his offered hand, he drew me in closely for an unexpected kiss.

I looked into his brown eyes and saw them soften. Perhaps things were going to be all right between us after all.

Amanda was wrong about Man A.

Chapter Seven

The Royal Castle Hotel in Dartmouth had gradually become 'our' place and one we went to a lot. We even had a favourite table and tonight the sign said 'Reserved'.

Built in the 1600s, the building had a white castellated façade and overlooked the harbour. Inside there was ancient panelling and beams of hand-hewn timber reputedly salvaged from the wreck of a Spanish Armada vessel. Apart from the excellent food, the ambience was warm and the service always good. We were shown to our usual table in the corner. I made a beeline for the Ladies. I had to do something with my unruly hair.

I looked at my reflection in the mirror with dismay. There was a coffee stain on the collar of my white shirt. Why hadn't I noticed it before? In the old days when I was the host of *Fakes and Treasures*, my wardrobe malfunctions used to grace the front page of the trashy tabloid *Star Stalkers*. At least that didn't happen to me anymore.

I found an elastic band in my coat pocket and pulled my hair off my face just as a stunning woman in her late forties dressed in black entered the bathroom. She came straight to the neighbouring wash basin where she took out a velvet make-up bag and set it on the narrow counter between us. The woman was a head taller than I was with high cheek-bones and grey-green eyes. Dark brown hair cascaded in perfect waves to her shoulders.

I couldn't stop staring as she reapplied scarlet lipstick to perfect lips that any Hollywood actress would die for. She caught me watching her and raised an eyebrow.

'Sorry, I was admiring your hair,' I said, feeling unusually shy. 'I never know what to do with mine.'

'Ah, the hair,' she mused and, turning to me, her eyes raked in my appearance. I was instantly conscious of how scruffy I looked. She nodded. 'Of course. He loves long hair.'

'Excuse me?'

The woman smirked. 'I've got a laundry pen. I never go anywhere without it.' She delved into her make-up bag again and handed me a Tide-to-Go stain remover. 'Your collar?'

'Oh,' I said. 'I didn't have time to go home and change today.' I dabbed at the collar and miraculously the stain came off. 'Thank you.'

'No problem.' She took the pen from me. Even her scarlet nails were immaculate. I'd broken three of mine when I'd taken Mum's garden table out of the boot of my car.

Returning to the restaurant, my stomach lurched. Mallory was standing there talking animatedly to Shawn. Mallory looked smart in a black jacket with a collarless shirt, which made me even more self-conscious about my appearance. Draped over his arm was a Burberry trench coat.

'Here she is now,' I heard Shawn say as he got to his feet.

Mallory greeted me with a smile. 'I was just extending my congratulations.'

'Congratulations?' I looked from one to the other.

'I was going to tell you,' Shawn began but then I was conscious of a female voice behind me.

'There you are, darling.'

It was the woman with the scarlet lips, and it was obvious from the way she took her coat from Mallory that they were a couple. It was unexpected and I felt a twinge of something I refused to acknowledge.

Mallory made the introductions. The woman in question was called Stella Barlow but when Mallory said 'Barlow' she laughed and corrected him. 'Not anymore! It's Greenleigh.'

'Sorry. Greenleigh,' Mallory muttered before adding, 'We'll leave you to your meal.'

'Are you sure you don't want to join us?' Shawn suggested.

'No, but thank you.' Stella linked her arm through Mallory's and gestured to the table on the opposite side of the room where a waiter was signalling that their table was ready. 'Nice to meet you both.'

Of course, Mallory would have a girlfriend, but this woman was the last person I could ever imagine him with. As a couple, they were striking. He stood at six foot three and she reached his shoulder. They even had matching grey-green eyes. She was sophisticated. Elegant. A few years older than him for sure.

It wasn't until we both had a glass of wine in front of us that Shawn smirked. 'So, the rumours are true.'

'What rumours?'

'Mallory and Chief Superintendent Stella Barlow or, should I say, Greenleigh.'

I had heard the rumours that swirled in the village when Mallory first moved from Plymouth to the countryside. There had been a woman involved. I don't know what I had imagined this woman to be like, but I had never expected it to be someone like her.

'His superior officer and *allegedly* the reason for Mallory's transfer,' Shawn went on. 'Married, well, separated *allegedly*, but I'd heard she got divorced. It looks like they're back together.'

'What was her husband like?'

'I never met him,' said Shawn. 'Worked in Vice.'

I had to ask, 'Did Mallory know her husband?'

'He did,' Shawn said. 'And let's put it this way, they fought it out in the boxing ring.'

I was so shocked. I hadn't seen Mallory in that light at all. Maybe my mother was right about duels.

Shawn laughed again. 'I wasn't there but I heard that's what happened.'

'Allegedly,' I pointed out, reluctant to believe it could be true. 'Do you think Mallory will stay in the area now?' I reached for my wine and took a larger gulp than necessary and ended up coughing.

'I have no idea.' Shawn regarded me with curiosity. I looked away.

A couple came in with a new-born and took the table behind us. I glanced over and smiled at the mother who had the baby cradled in her arms, hidden by a mound of baby-pink hand-crocheted blankets.

'How old is she?' I asked.

'Three weeks.' The mother was ecstatic. Joy radiated from every pore.

'What's her name?' I asked.

'Emily,' said the mother. 'I could do with a proper night's sleep though.'

'So could I,' added her partner and leaned in to kiss little Emily on her matching pink crocheted cap. 'But it's worth it.'

'What about you?' the mother asked.

'Me?' I smiled again. 'Not yet.'

I turned back to Shawn with a silly grin on my face. 'She's so tiny.'

Shawn gave me a strange look and then studied the menu. I felt as if I had missed something.

We placed our order, but it wasn't until we started on our appetisers – steamed mussels for Shawn and beetroot and goat's cheese for me, that I asked, 'What did Mallory mean by congratulations?'

'Oh, just a high-profile case that we solved,' he said. 'But . . .' Shawn took a deep breath. 'I've put in an offer on a house in Exeter.'

I stopped eating. 'You're moving?'

'I was hoping you'd move with me.'

I felt my jaw drop. This was totally unexpected, especially given how strained our relationship had been since Christmas. This wasn't a marriage proposal – not that I expected one.

Shawn had told me from the beginning that he didn't think he could marry again, and I had accepted that.

I felt confused. 'But my life is here,' I said. 'My business is here.'

'Exeter is thirty miles away,' Shawn said. 'You can drive back and forth. That's what I've been doing for the last few months.'

I hesitated. Exeter was a beautiful city, but it was still a city. I was happy where I lived. I'd grown to love the countryside and being surrounded by nature, woods, fields, streams and wildlife.

And then there was my mother.

Shawn leaned back in his chair. I could tell he was disappointed by my reaction. 'Well, think about it.'

'You just sprung it on me, that's all.' I pushed my half-finished starter away.

But it wasn't just that.

For some time, things hadn't been good between us and, subconsciously, I knew that, as a way of self-protection, I had begun to withdraw from our relationship.

The waiter cleared our plates and brought out our main courses but I'd lost my appetite completely.

'I've taken a few days off so we have plenty of time to talk about it,' said Shawn. 'The twins are away on a camping trip. I thought we could have a good look around Exeter. Maybe go up to Exmoor. It's a very different moor from Dartmoor. For a start, there's no prison.' It was an attempt at a joke.

I had a full week of valuations, to say nothing of my regular stint at Dartmouth Emporium and my Tuesday ride with Edith. I couldn't just drop everything, and I told him that.

Shawn stiffened. 'I wanted it to be a surprise.'

'It is!' I protested but another wave of irritation swept over me. How could he not think of my life and my commitments? 'I just . . .' I stammered. 'You've been so remote recently.'

'Remote? What do you mean?' Shawn demanded, so I told him exactly how I'd been feeling and how torn I'd felt over the relationship between him and my mother.

Shawn seemed incredulous. 'What's your mother got to do with it? I was working a case. I was house hunting—'

'Without me,' I put in.

'I didn't have time!' Shawn was exasperated. 'I'm sorry. Truly sorry if you felt I was neglecting you.'

I was stunned. 'So . . . are you telling me that your . . .' I struggled to find the right word. 'Remoteness . . . has nothing to do with my mother?'

'Iris?' Shawn looked surprised. 'I admit I was pretty fed up with her over Christmas, but I knew it wasn't your fault. Iris has always been a law unto herself. I've just been busy.'

Busy! I felt a rising sense of anger. I'd tormented myself for weeks over what I thought was Shawn's reaction to my mother's secret life and all the time he had just been busy!

'What about the twins?' I managed to say.

'I've found a good school for them,' said Shawn. 'They'll start in September. Lizzie has already had an offer on her house.'

'Lizzie is moving too?' I shouldn't have been surprised. After all, Lizzie was their grandmother, but it seemed as if things had moved quickly without my knowledge and I didn't like it one bit.

'You didn't tell me any of this, Shawn.' I reached for my wine glass to take another sip. It was empty.

And then the waiter arrived carrying a bucket holding a bottle of champagne and two flutes. 'From the couple over there.'

Shawn looked up and waved a thank you. I stole a glance and saw Stella holding onto Mallory's arm.

Neither Shawn nor I spoke as the waiter popped the cork and poured the bubbling liquid into our glasses.

'What's this for?'

'Solving the case,' Shawn said. 'I told you.'

'Yes, you did,' I said. 'But not what sort of case you solved!'

It was a bone of contention between us. Shawn never discussed work and if I asked a question, he'd just trot out the old line, 'I'm not at liberty to say.' On more than one occasion I'd discovered what he was up to because he'd been interviewed on *Devon Live* or his name would appear in the newspaper.

'Come on, Kat,' said Shawn quietly. 'I'm sorry I just went ahead without you, but I thought you'd be pleased.'

'I am,' I protested again but it sounded insincere. 'But I'd still like to have been involved.' I sipped my champagne. It was Bollinger, not Prosecco. Stella had expensive tastes.

When the waiter came to top up our glasses, Shawn put a hand over his. 'I'm driving,' he said.

'We'll take whatever is left home,' I said to the waiter. 'It's too good to waste.'

Shawn chattered away about the merits of living in Exeter. Somehow I got through to the end of the evening. Mallory and Stella left before us, for which I was glad.

Shawn didn't even seem to notice my mood as we walked back to the car with the half-drunk bottle of champagne in hand. He put his arm around my shoulders and pulled me close. 'I know we've got the plaque-unveiling tomorrow morning but how about we drive to Hound Tor and have a late lunch at The Rugglestone Inn in Widecombe in the Moor? I know you like it there.'

I knew Shawn was trying to make it up to me and that made me feel even worse. I wasn't sure why I felt so conflicted. A few months ago, I would have been ecstatic. I had to pull myself together.

I reached over and kissed his cheek. 'That would be lovely.'

He drove with one hand on the steering wheel and the other holding my hand. I tried to feel enthusiastic about the house he'd put an offer on. It was in the St Leonard's area and supposed to be lovely. It was a four-bedroomed, detached Regency property with a large garden. It suddenly occurred to me that Shawn couldn't possibly afford it on his own. I started to feel anxious. This was a life-changing commitment and I just wasn't ready. Shawn didn't seem to sense my discomfort either, which made me even more concerned. I knew I'd have to say something. And soon.

But as we joined the main road, we had to stop at a police accident sign. A few hundred yards ahead were flashing blue lights, a fire engine and an ambulance.

The scene was bustling with people in high-vis vests. I recognised Clive Banks and, to my surprise, Mallory was there. I couldn't see Stella.

Shawn pulled onto the grass verge and got out. 'Stay here.' But I didn't. I got out too and started after him.

A hot pink Fiat had gone off the road and hit a belt of trees.

I didn't even need to get any closer to know that the driver couldn't have survived. A pool of dread began to form in my stomach. Surely it wasn't Staci Trotter.

I looked up and down the road for another car, another wreck, but there was none. The road was deserted. It was an old Roman road. Dead straight.

Shawn returned to my side. I could tell by the look on his face that it was bad news.

'She's dead, isn't she?'

Shawn nodded. 'There are no skid marks or signs of another vehicle being involved. Mallory thinks it could have been a burst tyre. We'll know more when the car's towed.'

'You do know who she was, don't you?' I whispered.

Shawn gave me a sideways glance. 'No.'

'Staci Trotter. I'm sure of it,' I said. 'We saw her car parked outside Eric's scrapyard this evening, remember?'

'We saw a similar car, yes—'

'Her sister is terminally ill. Her poor parents!' I felt sick. 'Her partner, he'll have to be told. She was pregnant. Did you know that?'

Shawn shook his head. 'Let's not jump to the conclusion that it is Staci Trotter until there has been a formal identification,' he said in a slightly patronising tone. 'And of course, her next of kin must be notified first. So please don't go sharing your theories.'

Sharing my *theories*? Sometimes Shawn could be so callous.

We didn't speak again until we stopped outside Jane's Cottage. Shawn reached into the back seat and picked up a small overnight bag. He followed me inside and started talking about the pros of moving to Exeter yet again, but I wasn't listening. I kept seeing the mangled wreck of the little pink car.

The tragedy had put a damper on our evening, at least for me. I put the bottle of champagne in the fridge. It would be flat by the morning.

As we climbed into bed, Shawn finally sensed my mood. He gave me a chaste peck on my cheek and turned over on his side.

Chapter Eight

It wasn't even nine the following morning when I heard the doorbell. I threw on my dressing gown and hurried down the spiral staircase, leaving Shawn in bed.

It was Clive. He was in uniform, and it looked like he hadn't slept all night. Dark circles bloomed under his brown eyes and his heavy black beard, that had garnered him the nickname Captain Pugwash, stuck out in all directions.

'Shawn here?' Clive asked.

'Good morning to you too,' I replied. 'He's still asleep. Is this about the accident last night? Do you know what happened?'

Clive looked over my shoulder, dodging the question, and yelled, 'Shawn! Need a quick word!'

'Be right there!' Shawn appeared, still doing up the zip on his jeans as he joined us at the front door. A navy sweatshirt with the Flying Scotsman steam train was emblazoned across his chest. 'Kat, can you make us some coffee?'

'Let's *all* go into the kitchen,' I said, remembering Olive's old-fashioned remark about a woman's place. I deliberately suggested they sit at the counter so I could hear what on earth warranted a morning call to Shawn about a case he had nothing to do with.

I handed out mugs of coffee, a bowl of sugar and some milk. I'd already bought some croissants for our breakfast so I set those out too.

'I can't stay long,' said Clive as he put two teaspoons of sugar in his mug. 'I've got to take Mum to visit Dad in hospital before Granddad's plaque-laying ceremony.'

'How is Dickie?' Shawn asked.

'They put in a pacemaker. He's stable,' said Clive. 'It's just bad timing. Dad missed Granddad's funeral and now he's missing this, too, but maybe that's a good thing.'

There was an unspoken prompt in Clive's comment. Surely he hadn't turned up here on a Sunday morning to talk about his father's health.

'It's Uncle Trevor again,' Clive blurted out. 'I need a favour.' He added more sugar to his mug and stirred it vigorously.

If Shawn asked me to leave the kitchen, I was going to refuse.

'What kind of favour?' Shawn said cautiously. 'Kat – perhaps you should—'

'I'm not going anywhere,' I said firmly.

Shawn and Clive exchanged looks of surprise at my tone.

Clive picked up a croissant and began to nibble at the edges. 'The car accident last night . . . ' He hesitated. 'She was the woman who was having an affair with my uncle.'

'Was her name Staci Trotter?'

Clive seemed shocked. 'You *knew* her?'

'Not really, but . . .' I was trying to process this new revelation. 'I thought your Uncle Trevor had run off with the carer who looked after your grandparents.'

'Yeah. It's the same person,' said Clive.

'But she told me she was a masseuse.' Although the nursing scrubs could easily double as a beauty uniform, I couldn't quite wrap my head around the young woman I had met at Luxton's and Clive's uncle who – although I'd only seen him briefly at the funeral – had to be a couple of decades her senior.

Clive dismissed my comment with an impatient wave. 'It doesn't matter. I'm just worried that someone might have done something,' he licked his lips, 'stupid.'

'Like what?' said Shawn.

'You know Uncle Trevor,' Clive said. 'He's got a bit of a temper.'

'I think we all know about Trevor's temper,' Shawn said coldly.

'I don't,' I chimed in.

Clive nibbled some more of his croissant. 'I just want you to find out if—'

'The answer is no, Clive,' said Shawn. 'I won't get involved. Period.'

'I suppose it's because you're too important now,' Clive said bitterly.

'Maybe she had a burst tyre,' I suggested.

'No. It wasn't a burst tyre.' Clive frowned then

brightened. 'Or perhaps she'd been drinking and fell asleep at the wheel.'

'I doubt she would have been drinking,' I said. 'Staci was pregnant.'

Clive turned white. 'Good grief. How do you know?'

'Because she told me.' I filled Clive in on what had happened at Luxton's and that, when she'd carried out my box of bears, she felt a warning twinge. 'I suppose when she mentioned her partner, she must have been talking about Trevor.'

Clive blanched. 'That's even worse.'

'If you want my advice, Clive,' said Shawn, 'I'd keep out of it. It's really none of your business.'

Clive shook his head. 'I know, I know. But . . .' He hesitated again. 'There's something not right about it. Her face. It was . . .' He gave a shiver of revulsion. 'You're right. That's what the missus tells me, but it's still family, isn't it? And besides, I'm worried about Gran. I don't know how much more grief she can take.'

I thought of Olive in the cramped cottage and felt sorry for her.

'Gran was devastated when Granddad drowned, and then my dad had to go to hospital and now Trevor's causing all sorts of problems again.' Clive added even more sugar to his mug. 'Dad said he'd never forgive his brother if he sent Gran to an early grave.'

I didn't mean to sound heartless, but by my calculations, Olive's advanced age could hardly qualify as early grave material.

'The thing is, if you were still in charge,' Clive went on. 'We could have er . . . gone in a different direction.'

'You mean, you would have hushed it up,' I said.

Shawn gave me a filthy look.

'Mallory does everything by the book,' Clive whined. 'He's even ordered a toxicology report!'

'I think you're overreacting,' Shawn declared.

Clive started playing with his beard, releasing a few crumbs in the process.

Shawn regarded his former partner with suspicion. 'What aren't you telling me? Why are you so worried?'

Clive hesitated yet *again*. He looked at me, and then at Shawn.

'This is my house and I'm not going anywhere,' I said.

'I saw her face,' Clive shook his head, as if trying to get rid of the memory. 'I'll never forget it. Not as long as I live. It was . . . as if she was laughing.'

A shudder ran down my spine. 'What do you mean by laughing?'

Clive didn't answer but Shawn turned to me. 'Are you *positive* that she was pregnant?'

'That's what she told me,' I said.

Clive looked miserable. 'The thing is . . . when we got her mobile phone to notify her next of kin, it turns out that she was living with someone called Brock Leavey.'

The name meant nothing to me but I thought of the man in motorcycle leathers that I'd seen arguing with Staci yesterday. Perhaps he was Brock Leavy.

'I see,' said Shawn. 'So are you saying that the baby might not be Trevor's after all and that's what's worrying you?'

'That is, if Trevor knows she's pregnant,' I said. 'Maybe Staci hadn't told him.'

Clive looked hopeful for about two seconds but then his face fell. 'The thing is, no one can find Brock Leavey. He seems to have disappeared. The neighbours haven't seen him since yesterday morning.'

Shawn grunted. 'Then you've got every right to be worried.'

'And now Trevor's disappeared.' Clive said. 'No one's seen him since the funeral.'

I remembered seeing Trevor. I couldn't forget it. He was wearing a trendy black leather jacket and too-tight jeans instead of a formal black suit. I'd also noticed he'd grown a bushy soul patch which, far from looking cool, gave the impression of having a moustache under his lip instead of above it.

'But surely he'll come to your grandfather's plaque-laying ceremony today so you can arrest him there and then take him in for questioning,' I joked. My joke fell flat.

Clive took a deep breath. 'And then there's the money.'

'Money?' Shawn and I chorused.

'Uncle Trevor had promised Aunt Paula she could lease the old tea shop for her new business—'

'Violet Green's place? Next to the post office?' I said. It was owned by the Honeychurch estate and it had been standing empty for a while.

Clive nodded. 'Anyway, instead of using their joint savings for that, Uncle Trevor paid for Staci's massage diploma *and* bought her a new car. He'd also been giving money to Gran to pay for the funeral.'

No wonder Paula was upset.

'Well,' said Shawn with a heavy sigh. 'It's a mess and I've already told you what I think.'

'But . . . what do I tell Mallory?' Clive looked as if he was going to cry.

'The truth,' I put in. 'Isn't that always the best way?'

There was the ping of an incoming text. Clive brought out his mobile and groaned. 'It's the missus. I've got to go. See you at the church, yeah?'

'Don't forget your handcuffs!' I said lightly.

And with that, Clive left.

Shawn and I looked at each other.

'What was all that about?' I asked. 'I don't see what the problem is. Surely Clive doesn't think there was something suspicious about Staci's death? You said yourself that there was no indication of another car.'

'Maybe,' he said. 'But unfortunately, Trevor has always been a bit of a loose cannon. Picking fights in pubs – he's still banned from the Hare and Hounds.'

'That's going to be awkward,' I said. 'Isn't that where they're having the reception after today's ceremony?'

'He's getting a special dispensation,' said Shawn.

'From the Pope?' I joked but that comment fell flat, too.

Shawn stood up and pulled me into his arms. 'Let's forget about the village drama just for once.'

'You don't miss it?' I teased.

'Nope,' said Shawn. 'And I definitely don't miss all the interlocking relationships and misplaced loyalties that are at the heart of any small community. Give me a straightforward drug case any day.'

When I first moved to Little Dipperton, I couldn't believe how everyone was related to everyone else, mainly because those five main families still lived in the area. True, some no longer worked in the house or in the grounds, but there was almost an incestuous understanding of sticking together no matter what. Having come from a city, I'd found it strange to begin with. The only time I'd speak to my neighbours was if the rubbish men hadn't turned up to collect the bins or if the weather had turned cold but here, everyone knew everyone else's business.

'I don't know what Trevor has been up to,' Shawn said. 'But I'll tell you something. It'll all come out in the end. There are no secrets in a village.'

Chapter Nine

I will say one thing for the new vicar, he certainly knew how to draw a crowd. There wasn't a spare pew in the Norman church, and you could have heard the proverbial pin drop when Danny delivered a sermon with the theme of sacrifice, bravery and selflessness to honour George Banks's memory. But then, true to form, Danny had to throw in his pet topic about the sanctity of marriage, looking directly at Trevor – who, as I had predicted, did show up – reiterating with evangelical zeal the importance of 'til death do us part.'

It had been a little chaotic when Mum and I first arrived at the church. Those aforementioned families all seemed to know which pews were theirs and had taken their places automatically. There was no space in the Cropper pew for us. In the end Gladys – wearing a jaunty red fascinator – my mother and I ended up sitting in one of the small pews at the side of the nave. As Mum whispered, it gave us a great view. I couldn't see Delia.

Trevor looked pale and distraught and yet Paula, who was

clasping his hand, seemed radiant. It looked like with Staci out of the picture, Paula was able to follow her marriage vows to a T.

There was a good turnout from the Honeychurch family who were crammed in the front pew bearing the Grenville coat of arms. The bone-thin dowager countess, Lady Edith Honeychurch, had forgone her usual side-saddle attire for a fitted black calf-length coat and wore her hair in tight pin curls; her daughter-in-law Lavinia's black suit had strands of straw stuck to the back and the hem of the skirt had partially come down. The current earl, Lord Rupert, looked every inch the country gentleman with his neat moustache and charcoal grey suit. I had to look twice at the young man sitting next to him in a navy suit. It was ten-year-old Harry. Every time I saw him he seemed to have grown taller.

And, just as Delia had said, Guy's banns were read out in church. Mum nudged me and nodded to a side pew directly opposite from ours. Delia waved and elbowed her son, who was with his fiancée, a pretty woman with long dark hair. There had been no love lost between us – it certainly hadn't been a great love affair. We exchanged polite smiles that did not go unnoticed by Shawn, who just happened to glance in my direction at the wrong time.

The service ended with Danny reminding everyone about the upcoming village fete and tomorrow's movie night that would be screening George's favourite war film in the function room at the Hare and Hounds. Tickets were still on sale for £5 with the proceeds – as always – going to the restoration of the church clock.

As we poured out into the spring sunshine, I recognised Ginny Riley with her cameraman for *Devon Live*. Polished and immaculately turned out in a tailored suit and high heels, she had been a good friend of mine once, but her ambition had got in the way of our friendship. Even so, we greeted each other politely and she asked after my mother before turning away to interview Olive and Trevor.

'Shall we?' Shawn pointed in the direction of the pub where refreshments had been laid on.

Landlords Stan and Doreen Mutters had run the Hare and Hounds for over forty years. They were almost caricatures of what you would expect good publicans to be. My mother nicknamed them Tweedledum and Tweedledee owing to their corpulent figures, cheerful demeanour and the fact that they never contradicted each other – at least, not in public.

I loved the Hare and Hounds. It was a typical Devon longhouse with a low, heavy beamed ceiling and a massive inglenook fireplace. The fireplace was so enormous that seats had been cut into the bricks of the enclosed hearth that flanked the grate. Today, a roaring log fire burned in front of a decorative cast-iron fireback bearing the date 1635.

The pub was one of the oldest in the county and smelled of a mixture of dust, mould and mildew. It was steeped in history. Two threadbare tapestries depicting battle scenes from the Civil War jostled with a plethora of pikes, maces and swords. Dozens of heavy antique keys dangled from wires along the beams overhead and copper pans, brasses and platters of all shapes and sizes filled what little wall space remained.

Tables and oak chairs were grouped in clusters or embraced by high-backed curved oak benches to provide intimate settings. Through a low arch was a tiny room known as the snug – where the mistletoe incident had happened with Mallory – and another arch that led to a passage with a staircase, the kitchens, the toilets and a small function room.

The pub was heaving.

The refreshments were from Paula's Field Pantry – she must have been up half the night cooking. They were a far cry from the general fare expected at such a gathering. Flags identifying the various dishes boasted such delicacies such as hedgerow beignets, nettle and morel mini-quiches and salmon and yarrow tartlets, to name just a few. I was impressed. Paula had left out promotional postcards with a beautifully illustrated wildflower border. Her mission statement claimed she was committed to only using 'locally sourced ingredients from the fields, shoreline, rivers and hedgerows of the South Hams.'

Since Shawn and I had planned a late lunch, I limited myself to just one slice of bruschetta topped with 'braised hogweed shoots and crispy sorrel crumbs'. It was delicious. Even though I'd only exchanged two words with Paula, I was happy to see her food was getting plenty of praise. It was hard to start your own business, especially given her personal circumstances and having to work at the Hall.

Shawn waved from the crowd at the bar and indicated that he'd bring me over a drink.

'Kat!' came a voice. I turned to see Clive, in a black suit that was far too tight for his portly stature. He looked hot and flustered. 'A word, please.'

'I thought the unveiling was lovely,' I said. 'How is your father? Did you manage to see him this morning, after all?'

'Yes. He should be home on Friday.' Clive took a deep breath. 'The thing is . . .'

I waited as Clive searched around for whatever the thing was.

'Gran says there is a very valuable item missing from Granddad's memorabilia. She's very upset.'

I frowned. 'I don't see how that's possible, Clive. The crate had a lid and it was secured by a leather luggage strap. Why? What's missing?'

'She won't say,' said Clive. 'Only that it's very, *very* valuable. Like . . . worth thousands of pounds. You'll need to go back to Luxton's and find it.'

'I need to?' I was amused. 'Why can't Trevor? And besides, if you don't tell me what is missing, I won't be able to find it.'

Clive ran his fingers through his beard. Luckily he'd trapped whatever crumbs that lurked within with plenty of cedarwood scented beard oil.

I relented. 'I'll drop the catalogue over tomorrow,' I said. 'Then your grandmother can point out the missing item to Trevor and he can go to Luxton's.'

Janet joined us. Clive and Janet had been married for years. Bright-eyed and inquisitive, Janet talked too fast and had boundless energy. She made me feel tired.

Janet launched into a full recap of the ceremony before changing tack. 'It's always Trevor causing problems in Clive's family,' she burbled on. 'And now that girl is dead, it's made it very awkward for everyone!' Janet stepped closer. I took a step back and hit the wall. She had me cornered. Another Gladys who seemed clueless about personal space.

'Awkward,' I managed to say. 'Why?'

'We all picked Paula's side and now they're back together!' Janet made a face. 'I spent hours listening to her moans about Trevor and agreed with everything she said about him being a boorish twit – because it's true – and she went and told him what I said!'

'Janet,' Clive protested weakly.

Janet shrugged. 'I'm just saying. Although if you ever did anything like that, I wouldn't take you back. Trevor has been snivelling like a baby. Cried all through the service.'

'Because Granddad died,' Clive mumbled. 'That's all.'

'Well, let's hope Trevor shaves off that silly little mouche or whatever it's called,' Janet sneered. 'It looks like he's been playing in a coal scuttle. It's bad enough waking up to that every morning.' And she gave her husband's beard an affectionate pinch.

Thick black hair seemed to run on the male side of the Banks family. I stifled a smile.

Janet gave a snort of disgust. 'Let's go and eat. The least we can do is support Paula's business although I'm not too keen on the sound of some her fungal offerings. It seems that everyone is into foraging these days, aren't they – until someone eats a poisonous mushroom.' And she bore Clive away.

'What was that all about?' said Shawn as he handed me a glass of white wine spritzer. He was drinking Perrier.

Suddenly the room fell silent.

Peter Becker stood in the doorway. He looked so obviously out of place that I whispered to Shawn that we should rescue him. So we did. I made the introductions.

'What happened to the keys to the motorbike?' Peter asked. 'Did the rider ever collect them?'

'I took them to the community shop,' I said. 'But other than that, I don't know.'

'It's strange,' he mused. 'The motorbike is still there. I drove by early this morning.'

All too late I realised I had forgotten to report the motorbike to the police. I hadn't even told Shawn! Quickly, I brought him up to date.

Shawn spied Bethany. 'Let's ask her if she's heard anything.' He caught her eye and Bethany came over with half a pint of cider in hand.

'I've still got the keys,' Bethany said in answer to Shawn's questions. 'No one came to claim them. Since we're closed today out of respect for dear old George, I left a note pinned on the door with my mobile number.'

Shawn nodded. 'I'll inform Mallory, and he can get down there and run the number plate. I assume you have it.'

I withdrew a scrap of paper from my tote bag and handed it over.

Danny approached us, all smiles, with Shawn's grand-mother Peggy Cropper in tow. Peggy wasn't that much older than my mother but, unlike Mum, Peggy had always had a matronly air about her. She seemed to be thriving ever since retiring as cook at Honeychurch Hall. Danny greeted us with his usual vicar handclasp and laser-like scrutiny. I wondered if this was something vicars were taught to do at theology college. Danny did the same to Peter, who returned the intensity with his own.

'I hear you are our man for the clock,' Danny began cheerfully. 'When Kat told me all about you, I immediately came here to hunt you down, but you were out. Didn't you get my note?'

'Yes, sorry about that,' said Peter. 'But Doreen told me you would be here today along with every man and his dog.'

There was a yap and Edith's little Jack Russell bounded in, nipping at everyone's ankles, and tearing around in circles. We all laughed.

'That's Mr Chips,' I said. 'And let's not forget Fred!' I gestured to the Indian Runner duck wearing a green bow-tie standing proudly on the bar. He was enjoying plenty of attention from those waiting for their drinks. 'Fred is the pub's lucky mascot.'

'There was a ferret called Deidre before,' Shawn put in. 'She was fourteen when she died.'

I caught Peter and Danny exchange startled looks. To an outsider, I suppose we did seem like an eccentric bunch.

'Kat mentioned you're connected to the Churches Conservation Trust.' Danny's enthusiasm was contagious. 'Excellent! Excellent!'

Peter retrieved another of his business cards and gave it to Danny, who slipped it into his trouser pocket. He had removed his surplice and was wearing a black shirt and a clerical collar.

'I don't know what Kat told you,' said Peter, 'But I'm

doing a census on all the chapels in the area – specifically those that are no longer in use.'

'Ah, the power corner,' Mum trilled happily and joined us too. She smiled at Peter, then back at Danny, then winked at me. Two handsome men in her ball-park age group.

If we were in a cartoon there would be halos of sweethearts hovering over her head.

Mum thrust out her hand. 'I'm Iris, the family historian and you must be Peter. We spoke—'

'On the phone last night, yes.' Peter smiled. 'That's right. And you mentioned there is a chapel on the Honeychurch Hall estate.'

Danny's ears perked up. There is no other description for it. He seemed like a hound who had just found the scent of a fox. 'A chapel. You're certain?'

Peter frowned. 'You didn't know?'

'I'm new to the area,' said Danny. 'There hasn't been a vicar here for twenty years. I'm just getting up to speed on my flock.'

'I'm afraid the chapel is beyond repair,' Mum said. 'There is only the bell tower left.'

'Yes, Kat mentioned that,' said Peter. 'Would you show it to me?'

'Let's go now,' Mum said quickly. 'It's on the north-west boundary. Too far to walk. Do you have a car?'

'Not today,' Danny cut in firmly. 'I am going to take Peter up the tower to show him my clock!'

'And besides, the chapel is dangerous,' Shawn said. 'It's out of bounds, I'm afraid.'

'According to who?' Peter demanded.

Shawn seemed taken aback by Peter's direct question. 'The dowager countess, Lady Edith Honeychurch.'

'Then we need to talk to her. It's very important.' Peter scanned the busy bar. 'Is she here now?'

'I thought I saw her leave,' I said.

'Clocks are my forte,' Danny went on regardless. 'I just love them. They have so many stories to tell. Iris, did you tell Peter here about my lovely clock?'

I thought of Ruby's typewriter with the missing key and a word flashed into my head and just wouldn't go away. I heard a snigger and knew the same word had flashed into my mother's head, too. Perhaps flashed wasn't the right word either. It was all I could do not to snigger, too.

Shawn nudged my elbow and raised a questioning eyebrow.

'Um. We were . . . excuse me,' Mum snorted. 'I've got something in my eye. Oh – there's Lady Lavinia! Perhaps she's seen the dowager countess.' And my mother scurried away.

I struggled to compose myself.

'My father was a clockmaker,' Danny enthused. 'Did you pick up a copy of this week's church circular? If not, let me give you some historical information on our clock!' He didn't wait to see if we had either picked it up or read it. 'The clock was built by Gillett and Johnston of Croydon, a family firm which started making clocks in 1844. Did you know that in their first hundred years they made over ten thousand tower clocks! They also made bells but not the ones at St Mary's which, in fact, date from 1762. Don't you think it extraordinary?'

'Very,' said Peter. 'But I'm not here about the clock—'

'Our clock is called a Westminster quarter chimes, number two size.' Danny cut in. 'It is gravity driven by three weights with a fall of eighteen metres which are still wound by a hand-cranked handle twice a week. Sadly, this is where we have run into trouble. No one is willing to go up the tower these days. Health and Safety, you see. There are one hundred steps that ascend in a steep spiral – imagine the feet that have graced that old stone.'

'A hundred? That's a lot of steps,' I said lamely.

'And did you know that to look in proportion and aesthetically correct, all church clocks should be one tenth the height of the tower?' Danny paused to allow us all to absorb this phenomenon. 'Did you know that our clockmaker made clocks for important places all over the world, including our own Royal Courts of Justice, Windsor Castle and Exeter Cathedral. Just imagine!'

'Very interesting,' Peter said politely. 'But as I told you, I'm not—'

'Many of the men and women of the village have wound this clock over the years,' Danny continued. 'It's part of our village tradition which it is why it's vital—' He was back in the pulpit again, despite having lived in Little Dipperton for all of five minutes. His eyes blazed. He slapped one hand over the other to make a point. 'Yes, it's *critical* that we get our clock working again and modernised! Digitised! With the support of *your* organisation, *you*, Peter, are going to help us!'

Peter seemed uncomfortable. 'It isn't really my department—'

'Lavinia,' Danny called out – he had clearly dispensed with any form of title in his attempt to be modern. 'Lavinia, do join us! We're talking about our lovely clock.'

Lady Lavinia Honeychurch joined us with Harry in tow. More introductions were made all round and Danny filled her in about his wretched clock.

'Gosh. How ab-so-*lutely* thrilling. Going to give us a face?' Lavinia looked earnest but seeing none of us knew what she was talking about, added, 'Feud. Feud between the Honeychurches and the Carews?'

Everyone looked blank, which was hardly surprising since along with the strangled vowels of the upper classes, Lavinia spoke in short sentences that often seemed to have no context at all.

'Families at loggers,' Lavinia went on. 'Carews for Cromwell. Honeychurches for the King. The war.'

The feud between the clans was the stuff of legends, not helped by the Carews who successfully ran a twelve-square-mile estate – having kept their fortune intact – whilst the Honeychurches were gradually having to sell off bits and pieces of theirs to keep their heads above water.

'Clock installed by my husband's ancestor,' Lavinia burbled on. '*Huuuuge* falling out. Earl insisted clock face only south and west sides of the tower so that we,' she gestured wildly behind, 'wouldn't be able to tell the time. Hilarious.'

We all turned to look in the direction she was pointing but of course, it was just the wall.

'Do let us have a face,' Lavinia begged. 'Piers – that's my brother, he's the thirteenth Earl of Denby – would be *frightfully* excited, wouldn't he, Kat? Kat knows Piers really, *really* well.'

I felt Shawn stiffen beside me. Honestly, I had only dated two men – Piers Carew and Guy Evans – since I'd arrived in Little Dipperton. My long-term relationship with David had already ended and that was well before Shawn and I got together. At the same time, I quite liked Shawn showing a bit of jealousy,

'What a fascinating story,' Peter said courteously.

'Granny Pole was—'

'Pole?' Peter said sharply. 'I thought you said Carew.'

'Oh,' Lavinia looked startled. 'Yes. I'm a Carew but Mummy was a Pole.'

'What was your grandmother's name?' Peter demanded.

'Geraldine,' said Lavinia.

'Did she have any siblings?' Peter sounded eager.

'Six,' Lavinia said. 'Great Uncle James, Great Uncle Christopher, Great Uncle—'

'Any sisters?' Peter said. 'Perhaps someone with the nickname of Fudge?'

Lavinia looked blank. 'Fudge? You mean? As in fudge-fudge?'

I caught Shawn's eye. It was an odd question.

'Have you been here before, Peter?' Danny asked the question I suspected we were all beginning to wonder.

Peter shook his head. 'As I already told you, I'm with the Chapel Restoration Trust of Great Britain and I'm doing a census on disused chapels.'

'Honeychurch Hall has a disused chapel,' Lavinia said.

Which is where we all came in. I felt I was caught in a loop.

'I'd love to know where it is,' said Peter.

'That's easy,' said Lavinia. 'It's in the woods. The ha-ha. Formal gardens, past the topiary. Chestnut walk and stumpery. Woods. Nothing to see.'

'The bell tower is still standing and a few walls,' Harry spoke suddenly. 'But the roof has gone and the trees have done the rest. A stray bomb caught it when the Germans were bombing Plymouth during the war.'

'A bomb, you say?' Peter said eagerly. 'It sounds like you're interested in the war.'

'Very much so,' said Harry.

'Dressed as Biggles. Small.' Lavinia said. 'White scarf and flying helmet. Goggles. Ab-so-*lutely* adorable.'

And Harry had been and still was but I still missed that seven-year-old little boy and his over-active imagination.

Harry groaned. 'I was really, *really* young.'

'I'm interested in the war, too,' said Peter. 'You mentioned that Plymouth was bombed. That's not too far from here, is it?'

'It's about half an hour,' I said.

'Did you know that between July 1940 and April 1944 Plymouth had 602 alerts and 59 bombing raids?' And Harry was off. 'There were 1,174 civilians killed and another 3,209 were injured. More than 4,000 properties were destroyed and another 18,000 damaged.'

Peter grinned. 'You really are interested in the war, aren't you?'

'Hobby of his,' Lavinia said proudly.

'It was the naval dockyard at Devonport, you see,' Harry went on. 'Also, the air force and the army were in the city. They were a huge target for the Luftwaffe.'

'Hence the Home Guard.' Peter smiled. 'It sounds like George Banks was quite the hero to have a plaque laid in his honour inside the church.'

Harry shrugged. 'I suppose so but the Auxiliary Patrol was more exciting. They were properly trained – I'm not saying that the Home Guard *weren't* trained,' he added hastily. 'But the AP were real soldiers. They had OBs – operational bases – in Larcombe Woods. I can show you them if you like.'

'And where's Larcombe Woods?' Peter asked. 'Is that near the chapel?'

'About a mile from here,' said Harry.

'Perhaps another time,' Peter said almost dismissively. 'Today I want to see the chapel.'

'Out of bounds,' Lavinia said. 'Too dangerous.'

'The chapel is supposed to be haunted by a Luftwaffe pilot who was shot down,' said Harry. 'But Father says it's an urban legend. The wreckage was never found.'

'A pilot? Is that so?' Peter said. 'Well, I'd still like to ask the dowager countess if I could look. Perhaps you would like to come with me, Harry.'

Danny had been listening intensely throughout this whole conversation. 'Let me show you the clock right now, Peter.' He clearly didn't want to let Peter and his Trust go.

'I think we're going to look at this chapel, aren't we Harry?' Peter said.

'Homework,' Lavinia said firmly. 'Not today.'

'To the tower!' Danny declared. 'And while you are up there, Peter, we could look at the roof flashings and parapet stonework. I've already listed the structural repairs that must be done immediately. Our roof could collapse at any minute.'

Peter didn't look very keen.

'I've never been up the tower,' I said.

'Then you must come too!' Danny exclaimed. 'Although it can be a little cramped.'

'I'll take Gran back and meet you at the car,' said Shawn. 'I've been up there many times and there is definitely not room for four.'

'I hope you don't suffer from claustrophobia, Peter.' Danny took Peter by the arm. 'I'll lead the way.'

Chapter Ten

The entrance to the clock tower was something that could easily be missed. Tucked behind a tapestry hanging to the side of the pulpit, it was necessary to turn sideways to get through the narrow entrance to the bottom of the steps.

Just a few feet further on was the vestry with a typewritten notice hanging from a sign on the door saying Consultation in Progress – without the letter l in Consultation.

'Wait here,' said Danny. 'I'll be right back.' He entered the vestry and my eye caught the red velvet curtain that Mum had mentioned. It was hanging from a makeshift pole on the diagonal. One end was wedged into a crevice in the wall and the other was balanced on a candle sconce. I couldn't help myself and had to quickly dart forward and draw the curtain back from the improvised nook. Sure enough, there was a chair inside.

Danny returned and handed me a pair of disposable gloves. 'But where is Peter?'

'He's here!' Gladys exclaimed and bundled her victim towards us.

'Are you coming up the tower, Gladys?' Danny enquired as he thrust a pair of gloves at Peter.

'No, thank you,' Gladys declared. 'Once was more than enough for me. I'll wait here.'

I was beginning to have second thoughts myself. 'Why do we need these gloves?'

'Ah, it can be a little grubby,' Danny said. 'What we need to do is use one shoulder to brace against the outside wall and the other to hold the central pillar. As we get higher, you'll find it easier to use your hands to climb upwards.'

I gave a nervous laugh. 'It sounds like we're going up a mountain.'

'And you'll also want to place your feet sideways on each step because they are a tad narrow,' said Danny. 'Any questions? Good. I'll go first. Kat, you follow me and Peter can bring up the rear.'

'I'll make sure he does, Danny,' Gladys said and turned to Peter. 'Don't look up and don't look down. Just keep your eyes focused on the step in front of you.'

I couldn't be certain but I thought I heard Peter whimper.

There was very little light inside the tower and I had the immediate sensation that the walls were closing in. It smelled of dust, old wood and damp stone. No wonder Danny had asked if we were claustrophobic.

Our ascent was lit only by the dirty glass slits in the tower wall. The staircase was treacherous and curved tightly and steeply upwards. It was so narrow that you couldn't *not* brace your shoulder against the outer wall. The steps were uneven through the constant wear of centuries. Danny wasn't joking when he told us we had to place our feet sideways and climb, one foot over the next, clinging to that central pillar.

Danny climbed like a gazelle. He was so lithe and graceful. In a matter of seconds, he had disappeared. I was slower because I had to watch every single step. Twice I glanced back to check on Peter, who was breathing heavily.

It was hard to calculate just how far up we had climbed when Danny popped his head out of a gap in the wall which opened into a basic platform with a single wooden railing. We'd reached the top of the stone flight of stairs. From now on, a series of narrow wooden ladders continued up into the darkness.

Noticing my upward glance Danny said, 'That goes to the roof for the final push. Bit tricky. Would be excellent to have new steps installed. We should talk to Peter about that too.'

Even if I was paid a million dollars, there was no way I was going up any further.

'Come and see this, Kat.' I followed Danny onto the platform that stood flush to the bell chamber. There were four bells and clappers, suspended from wooden crossbeams on hinges. Thick red and blue bell ropes dangled into the void below.

'I'll be putting the word out for bellringers soon,' Danny said cheerfully. 'Perhaps you might like to join?'

I was frozen to the spot. Below to my right was an open trap door with another long ladder that dropped into the clock room where the mechanism was housed.

I had never felt so unsafe.

Danny must have guessed I was nervous. 'Don't worry,' he grinned. 'The platform isn't going to collapse quite yet.' Then, to my horror, he jumped up and down three times. The platform quivered. I lunged for the railing. From below came a cry of fear.

'Where is Peter?' asked Danny.

Peter appeared. His face was grey and slick with sweat.

I was concerned. 'Are you feeling all right?'

Danny regarded him keenly. 'You can't be a church clock restorer and not have a head for heights, man!'

'A census,' Peter said weakly. 'Not clock.'

'Perfectly safe in here.' To my dismay, Danny leapt up and down three times again! I thought Peter was going to faint from fear. The poor man was clearly terrified. He sank to the floor and shook his head. 'I can't move.'

Danny and I exchanged worried looks.

'Can I get picked up by helicopter from the roof?' Peter said with a tiny smile.

'You don't want to do that,' I said quickly as I thought of those wooden ladders disappearing into space.

'This is ridiculous!' Danny's sense of humour seemed to be deteriorating by the minute. 'We'll go down to the clock room.' He practically manhandled Peter towards the trapdoor.

Somehow, Peter and I climbed down. I was just as nervous as Peter, who was holding on to the sides of the ladder so tightly that his knuckles were white.

Danny then gave us a lesson about the mechanism of the clock: the three winding shafts for the 'going train', whatever that was, the quarter and hour chimes, and the flat-bed frame mechanism, which looked like a series of levers, dials and metal bits and pieces.

'Right!' Danny commanded. 'Did you bring a camera? You'll need to take photographs.'

Peter shook his head, which seemed to annoy Danny even more.

'I've got my iPhone,' I offered and retrieved it from my pocket. 'Peter, just tell me what to photograph and I'll do it. I can put them on a thumb drive.'

'I'm sorry,' whispered Peter, shaking his head. 'Give me a minute.'

Danny muttered something derogatory under his breath and took charge. He was very clear on what he wanted photographed. I followed his commands and, finally, it was all over.

'In the future,' Danny said coldly, 'the Trust should send out someone who isn't afraid of heights! I wanted to take you out onto the roof and show you the flashings. Well, we can't do that now, can we?'

'I keep trying to tell you!' Peter exploded. 'I am not here for your clock! I am here to take a census of disused chapels. I never said anything about clocks!'

A sick feeling began to grow in my stomach as I replayed our initial conversation at Bridge Cottage. Had Peter mentioned clocks? I could have sworn he did but perhaps he hadn't. Come to think of it, Peter kept repeating that he was doing a census on disused chapels. He must have told everyone half a dozen times.

I began to feel horribly embarrassed. This was all my fault and now we were stuck up the church tower for God knows how long. I stopped myself – why did I use that figure of speech? It was disrespectful. I made a mental note to watch my language in the future.

The more immediate problem was how to get down.

I brandished my phone and said lightly, 'Shall I call the fire brigade?'

'There is a wooden shutter a few feet down,' Danny nodded. 'We could open that. The ladder might reach.'

Peter turned even paler. 'No.'

'You'll want to go down feet first and backwards,' said Danny. 'Hence the gloves. Imagine you're scaling down a cliff.'

Now it was my turn to balk but there was no other way out.

'I'll go first, then you, Peter,' Danny said. 'Kat, you're small. You could probably shifty down on your rear and that way you can lean down and keep hold of Peter's shoulders.'

The descent was one of the most horrible experiences of my life.

Finally, we were out into the March sunshine. The only person waiting was Shawn, who was sitting on a wooden seat. He sprang to his feet.

'I was about to give up on you!' He raised an eyebrow in Peter's direction. Peter looked as if he had just escaped death. 'Is everything all right?'

'Not really,' I said in a low voice. 'Where's Gladys? I think we could do with some of her medical assistance.'

'She had to go back to her cottage,' said Shawn. 'Something about having a cake in the oven that she was making specially for Danny but that she would be right back.'

Peter staggered to the bench and sank down. 'Sorry.'

'This is too bad,' said Danny, no longer bothering to hide his irritation anymore. 'I was hoping since we were up there that we could have continued up to the roof to look at the flashings.'

'At least we've got the photographs.' I desperately wanted to make amends. 'I will put them on a thumb drive and you can have them this afternoon.'

'Don't you remember we're going to Dartmoor?' said Shawn. 'The Rugglestone Inn stops serving food at three. Unless you've changed your mind.'

'Of course I haven't,' I said. 'I will drop the thumb drive off to you tomorrow and I'll give you a copy too, Danny.'

'We'd better go,' said Shawn and bore me away.

I took a backward glance and saw my mother hurry along the path with Gladys bringing up the rear. Quite the foursome. I left them to check pulses and blood pressures.

At last, Shawn and I were on our way. I managed to push the clock tower fiasco to the back of my mind. It was a beautiful afternoon with the smell of spring in the air. But no sooner had we left Little Dipperton behind us and descended the hill to Bridge Cottage, we saw the flashing blue lights of an ambulance and a police car. Mallory was standing next to the motorbike.

'That's the motorbike I told you about,' I said. 'But why is there an ambulance?'

Shawn cut the engine. 'Let's go and find out.'

The rear doors of the ambulance were wide open. I glanced inside and saw the Cruickshank twins attending to a figure on a gurney.

'What's happened? Anyone hurt?' Shawn asked Mallory.

Mallory gestured for us to follow him. 'He'll live. Two broken ankles, a broken pelvis. He's got a concussion to his head which he must have struck on something as he fell. He's also got hypothermia for having lain there all night.'

Shawn frowned. 'Fell? You mean, fell off his motorbike?'

I was puzzled. 'Lain where?'

Mallory seemed mystified. 'He was in the cellar.'

'You mean, here?' I was shocked. 'The Bridge Cottage cellar?'

Mallory shrugged. 'For some reason he had decided to go into a dangerous building and ignore the warning signs which, I admit, aren't very visible, missed his footing and fell through the floor and into the cellar.'

'But . . .' I stammered. 'I looked for him yesterday.' It had never occurred to me to look inside the building.

'He probably knocked himself unconscious,' said Mallory. 'The drop must be a good fifteen feet. He'll recover but he'll be going into surgery straightaway.'

'Next of kin?' Shawn asked.

'We recovered his mobile which should help us identify him.'

I looked at Shawn, bewildered. 'I feel terrible. I just . . . I didn't think to look in the cellar and neither did Peter.'

Mallory whipped out his police notebook and pencil. 'Peter—?'

'Becker,' I said. 'He's from the Chapel Restoration Trust. He's staying at the Hare and Hounds.'

'I'll have a word with him.' Mallory made a note of it.

I thought for a moment. 'You know that man, the rider, nearly caused an accident yesterday.' I told Mallory he had cut in front of me when I was trying to make a turn against the traffic. 'I can't have been more than five minutes behind him.'

'Ha!' Shawn exclaimed. 'Look up there!' He pointed to the blackened timbers beneath the gable end of the roof.

It was a CCTV camera.

'Well, I never!' Mallory grinned. 'The question is, does it work?'

'It works all right,' Shawn declared. 'Why else do you think we've had no reports of fly-tipping here for months!'

'Good.' Mallory clapped Shawn on the shoulder and scribbled something on his notepad and closed it with a snap. A fresh-faced officer who I had never met before approached. He was holding a motorbike helmet with a distinctive purple zigzag on the back. 'I found this, guv. It was around the back of the building.'

'I know where I've seen it before,' I blurted out. 'He was in the car park at Luxton's saleroom.'

Mallory inhaled sharply. 'I don't believe in coincidences.'

'Nor do I,' said Shawn.

'Would you mind coming back to the station, Kat?' Mallory said. 'There's more to this than meets the eye.'

Shawn scowled. 'I guess we won't be going to Dartmoor, after all.'

Chapter Eleven

Shawn and I followed Mallory to the small satellite police station which was on the outskirts of Dartmouth. Usually it was closed on a Sunday but today Mallory seemed to be making an exception.

The police station was tiny and furnished with an uncomfortable-looking bench and two hard chairs.

Shawn's first comment when he stepped through the door was, 'How could I have worked from here? It's a shoebox.'

Not for the first time did I think of Mallory's request for a transfer from the big city lights of Plymouth to a rural . . . shoebox. And then I saw him with Stella again. Would things change now they were back together?

Shawn had stopped at a service station and bought sandwiches and crisps, complaining bitterly of having missed out on Sunday lunch at the Rugglestone Inn.

The smell of freshly brewed coffee greeted us. I didn't usually drink coffee in the afternoon but I was in dire need of a boost.

'Well, while I've been waiting for you I've been busy,' said Mallory. 'The Kawasaki belongs to a Brock Leavey.'

I gasped. 'Are you sure? But he's . . . he's Staci Trotter's partner.'

'Staci Trotter?' Mallory's tone was sharp. 'The driver of the pink Fiat?'

'Yes but . . . Oh no.' I was appalled. 'How awful. Does Brock know that she's dead? Oh! And she was pregnant, too.'

'Kat,' Shawn sounded impatient. 'It's not as if you knew her!'

'But I spoke to her yesterday at the auction.'

'Whoa!' Mallory exclaimed. 'Let's start at the beginning.'

'I met her at Luxton's when she was bidding for the same lot as me,' I said and went on to fill Mallory in on our rival bids for a box of bears. 'I repair them and donate them to children's hospitals. I've been doing it for years.'

'And you say Staci Trotter offered to buy these bears from you?' Mallory asked.

'Yes. But I'd already promised them to Gladys – she's the retired matron in the village. Apparently, Staci's sister has terminal cancer and likes to collect bears. Oh. This is just so sad.' I was surprised by just how much this news had affected me.

Mallory turned to a fresh page in his notebook. 'And you're saying you met Staci Trotter on Saturday afternoon at Luxton's. Was Brock Leavey there?'

'Only in the car park when I was leaving,' I said. 'Not the saleroom.'

'Wait a moment, Kat,' said Shawn. 'So what you are saying is that this Brock Leavey passed you on the main road and then stopped at Bridge Cottage where he left his motorbike. For some reason he went inside the cottage and fell through the floorboards.'

It sounded bizarre hearing Shawn say it aloud. 'And Brock Leavey was in the cellar all night?'

'It would appear so,' said Mallory.

'And what about Trevor Banks?' Shawn asked. 'Do we know where he was on Saturday evening?'

'Why?' said Mallory. 'What has Trevor Banks got to do with this?'

'No reason,' said Shawn.

'Because he was having an affair with Staci Trotter,' I said at the exact same time that Shawn said, 'No reason.'

Shawn shot me a furious glare. 'It's just a rumour. Clive's Uncle Trevor—'

'Clive? You mean Detective Sergeant Clive Banks?' Mallory asked. 'And what was this rumour?'

'Trevor had been messing about with the woman from the care agency who visited his grandparents,' said Shawn dismissively.

'Messing about?' I was outraged. 'Hardly messing about. He got her pregnant!'

Shawn tensed. 'As I said, a rumour. I'll deal with Trevor Banks if that's okay with you, Mallory.'

Mallory's jaw hardened. 'I'm afraid not, Shawn. There's something suspicious about this young woman's accident.'

I gasped.

'What do you mean!' Shawn said quickly. 'Suspicious? Why haven't I been informed?'

'It's not your case.' Mallory's tone surprised me. It wasn't friendly. He turned to me.

'Did you see Staci Trotter after you left the saleroom?'

'I didn't see her,' I said. 'But I did see a pink Fiat parked outside Eric's scrapyard.'

Mallory frowned again. 'She was at Honeychurch Hall? When was this?'

Shawn didn't answer. I could tell he was sulking.

'I don't know if she went to the Hall,' I said. 'But her car was still there after I left my mother's house around six – the entrance to Mum's courtyard is opposite Eric's gate.'

Mallory wrote it down.

'And when we left for Dartmouth,' I went on. 'The Fiat was still there, wasn't it, Shawn?' When Shawn didn't comment I added, 'I'm assuming that Eric must know Staci.'

'He doesn't,' Shawn snapped.

Now it was my turn to glare at him. It was another bone of contention between us that Shawn protected anyone connected to the Honeychurch family no matter what they did.

'Perhaps that's a question for Eric,' Mallory said.

'You're wasting your time.' Shawn's voice was pleasant but I detected a distinct edge to it.

'And if I am,' said Mallory, 'that's on me.'

The tension between the two men was hard to ignore.

'It wouldn't surprise me if Iris had something to do with it,' Shawn said suddenly.

I felt a flash of anger. 'How come?'

Shawn shrugged. 'If there's any trouble, you can bet that Iris is involved in some way.'

'If you must know,' I said coldly, 'my mother had a parish meeting with Ruby – that's the vicar's mother – and Gladys Knight, the matron I'm giving those bears to. So, it's highly unlikely, isn't it?'

'All right, okay,' Mallory said in a soothing voice. 'We're going off track here.'

I thought for a moment. 'But surely Staci must have seen Brock's motorbike when she drove by Bridge Cottage!' I exclaimed. 'Why didn't she stop – oh wait, she wouldn't have seen it. Peter had moved it off the road.'

'We'll see what comes of the CCTV footage and what else we can glean from Staci Trotter's mobile.' Mallory stood up and closed his notebook.

'And what about Brock Leavey's mobile?' I asked.

'Technically we can't look through it, other than to find his next of kin,' said Mallory. 'In the meantime, I'll speak to Peter Becker and find out if he noticed anything unusual after you left Bridge Cottage.'

Shawn and I got up to go too but as we reached the door I remembered something. Clive had mentioned that Mallory had ordered a toxicology report on Staci Trotter so I asked him about it.

Mallory nodded. 'We're expecting the results back from the lab tomorrow.'

'So soon?' Shawn sounded surprised. 'Oh yes, of course! It's handy to have friends in high places.' He laughed but

there wasn't any kindness there. I had never seen Shawn act
like this before, but if it bothered Mallory, he didn't show it.

Shawn drove me back to Jane's Cottage in barbed silence.
When he stopped the car outside, he cut the engine but made
no attempt to get out.

'I don't think I'll stay tonight,' he said quietly.

My heart sank. 'But why? I thought we were going to do
something tomorrow. I thought you wanted to show me that
house in Exeter.'

'You told me you've got a busy week,' said Shawn. 'So I
don't really see the point, do you?'

I felt the anger rise again. 'And I told you that I would
change my plans.' I studied his face and, to my dismay, saw he
looked desperately sad. 'What is it?' I whispered. 'Is it because
I was too opinionated at the police station?'

Shawn shook his head. He seemed to be struggling to
speak.

'Is it because I said too much in front of Mallory about
Trevor? Or Eric?'

There was still no response.

'What is it, Shawn!' I felt scared. 'Please talk to me.'

'Kat . . .' Shawn finally looked at me. I was horrified to see
he looked close to tears.

My stomach turned over. It was his expression that made
my blood run ice cold. 'What's the matter? You've got a
weird look on your face.'

Shawn looked down and studied his hands.

'This isn't working, is it?' he said. 'Us. We're not
working.'

I felt blindsided. Where was this coming from? 'I don't understand. What have I said? What did I do?'

'I've tried and tried,' said Shawn. 'I was looking forward to spending my days off with you but . . . I can see it's no use. We bicker all the time and you're so defensive.'

'I'm not defensive,' I said, being defensive. For the most awful moment I thought of that stupid letter to 'Dear Amanda'. Had Shawn read it? Did he know it was from me? Was that why he was so rude to Mallory?

'Kat, I love you but—'

'You're not in love with me.' I was incredulous. Had he actually trotted out that old cliché?

'I *am* in love with you,' Shawn said quietly. 'I adore you. I know we argue but it's not that.'

I felt a wave of hope. 'Then what? It can't be my mother anymore. She's given up her writing! Turned to God.' It was a stupid flippant remark, but Shawn didn't smile. He wouldn't look at me.

'If you love me and I love you . . . then why can't we work things out?' I said desperately.

There was a hideous silence. My heart was racing and I felt sick. Of course I'd known we had been having problems. None of this should have come as a surprise and I was obviously deceiving myself that our relationship could be saved. The awful thing was that I didn't even know if I wanted it to be saved. I felt so confused.

I had always thought it would be me who would have ended things between us. How arrogant and selfish was I?

When Shawn finally turned his face back to mine, his look of utter despair just cut my heart in two.

'It's Helen, isn't it?' I said. 'You can't let go of her memory. But I told you I don't want to replace her. I never have.'

'It's not Helen,' he said.

'I've never tried to be a mother to the twins.' I rushed on. 'You know that.'

'The twins. Yes. Kat—' Shawn hesitated before taking a deep breath. 'I can't give you what you want.'

'What do you mean? I don't understand.'

'Children.'

There. He'd said it. He'd mentioned the elephant in the room. I knew I had told him how important having kids was to me, and, as my fortieth birthday came and went, the chances of that happening were getting smaller and I was okay with that. I really was.

'But, it's fine if we don't or I can't,' I stammered. 'Mum says what you haven't had, you don't miss.'

'No. You don't understand.' Shawn's tone was stronger now that the cat was out of the bag. 'I don't want any more children, Kat.'

'You don't?' I was shocked. 'But . . . I thought . . .' We had spoken about children but perhaps it was one-sided. My side. I thought we'd talked about it or maybe I had talked about it and assumed, just as I had assumed that Peter Becker was a wretched clock specialist, that Shawn wanted more children, too.

'I've been thinking about this for a long time,' Shawn went on. 'I saw how you looked at that baby yesterday. It's just not fair on you. I will never stop loving you. Ever. You're a beautiful woman, inside and out, and one day the right man will come along to give you all those things. Someone like . . . like Mallory. But it isn't me.'

I was speechless and felt dizzy and bewildered. And why would Shawn have mentioned Mallory?

He reached for my hand, 'Kat . . .'

I snatched it away and got out of the car, stumbling blindly to the front door as tears spilled down my face.

I fumbled for my house key and dropped my tote bag. I expected Shawn to come after me, but he didn't. I heard his car start and drive away.

I knew that this time our relationship was really over. All I wanted now was my mum. I ran back to my car and sped to the Carriage House.

Unfortunately, my mother wasn't alone.

As I drove into the carriageway, a Skoda Scala was parked next to my mother's red Mini. There was no way I wanted to see anyone else – especially a stranger.

The back entrance opened and two figures emerged. It was too late. I'd been spotted.

I glanced in the rear-view mirror to check my reflection. It was worse than I thought. I looked a wreck. My mascara had run, my eyes were small 'like piss-holes in the snow' – that's what my dad would have called them – and my skin was blotchy.

I wiped what mascara I could off my cheeks, straightened my shoulders and got out of the car.

Chapter Twelve

Peter smiled. 'Your mother is an excellent historian and . . .' He stopped, worried. 'Are you all right?'

'Whatever's happened?' My mother's face fell. 'You look dreadful. What is it?'

'Nothing,' I said brightly. 'How are you? Excuse me.' And I pushed past them and into the house.

Mum – thankfully alone – found me eating the last three of Paula's chanterelle and watercress picnic puffs. I hadn't even tasted them.

'I'm glad someone is eating those,' she said. 'Peter is gluten intolerant. I must tell Paula she needs to make a gluten-free range.'

'Where have you hidden the brandy?'

'It's in the sideboard in the dining room.' Mum frowned. 'I'll get it for you. Just sit down and perhaps try to breathe a little. You have gone a very odd colour. Have you found another body?'

At that comment, I just burst into noisy tears. My nose

ran, I start hiccupping and the sobbing just wouldn't stop. I reached for the box of tissues on the dresser. 'I didn't think I'd be this upset.'

'Oh, dear,' said Mum. 'Sit down. I'll be right back!'

She dashed out of the kitchen and returned with two crystal balloons and poured us each a hefty slug.

'Do you want to start at the beginning?' Mum said and, as the whole sorry story just came out, she knelt beside me on the flagstone floor and took me in her arms. I bawled like a baby. She patted my hair and stroked my back and just whispered, 'It'll be all right, just you see.' She didn't say it was for the best or do-a-Delia and say that there were plenty more fish in the sea or that Shawn was an idiot and that made me love her all the more.

Slowly, the tears subsided and apart from a few sniffles and a last hiccup, I began to recover my composure and when Mum attempted to stand up and couldn't, I smiled.

'Getting too old to kneel on a flagstone floor,' she said with one last successful effort.

'I sort of knew it was coming,' I said miserably. 'It's never been an easy relationship.' And it hadn't. Apart from having to deal with the ghost of his dead wife there was the ongoing practical management of his twins – even though I loved them. The twins! Perhaps that was why Shawn had never truly included me in everything. The odd thing was that now I knew where I stood, I felt a little better.

'It was the not knowing,' I said as Mum poured out two more shots. 'Now I know, I can move forward. I've been in such a strange place with him for so long.'

Mum gave a mischievous smile. 'And now you can crack on with Man B!'

'Very funny,' I said drily. 'Man B – and I'm not admitting I wrote that letter to "Dear Amanda" by the way – is back with his girlfriend.'

'Oh. What a shame. How do you know?'

'Because I saw them together on Saturday evening,' I said. 'We were in the same restaurant in Dartmouth.'

'And?' Mum demanded. 'What's she like?'

'She's his old boss. And by old, I mean older,' I said. 'Sophisticated, elegant, and utterly terrifying. She just doesn't seem his type. I really don't care. Honestly.'

'Oh.' For once, my mother seemed lost for words.

We fell silent for a few moments. Mum brightened. 'Never mind. There are plenty more fish—'

'Don't say it!' I squeaked. 'Speaking of which, it looks like you have two fish swimming in your little pond.'

'If I had to choose, it would be Danny,' Mum declared. 'He speaks with such passion in the pulpit, it's easy to imagine what he would be—'

'No, it wouldn't!' I said quickly.

'Anything to get one over Miss Pips,' Mum said and topped up our glasses for the third time. 'Ruby says Gladys has taken to deliberately blocking Danny's car in so he has to knock on her door to ask her to move it. Invariably, she guilts him in for a cup of tea – he's too kind to refuse – and when he does, she's scantily clad.'

'Scantily clad?' I snorted. 'You're making that part up.'

'But it made you laugh.'

'I snorted. I did not laugh,' I said. 'It sounds like you and Ruby are becoming friendly. As you mentioned, a way to a man's heart is through his mother.'

'I know I said that,' Mum looked sheepish. 'But I genuinely like her. It's a pity about her scar. It makes her self-conscious. I'm sure that's why she doesn't go out much.'

'Do you know how Ruby got it?'

'I couldn't possibly ask her,' Mum sounded shocked that I would even suggest it. 'I don't think it helps that she didn't want to move down to Devon. She's lived with Danny since her husband died and what Danny says goes. Did you know he used to teach science in an all-girls school? He gave it all up for the Lord. He's very clever. Only reads things like—'

'The Bible?'

'Yes, that, but the *New Scientist*, *Christianity Today* and biographies of important people,' Mum said, clearly impressed.

'So probably not Krystalle Storm in that case,' I said. 'Well, I'm glad you've found a new friend and potential mother-in-law.'

I waited for the denial, but none came. I knew my mother well now. She was in the infatuation stage and until she saw his feet of clay, just-call-me-Danny would enjoy unfettered adulation.

'*Three Widows and a Widower*,' I mused. 'You, Gladys, Ruby – and Danny.'

'For someone with a broken heart, you can be quite amusing.' Mum's voice dripped with sarcasm.

I smirked. 'What did Ruby think of Danny's dead wife?'

'Caroline,' Mum says. 'I told you. We are forbidden to mention her name.'

'You're lucky,' I said. 'Helen was all Shawn could ever talk about. She was perfect in every way.'

Mum reached over and patted my hand again. 'I know. I'm sorry, dear.'

'I'm fine, really.' I forced another smile. 'What about fish number two?'

'Peter?' she said. 'Pleasant. Single. Not sure if he ever married. I haven't had that conversation with him.'

'I like him,' I said. 'He was very helpful at Bridge Cottage with that motorbike.'

Mum looked blank. I realised I'd been so preoccupied with Shawn that I had yet to tell her about Brock Leavey falling into the cellar and his connection with Staci Trotter and Trevor. So I did. 'A love triangle with a pregnancy thrown in for good measure. Right up your street.'

Mum's jaw dropped. '*The Mouche and the Masseuse*. Now, that's a good title.'

'I thought you'd given up writing.'

'I have,' Mum declared firmly. 'Force of habit. But, back to Peter. Yes, he's nice enough but . . .' She paused. 'There is something not quite right about him. Something off. He kept asking me who had lived in the village the longest and were they still alive.'

I shrugged. 'Edith, obviously. Olive Banks and some of her cronies that came to the funeral . . . Peggy Cropper perhaps. Why?'

'What's that got to do with a census on chapels?' Mum

said. 'He asked me the strangest question. Had I ever come across anyone called Fudge?'

'Peter asked Lavinia the same thing yesterday in the pub.'

'I kept telling him I was a blow-in,' Mum went on. 'I had to explain what that meant.'

I knew the derogatory term, of course. It applied to anyone who had not been born in the village or had lived in Devon for less than forty years. In Cornwall, non-locals and holidaymakers were called grockles.

'Well, I don't hold out much hope that he'll get to see the chapel,' Mum said. 'I'm not going behind Edith's back and I told him that.'

I sat back in my chair and wailed. 'Why didn't I see my break-up coming?'

'I thought we'd moved on from Shawn, dear.'

'I don't believe he dumped me because of the children thing.'

'Children thing?' Mum sounded surprised. 'Don't give up hope, dear. I believe the oldest woman to naturally conceive is sixty-seven.'

'Not helpful, Mum!' I exclaimed. 'Shawn doesn't want any more children. He was very clear on that.'

Mum shot me a sympathetic look but I could tell she wasn't sure what to say. And then, 'Come along. Stop being maudlin. Do you have a cupboard to clear out? Or a drawer?'

'Not really,' I said.

'What about those bears you mentioned?' Mum said. 'Go home now and get them sorted out for Miss Pips. Manual work is good for broken hearts.'

'I don't feel like it,' I grumbled.

'You look exhausted,' Mum said. 'Sleep here tonight darling. It will be like old times.'

'No. You're right. The bears must be sorted out,' I said. 'I told Gladys I would drop them over tomorrow. I also have to go to Luxton's in the morning for Olive Banks.'

Mum raised a quizzical brow.

'Clive said that an item was missing from the lot I picked up on Saturday.'

'Surely that's not your problem,' Mum pointed out. 'You've got to learn to say no.'

'And I have to download the photos I took in the clock tower for Danny and Peter and that's not my problem either but somehow it is.'

'Generous persons will prosper; those who refresh others will themselves be refreshed,' Mum smiled. 'Proverbs 11:25.'

'Did you really just quote from the Bible?'

'I'm taking Bible study classes on Tuesday evenings,' Mum said. 'You should come!'

'Thanks. But no thanks.' I got up to leave.

Promising to call Mum first thing in the morning 'to make sure I didn't die of a broken heart in the night,' I set off for home feeling marginally better.

When I got into bed, I felt a wave of sadness that was followed by an unexpected feeling of relief. The worst had happened and I was still in one piece. To use one of my mother's favourite quotes from *Gone with the Wind* – as Scarlett O'Hara would say, 'Tomorrow is another day.'

Chapter Thirteen

I slept surprisingly well, given everything that had transpired over the past twenty-four hours, and was up just before six. It was still dark.

I sorted out the bears, mended a few paws and set aside two that needed serious surgery. I decided I would part with the French bulldog after all. I'd drop them off with Gladys after I had swung by Olive's cottage with the Luxton's catalogue for Trevor. Mum was right. Let them sort the missing item out between them.

I took a quick shower, put on some light make-up, black jeans and a black polo-neck sweater. A dark green peacoat and my favourite ankle boots completed the outfit. I put the box of bears on the back seat of my car.

Grabbing the Luxton's catalogue, I found the page that listed Lot 49 and marked it with a Post-it.

The lot was described as 'Home Guard Memorabilia' and listed: 6 percussion cap tins dated 1943, a water bottle with webbing cover, an ARP whistle dated 1940, a traffic lantern, a respirator, an ARP tin box, an MK11 steel Brodie helmet, a dagger, a Home Guard pattern leather equipment pouch, an ARP badge (solid silver), a hand bell, a screw lid bakelite compass (1930), an ARP gas rattle and a webbing British rucksack. I couldn't see any item that was worth thousands and thousands of pounds.

Ten minutes later I pulled up outside the terrace of three cottages. The U-Haul had gone. I hoped that I wasn't too early, but I needn't have worried. Delia emerged from next door just as I got out of my car.

'First day on the job and Paula is late,' Delia grumbled. 'I said seven-fifty sharp.'

I glanced at my watch. It was seven fifty-two.

The front door flew open. Paula was all teeth and smiles. Wearing the demure black uniform that Delia had given her, she had tied her hair up in a smart knot on the top of her head and had applied mascara and a pale pink lipstick. She seemed happy and I could easily guess why.

Her love rival was dead.

'I've brought the catalogue for Luxton's,' I said. 'Is Olive up?'

'Ma!' Paula called out. 'Kat to see you. Bye!'

She fairly skipped past and when Delia scolded her for being two minutes late, Paula just laughed.

I made my way past unpacked boxes and entered the kitchen. Trevor was boiling the kettle. He was a big man and filled the room. He had shaved off his mouche and was dressed in a grubby sweatshirt and dirty jeans. I wasn't remotely surprised to see the prodigal husband standing in his mother's kitchen. No surprise that Paula was cheerful.

I wondered if this latest development would change things between Delia and Paula now that they had nothing in common.

Olive was seated at a small table with her walker close to hand. She wore a chunky hand-knitted jumper in orange and navy stripes with a navy skirt. The remains of breakfast were set out on the table – a half-eaten piece of toast, butter peppered with crumbs and an open pot of marmalade.

Various baking tools, wire cooling trays, tins and other cooking paraphernalia took up most of the kitchen counter-top. An assortment of green leaves and what looked like weeds stood in jam jars along the windowsill.

Trevor made himself a cup of tea and leaned against the countertop. I thought of Staci, so young and vibrant – and pregnant – and wondered what on earth she had seen in him.

I commented on the lovely service and unveiling yesterday and how much everyone seemed to enjoy the reception at the Hare and Hounds, but Olive didn't seem to be listening. Her expression was dour and the tension in the kitchen was tangible.

I took the catalogue out of my tote bag and handed it to Olive. 'I marked your lot with a Post-it. It's Lot 49.'

Olive passed it back without even looking at it. 'Trevor is going with you this morning. He'll talk to them.'

'Excuse me?' I wasn't sure if I had heard correctly.

'Trevor lost his driving licence,' Olive said bluntly. 'He's not allowed to drive.'

'Only three more weeks, Ma,' Trevor whined.

There was no way I wanted to drive Trevor to Luxton's – Proverbs 11:25 or not.

I remembered Olive saying that she could drive but when I mentioned it, she looked at me as if I had suggested she run naked down the street. 'Oh, I can't possibly drive all that way,' she said in horror. 'No, it's much easier if you take Trevor. You'll be back before you know it. Now then, off you both go.'

I realised I was stuck. Trevor couldn't drive. Olive refused to and that left me.

'Right then,' I said. 'If we're going, we're going now. I've got a busy day ahead. Are you ready, Trevor?'

Trevor scowled and set his mug down. Tea sloshed onto the floor.

'It's very kind of you to help us,' Olive said suddenly. 'In fact, everyone has been so kind. Even strangers! I wondered about that man. The man connected with the Church Trust. Someone told him that George and I lived near the chapel. Do you know why he wants to see it?'

'He's doing a census for the Churches Conservation Trust,' I said.

'Oh, I see,' said Olive. 'Her ladyship won't like him snooping around and I told him that.'

'I think everyone has told him that,' I said. 'But whether he listens or not is another matter. Are you ready, Trevor?'

Trevor just grunted.

'And take a jacket,' Olive scolded. 'It's going to rain. And mind you don't come back without it. Your father would turn in his grave if he knew what you'd done.'

And with that, I led the way to my Golf. Trevor, bundled up in a padded anorak, was a shadow of the stylish man with the leather jacket and the mouche I had seen only yesterday.

I tried to make small talk but the only answers I got were grunts. He seemed preoccupied with his mobile. Uncharitably, I thought that Paula was better off without him. But then I remembered that his pregnant lover had just died and that his whole life had to be in turmoil. It was hard to find compassion but I was determined to try.

We entered the village.

'I have to make a quick stop at Blackberry Cottage.' I turned into Church Lane and gave a cry of annoyance. 'Oh! I don't believe it.'

Gladys had parked her yellow Peugeot so badly – on the diagonal in fact – that it was impossible for anyone to get past.

I stopped where I was, left the engine running and told Trevor that I would be right back – he made no sign of having heard anything I said – and, grabbing the box of bears from the back seat, I headed for Blackberry Cottage.

Gladys answered the door straight away. 'Oh, it's you.' Her disappointment was plain.

It was very difficult not to stare. Gladys had applied a dark red lipstick and was wearing a peach tiered floating skirt and a floral blouse with the top three buttons undone revealing the top of a black lacy bra. Mum was right.

I passed Gladys the box. 'I've brought the bears for the children.'

Gladys's face lit up. 'What a sweet little French bulldog.

Someone is going to love that!' She stepped outside and scanned the lane. 'Have you seen the vicar this morning?'

I told her I had not.

'Hmm. How strange.' Gladys frowned. 'He went out last night and hasn't come back yet. I called the police to report a missing person, but they said for someone to be reported as missing, they had to have gone for at least twenty-four hours. And what with that young woman who had that car accident – you know, Trevor Banks's mistress – it seems that the roads just aren't safe. He could be lying in a ditch!'

'Perhaps he takes services at another church?' I suggested.

'Oh. I hadn't thought of that.' She thought for a moment. 'I'll ask Ruby. And if she doesn't answer that door, I'll break it down if I must!'

I was going to ask Gladys to move her car but by the time she'd found her car keys it would be quicker for me to reverse the short distance to the main drag.

Trevor and I set off once more for Newton Abbot.

After what had to be fifteen long minutes of silence, Trevor finally spoke. 'Shawn Cropper's your boyfriend, isn't he?'

I didn't want to explain that twenty-four hours ago I would have agreed, but not now. 'Why are you asking?'

'I just wondered if he'd heard what happened to . . .' Trevor swallowed hard and made a peculiar strangling noise. 'That girl. You know. The one who,' he swallowed again, 'had a car accident.'

I stole a glance and saw a stray tear trickle down his cheek.

'Sorry, I haven't,' I said, which was true.

'Clive told me there was nothing wrong with her tyres,' Trevor went on. 'He said she must have fallen asleep at the wheel, which can't be right.'

'Why?'

'Because Staci suffered from insomnia, that's why,' said Trevor. 'She could survive on four hours' sleep and before you say anything about drugs, she didn't believe in all that either.'

I hadn't been going to mention drugs but now Trevor had brought it up, it did make me wonder.

'The police are conducting a toxicology report,' I said. 'Perhaps something will come out of that.'

Trevor gave a snort of disgust. 'Yeah. They'd think the worst, wouldn't they? And she wouldn't have been drinking because . . .' He paused to compose himself. I waited patiently. 'Because she was pregnant with . . . with our child.'

This was awkward. 'Yes, I know. She told me.'

'What? You *knew*?' Trevor exclaimed. 'How? When?'

'I saw her at Luxton's on Saturday afternoon.'

'Luxton's?' Trevor exclaimed again. 'You mean, where we're going now?'

'Yes,' I said.

'No, that can't be right,' said Trevor. 'She always visits her sister on a Saturday afternoon. Her sister's poorly, you see.'

'Maybe she missed last Saturday,' I suggested. 'Or went there later.'

'No. She'd never miss seeing Carrie.' Trevor was adamant. 'Never.'

I stole a sideways glance. 'When was the last time you saw Staci?'

Trevor's face crumpled. He made the same strangled sound again. 'Saturday morning. We'd argued. I don't want to talk about it.'

Staci was not only *not* seeing Carrie on Saturday afternoon, but she was also seeing Eric on Saturday evening. And then there was Brock. Perhaps Staci had a slew of boyfriends.

'Staci had so much to live for,' Trevor whispered. 'She was just getting started with her new business. She'd only been doing it for a week.'

That certainly explained Staci's insistence that she was a masseuse but not the practicality of driving a small Fiat.

I was positive Staci was the same carer who had found Trevor's dad in the bath, but I just wanted to make sure. 'What did Staci do before she qualified as a masseuse?'

'She worked for the Nightingale Care Agency,' said Trevor. 'Just A Wing Away. That was their slogan. You know, visiting the elderly, taking them meals and playing cards and games with them. She was a real hard worker.'

I felt uncomfortable. Perhaps I had misjudged Staci. It took a special type of person to do that kind of job.

'That's how we met,' Trevor went on. 'She visited my folks every day. Did a bit of shopping. Just checked in to see how they were.'

'Was that when your parents lived at Ivy Cottage?'

'That's right,' Trevor said. 'Staci didn't even mind the drive. The track to the cottage was a quagmire in the winter but she didn't care.'

'Staci sounded lovely.' I didn't know what else to say.

'She was.' Trevor wiped away a tear. 'The nicest girl I ever knew. So kind. So willing. She'd give you the shirt off her back.'

I bet she would, I thought to myself and then felt awful. What was wrong with me? When had I become so cynical?

'I just wanted to help her fulfil her dreams,' Trevor droned on. 'I paid for her to get her massage diploma. I don't know of anyone else who has strong fingers like Staci.'

Surely he knew that Staci had a partner?

'I bought her that Fiat,' Trevor continued wistfully. "I want hot pink, Trev." That's what she said and that's what she got.'

I tried to think of something to say but I couldn't think of a single thing.

'So . . . what happens in situations like this?' Trevor had suddenly snapped out of his lovesick monologue.

'Like what?'

'As I said, I bought her the car – insured it for her and everything. I should get the insurance money, right?'

'Was her name on the title?' I asked.

Trevor nodded.

'Then presumably it would go to her next of kin,' I said. 'Her sister Carrie or . . . maybe . . .' I took a breath. 'Her partner.'

There, I'd said it.

'Partner?' Trevor said sharply. 'What partner?'

I didn't care much for Trevor, but I suppose I could have been a bit more tactful. 'Her . . .' I hesitated. 'Male friend. The man she lived with.'

'Staci lived alone. She told me she lived alone.' He sounded panicked and grabbed my arm. 'She swore she did. Who is it?'

'Please let go of my arm.' Trevor was beginning to scare me. 'I'm driving.'

Trevor increased the pressure. It hurt. I should have remembered Trevor's reputation for picking fights in pubs. I hoped he wasn't going to pick a fight with me.

'Ask your nephew,' I said quickly. 'Clive knows more than I do. Please, I don't know anything.'

Trevor dropped his hand and gave a bitter laugh. 'You know what we call our Clive in the family? The wooden spoon. Because he's always stirring up trouble.'

Trevor's reaction had alarmed me. It had also thrown up more questions. Trevor had been prepared to leave Paula for Staci. Had Staci been prepared to leave Brock for Trevor? It was something we would never know.

Trevor had mentioned he and Staci had argued on Saturday morning. I wondered what it had been about. So I asked him.

Trevor huffed and puffed. 'I didn't understand why Staci was making such a fuss over Dad's military stuff being withdrawn—'

'Staci knew about the Home Guard memorabilia?' This was interesting.

'Yeah,' Trevor nodded. 'Staci used to love hearing my dad talk about his wartime adventures. Sometimes he showed her his equipment.' He sounded wistful again. 'She used to put on his helmet and make him laugh.'

I glanced over at Trevor, who continued to look mournful.

I had a thought. 'Did your father promise her anything – maybe he left her his helmet in his will? Assuming he made a will.' I'd not considered this idea. 'And Olive remembered and had the lot withdrawn so she could give whatever it was to Staci as a memento?'

'Are you kidding?' Trevor said with scorn. 'Ma got angry when Dad showed Staci his stuff. Said the past is the past. That's why Dickie and I thought Ma would be happy to see the back of it all. Ma could do with the money, too. What with the funeral and the coffin and then the reception. She'd told us she'd bought a funeral plan but it turned out she hadn't. It cost us thousands!'

I was sure it must have done. Funerals don't come cheap and from what I'd observed, there wasn't a lot of money in the Banks household.

'Staci hung up on me.' Trevor was back to their argument. He made a snuffling noise. 'I never spoke to her again.'

I thought of Staci's Fiat parked outside Eric's scrapyard and tried to sound casual. His reaction to Staci having a partner was enough of a warning to tread carefully. 'Did you see her at all on Saturday?'

'No. Never saw her again.' Trevor said. 'I got my mate to pick me up and we went fishing in Brixham and then to the Sprat and Mackerel for a pint or two. Let her stew, I thought. Didn't get back until midnight.'

His story would be easy to check and besides, I believed him.

Never had I been gladder to reach a destination. I pulled up on the double yellow lines outside the entrance to the forecourt. I really did not want to go in and find myself embroiled in an unpleasant scene with people I liked and respected.

I reached into the central console for a business card and handed it to Trevor. 'I'll go and find somewhere to park. Call me when you're ready.'

Trevor shifted in his seat. 'You're not coming in?'

'Your mother wanted you to handle it,' I reminded him. 'You've got the catalogue. Tell any of the porters in a hunter-green uniform that you want to speak to Johnny. He's the floor manager.'

Trevor got out of the car and slammed the door hard.

I retreated down a residential side street lined with Edwardian bay-fronted semi-detached houses and reversed into a space behind a red Harley-Davidson motorcycle and a sidecar with the personalised number plate PRZ HM.

And then, moments later, Danny emerged from the house on the opposite side of the street.

I watched in astonishment as a voluptuous woman in her sixties joined him on the doorstep. She was wearing a flimsy dressing gown and had her hair up in a towel. She looked angry and slammed the door in his face.

It didn't need a brain surgeon to guess the nature of their relationship. Panicked, I slid down in my seat, terrified of being seen as Danny, with an expression I can only describe as stricken, passed me by and climbed onto his Harley.

I was shocked. Our holier than thou vicar did not practise what he preached.

My mother was going to be very disappointed.

Chapter Fourteen

As I was trying to process this startling bit of information, my mobile rang. It was Trevor and he didn't sound happy.

'You need to come and talk to these idiots,' he shouted into my ear.

I suppressed a sigh. 'I'll be there in five minutes.'

Trevor was standing at the counter talking to Johnny. Even though Trevor had his back to me, I could tell by his stance that he was angry. His arms were hanging by his side but his shoulders were raised and his body was rigid.

Johnny exuded an aura of calm. He saw me coming and gave a smile of relief.

I joined them. 'Is everything okay?'

'No,' said Trevor rudely.

Johnny looked worried. 'You're making a very serious accusation, sir.'

'And that's why I want to talk to the manager,' Trevor said in a very loud voice that attracted more than a few stares from the public who were milling around.

I gave Johnny an apologetic smile. 'What's wrong?'

Trevor thrust out his jaw. 'They've nicked it.'

I gave another apologetic smile along with an eye roll, hoping Johnny would realise that I had nothing to do with this serious accusation. 'Perhaps Michael is in today?'

I knew that Johnny prided himself on being able to handle difficult customers, and fetching his boss would be something he would not welcome. But, in the short time I'd got to know Trevor, I was quite sure that only the boss would do.

Johnny left us waiting.

It was awkward, especially when Trevor started sharing his opinion with anyone who would listen. 'Bunch of crooks' and 'total rip-off' were his two favourite phrases. It was upsetting. I had a very good relationship with Luxton's and I wasn't about to jeopardise it for this odious man.

And then Michael Luxton appeared.

In his early seventies and wearing his hallmark black-rimmed glasses and a dapper suit and red bow-tie, he reminded me of an older version of Austin Powers.

'Are you this idiot's supervisor?' Trevor demanded, jabbing a thumb at Johnny.

'I'm the owner,' Michael replied with a broad smile. He nodded a hello to me. 'Johnny tells me that a dagger is missing from Lot 49.'

A *dagger*! So that was what all the fuss was about. Why couldn't he have said so in the first place?

Trevor glanced at me and in that split second I saw something unexpected. Panic.

Michael produced a leather-covered notepad and a

fountain pen. He removed the cap. 'Can you add any more details? If you want us to take a thorough look in our salerooms and warehouse, we'll need some specifics.'

Trevor looked blank. 'What do you mean?'

I leaned in. 'Size. Colour. Distinctive markings.'

Trevor hesitated. 'All I know is that it's a dagger.'

'Would you perhaps have a photograph?' Michael asked.

'No, I don't,' Trevor snarled. 'It's a dagger! You know what a dagger looks like!'

'Presumably it's British,' Michael asked. 'A Commando dagger? A Taylor Eye Witness dagger? A Fairburn-Sykes fighting knife?'

Trevor looked blank. 'In the catalogue it says it's a dagger.'

'So you haven't actually seen it yourself?' Michael said.

Trevor didn't answer.

'We get an enormous amount of traffic passing through here,' Michael went on calmly. 'Why, in the jewellery sale last week we had seven hundred and forty items listed. A description would be helpful.'

'One of your blokes took it,' Trevor said suddenly. 'It would be easy enough to do. Slip it into his pocket.'

Michael bristled at the accusation. 'Our staff are loyal and trustworthy. Our procedures and policies are strict.'

'They're not strict enough!' Trevor slammed his hand on the counter. Michael and Johnny continued to stay calm. I, however, just wanted the floor to open and swallow me whole. Just standing next to Trevor made it seem that I was on his side.

'Johnny tells me that when your . . . mother, is it?' Michael paused.

'Yes, Olive Banks,' said Trevor. 'She's very old and very upset.'

'And that's why we're going to sort this out,' said Michael briskly. 'When Mrs Banks called to ask for the lot to be withdrawn, it was immediately removed from the saleroom. It was a wooden crate with a lid, yes?' He looked at Johnny.

'The original leather luggage strap was secured around the crate,' Johnny declared. 'Nothing was removed.'

'But were the contents checked?' Trevor demanded.

'They were checked,' Johnny said.

Trevor's face was getting red. 'Maybe someone dropped it before they closed the lid and the dagger fell out.'

'Then we would have found it,' said Michael. 'But naturally, your satisfaction is key. I can assure you that I, personally, will make a thorough search today for this mysterious dagger. If you give me your mobile, I will call you when I have news.'

'You're not looking for it without me,' Trevor declared. 'It's very valuable.'

'I'm afraid that isn't company policy.' Michael forced a professional smile, but I could see from the coldness in his eyes that he was losing his patience. 'How do we know if we can trust *you*?'

Trevor's face darkened. He cracked and flexed his fingers and for an awful moment, I thought he was going to take a swing at Michael. But instead, he turned to me. 'Can't you say something?'

I wasn't exactly sure what he was expecting me to say so I just shrugged.

Trevor looked at Michael and then back at me. Suspicion oozed from every pore.

'Of course.' Trevor gave a snort of disgust. 'You're in on it as well, aren't you?'

'In on what?' I'd finally had enough. 'And frankly, I resent what you are implying.'

Trevor backed up and raised his hands in defeat. 'Well, it's got to be somewhere.'

Michael looked quickly at me. 'As I said, we will have another thorough search. We'll go through our CCTV cameras to see if they can provide a clue.' He gave another professional smile. 'That's all I can do. But in the meantime, why don't we start an insurance claim for you?'

Trevor seemed surprised. 'A what?'

'An insurance claim,' Michael repeated. 'If it turns out that this dagger is not recovered, then naturally you will want to file an insurance claim for compensation and by what you are implying, it was extremely valuable.'

Trevor bit his lip. 'It's not valuable enough for all that. It's . . . it's sentimental value, that's all.'

Which wasn't what he'd implied in the first place.

'I disagree,' said Michael. 'Military memorabilia are highly sought after. We have a few collectors who were disappointed when the lot was withdrawn. Two buyers had already placed their opening bids well over the reserve before we'd even started.'

Trevor thrust out his jaw. 'Well, my mum changed her mind. She's allowed to change her mind, isn't she?'

Michael gave a tight smile and our eyes met again. Thankfully I saw a glimmer of sympathy in them.

Trevor just stood there. For a moment, I didn't think he was going to let it go but with a loud huff and what sounded like an expletive under his breath, he turned and stalked out.

'I'm so sorry,' I said to Michael.

'And I'm sorry that you're somehow caught up in this,' said Michael grimly.

'It was just a favour to his mother,' I said. 'I hardly know the family!'

'Well, be careful.' Michael lowered his voice. 'I'd only say this to you in complete confidence, Kat, because we're friends, but I wouldn't be surprised if he's trying to pull an insurance claim on us. It wouldn't be the first time. He could have the dagger at home. After all, it's his word against ours.'

I thought of how Trevor suddenly backtracked when the topic of starting an insurance claim came up. Michael could be right.

We said our goodbyes and I set off in search of Trevor. He hadn't any idea where I'd parked my car and for some inexplicable reason, I got some pleasure from that. Sure enough, he was pacing up and down the car park, scouring here and there for me and when he finally saw me, he hurried over to accuse me of trying to leave without him. He really was the *end*!

On our way home I tried to find out what made this dagger so special, but Trevor answered with a series of grunts before muttering, 'Ma's going to kill me. She really is.'

Not for the first time did I wonder why Clive was helping his Uncle Trevor out. I also thought of Staci again and just couldn't fathom what she would have been doing with this ghastly man.

I was desperate to get home. I'd wasted most of the morning in Newton Abbot. I had a valuation at two at the gatehouse. And when we got stuck behind a line of cars waiting patiently for a herd of cows ambling along to their new field, I began to lose the will to live. Since when do cows move so slowly? Cow manure splattered up the side of my car. So much for living in the countryside! For a split second, clean pavements and the well-surfaced roads of city life seemed appealing.

I dropped Trevor outside Honeychurch Cottages. He didn't invite me in.

My phone pinged and Mallory's name flashed up on the screen. 'Outside your gatehouse. Can we talk? There's something I want you to see.'

Chapter Fifteen

When I pulled up behind Mallory's immaculately clean car – marvelling at how it was possible given the state of the roads – I realised just how filthy my own car was. The driver's side was coated in manure halfway up to the window.

Mallory wrinkled his nose. 'I think more rain is forecast this afternoon. Maybe it will give your car a good wash.' I noticed how his eyes twinkled with boyish charm when he smiled – something I hadn't noticed before.

My mother had persuaded her publisher to put Mallory on her next book cover. She'd sent the artist a newspaper clipping of a case he'd solved. Neither of us had yet to see the finished product but I admit that I was intrigued.

Mallory waved a brown paper bag. 'Sandwiches,' he said. 'Cheese and ham or egg mayonnaise. That's all I could get. You choose.'

Moments later we were in the galley kitchen at the back of the showroom. I flipped on the kettle and reached for two mugs, the coffee and the cafetière.

I was anxious to know what he wanted me to see but he just said, 'Let's eat first.'

As we did, we made small talk and I answered his questions about how Kat's Collectibles and Mobile Valuation Services came into being. I had never told him the story of how Mum had moved abruptly from my childhood home in Tooting down to the countryside after my father died. I kept to the truth about her spending summers with her adopted family's travelling fair and boxing emporium, which Mallory seemed to enjoy hearing about but, naturally, left out the Krystalle Storm saga. Now my mother claimed to have given up writing – presumably this next book would be her last – it was good to know I wouldn't have to keep her secret for much longer. But when Mallory asked why I had left London too, I was surprised that he knew far more about my old life as the host of *Fakes and Treasures*, as well as my relationship with David Wynne.

I found Mallory was easy to talk to – too easy, in fact.

'I don't believe in looking back,' I said, which wasn't exactly true. I seemed to look back a lot – especially thinking of Shawn. I didn't even know if Mallory knew that Shawn and I had broken up. Men didn't share that sort of news like women. Perhaps subconsciously my comment had been a trick of sorts. I wanted to see if he would mention his relationship with Stella.

Mallory gave a wry smile. 'Ah, in an ideal world it's best not to look in the rear-view mirror,' he said. 'But I am a policeman and I like to tie up the loose ends, dot the i's and cross the t's.'

His cryptic reply did nothing to answer my question and perhaps that was a good thing.

Mallory took the plates and cups to the kitchen sink.

'Just leave them,' I said. 'The house fairy will do them later.'

For a moment he was confused and then he laughed. 'Ah. My house fairy is very unreliable.'

I knew I was reading too much into things, but did he mean Stella was unreliable? Were they living together now?

'Let's go and sit down,' he said.

I'd made a point of making my office-cum-showroom as inviting as possible for people who came to see me for valuations. There was a two-seater sofa and a coffee table, and I'd put down a beautiful Persian rug. Even on this grey day, heavy with rain clouds, the three bay windows and gabled ceiling made the space light and airy. I was truly grateful to the dowager countess for allowing me to rent both gatehouses at the main entrance to the estate – not that I got footfall traffic, other than stray walkers or the occasional mob all at once if there was a random event in the adjacent parkland. But, along with my space at Dartmouth Antique Emporium, it worked well for me. Moving to Exeter with Shawn would have been difficult. Deep down I knew that our break-up had been a blessing.

Mallory brought out his mobile. 'Here,' he said. 'The wonders of technology. I was able to pull a few favours—'

'Ah, those kinds of favours,' I said and could have kicked myself. The words had been out before I could stop them. I felt my face get hot. 'That came out all wrong. I'm sorry. I just meant—'

'I know what you meant,' Mallory cut in quickly. 'There has to be some advantage to having friends in high places.'

He'd said friends. Not lovers. Kat! You must stop this!

'May I?' Mallory pointed to the seat next to me.

My stomach gave a peculiar lurch. I felt a rush of butterflies. 'Oh yes, yes of course,' I mumbled and smoothed my hands over my jeans, noticing that I had somehow got mustard on the knee from that ham sandwich.

Mallory sat down and came in close. I was acutely aware of the heat from his body.

He focused on his mobile and seemed to fumble with the keyboard. 'Ah, here.'

He tapped a button and handed the phone to me. 'It's the CCTV footage from Bridge Cottage,' he said. 'Take a look.'

I watched in growing astonishment as Brock Leavey pulled up outside the entrance. He dismounted and gently laid the Kawasaki down on its side in the middle of the road. Then he moved quickly, crossing the forecourt before going out of range.

'I don't understand,' I exclaimed. 'What on earth was he doing?'

'Keep watching.' Mallory fast-forwarded to the moment when my car came into frame. I watched myself get out and walk over to the motorbike before scanning the area. It was bizarre.

'I was looking for him,' I said. 'I called out.'

'We don't have audio. Keep watching,' he said again.

I entered the forecourt but didn't go any further.

'You didn't walk in,' Mallory pointed out. 'Why?'

'I didn't because I hate it there.' I told him about the fire and how Mum and I had almost lost our lives. 'And I got a weird prickly feeling as well. Something didn't feel right.'

Peter's Skoda came into view and stopped behind my Golf. We had a conversation. He strode over to inspect the motorbike, removed the keys and gave them to me. Then he wheeled the motorbike into the forecourt behind the low stone wall. I got in my car and drove away.

I watched as Peter checked the fuel tank then wrote a note, securing it under the windshield wiper. The CCTV followed him to the area which fly-tippers used as a dumping ground. He turned and then went in the direction of the cottage before moving out of frame.

'We don't know what happened after that,' said Mallory. 'Unfortunately, the CCTV camera is focused on the fly-tipping area not the cottage. There were no other visitors to the area at all. There was nothing until Shawn tipped me off about the motorbike and I went to check yesterday.'

'What made you look in the cellar?' I said.

'I made a thorough search of the area,' said Mallory, 'And heard moaning coming from inside the cottage.'

I was at a loss. 'I just don't understand what made Brock go inside in the first place.'

'I'll be heading to the hospital later this afternoon and plan on asking him,' he said. 'Unfortunately, I must tell him about Staci Trotter. Not a nice part of my job.' He thought for a moment. 'There is something else I'd like you to see.'

With a flurry of taps on his phone keypad, he found what

he was looking for. 'Ah. Here they are. We have the text messages between Brock and Staci.'

I was surprised. 'She was always texting on her phone.'

Mallory moved closer and showed me his mobile. It was a short exchange between the pair. To say I was shocked is putting it mildly.

Staci: Sorry, my fault. Sad emoticon.

Brock: Offer 50

Staci: Sad emoticon.

Brock: 80

Staci: Two sad emoticons.

Brock: 100

Staci: Skull emoticon

Brock: Get her address. Angry emoticon.

Staci: Thumbs up emoticon.

Mallory's eyes met mine. 'Presumably, you are the "her" in the text. Did she ask for your address?'

I nodded. 'I gave her my business card.'

'You said that Brock overtook you when you turned off the main road.'

'Yes,' I said. 'Why?'

Mallory raised an eyebrow.

A peculiar feeling began to pool in the pit of my stomach. 'What? You think . . . you mean he was waiting for me? Whatever for?'

'I was hoping you would be able to tell me,' Mallory said. 'Do you know anyone called Curtis Mainwaring?'

'Yes, I know of him in a professional capacity,' I said slowly. 'He's a dealer of high-end military memorabilia. Why?'

'We had to look at Brock Leavey's mobile to locate his next of kin,' said Mallory. 'Apart from having Staci listed, he also had Curtis Mainwaring, and Mainwaring was the last person Brock called on Saturday morning. Before lunch, in fact. The call lasted less than thirty seconds so it looked like Brock must have left him a message.'

'Brock *Leavey*? Sorry,' I shook my head. 'But I find that hard to believe.'

'In the last two weeks Brock Leavey had called Mainwaring four times,' Mallory went on. 'I can't keep the phone, of course, because it's an invasion of privacy and no crime has been committed but . . .'

He paused on the word but.

'*But* you think there could have been one.' I shook my head again. 'No, Curtis Mainwaring plays things by the book. He's an expert in his chosen field. He's a legend in the military weapon world—'

'A dealer, you say?' Mallory scribbled something down. 'Do you know where Curtis Mainwaring lives?'

'I know he used to have a shop in Knightsbridge, but he must be in his late seventies now. He might have retired.'

'Knightsbridge!' Mallory seemed impressed.

'I can't imagine why Brock would have been in touch with him,' I said. 'I viewed that sale, unless . . . the only box of military stuff belonged to George Banks.'

'And what was in it?'

'I wish I still had the catalogue,' I said. 'I can pull it up online if you'd like to look but I didn't see anything that would have appealed to Curtis's tastes. There were some Home

Guard items that although are worth something to a collector, they aren't necessarily worth a lot of money. I mean . . .' I shrugged. 'It's not like there was Hitler's watch for sale.'

Mallory's eyes widened. 'Excuse me?'

'Hitler's watch fetched over a million dollars in a private auction. It was believed to have been a gift given to Hitler for his forty-fourth birthday in 1933.'

Mallory gasped. 'Mainwaring was bidding for that?'

'No,' I smiled. 'But that's his level of interest in military weapons. As it turned out, he ended up buying some Wermacht toilet paper for one of his clients. He got teased a lot about that.'

Mallory smiled. 'Would George Banks have had anything that Mainwaring would have been interested in?'

'Home Guard stuff?' I shrugged again. 'It's hard to say who Curtis was buying for, but why all the secret phone calls from Brock Leavey? Curtis is a straightshooter – no pun intended. Michael – that's the owner of Luxton's – had told me that a couple of online bidders had already placed their bids above the reserve. He would have mentioned if Curtis was one of them. But then the lot was withdrawn.'

'Do you know why?'

'Trevor told me his mother never wanted to sell her husband's Home Guard stuff,' I said. 'When I returned the wooden crate, Trevor insisted that a dagger was missing. He even accused Luxton's of stealing it.' I frowned. 'But if this dagger was truly valuable, believe me, it would not be shoved in a box of Home Guard knick-knacks. It would have been headlining the sale.'

'So we're none the wiser,' said Mallory. 'And you? What were you buying at the auction?'

'Certainly not military memorabilia,' I said. 'I bought a box of raggedy bears and a stuffed French bulldog. Staci had been bidding for the same box. She believed she'd got it which is where my conversation with Staci all began at the counter when she realised that she had been outbid. Staci was very upset.'

'I see,' Mallory said slowly. 'And this flurry of texts between Brock and Staci was about buying this box of bears. Presumably, it wasn't to do with the crate that was also in your car. Correct?'

'She didn't mention that,' I said. 'Staci's sister is terminally ill and she'd wanted the bears for her.' I went on to explain that Staci had visited Olive and George Banks at their cottage on the estate regularly in her capacity as a carer and that was how she and Trevor had met.

'I see.' Mallory checked his notes. 'So we have a pregnant Staci who is having an affair with Trevor but living with Brock. But it's *Brock* who is contacting Curtis Mainwaring about this valuable dagger. Not Trevor?'

'I suppose so.' I wasn't sure. 'It sounds like Trevor had never seen the dagger. He couldn't describe it. He told me it was his brother – that would be Clive's father – who had dropped the lot off to Luxton's in the first place. Maybe you should talk to him?'

Mallory gave a heavy sigh. 'Not exactly straightforward, is it?'

'And Trevor didn't know that Staci had a partner,' I pointed out. 'Trevor was very emotional when he found out. Well, I told him. Maybe I shouldn't have done.'

Mallory drained his coffee cup and set it down on the table. 'Let's hope we get some answers from Brock Leavey.' He stood up and put on his coat.

His mobile rang on the coffee table. Glancing down at the Caller ID I read the name Stella. He grabbed it. 'Excuse me. I must take this.'

Mallory moved over to the window, not saying anything until a final, 'Thank you. Yes. I'll see you later this evening.'

When he turned back, he looked both thoughtful and grave. 'The lab results came back and confirmed two things. Staci Trotter was not pregnant—'

'Not pregnant!' I was shocked. 'Why on earth would she lie about that?'

'Women do strange things sometimes,' Mallory said almost to himself and then seemed to pull himself together. 'And secondly, there was a high level of alkaloids in her bloodstream.'

'I'm not sure what that means,' I said.

'Organic compounds of plant origin.' He took a deep breath. 'Staci Trotter was poisoned.'

Chapter Sixteen

'Poisoned?' I whispered. 'But . . . how?'

'That's my job to find out,' Mallory said. 'Stella has put a rush on her autopsy.'

I was shocked. 'You mean, deliberately poisoned?'

'We don't know,' said Mallory. 'She could have eaten something by mistake but we're treating it as suspicious.'

'Why?' I said. 'Why suspicious?'

'And that, I'm afraid,' he gave another wry smile, 'I really *can't* tell you at the moment. Do you have a few more minutes? I think you can help me with a timeline of Staci's movements.'

'I'll make some more coffee,' I said.

Mallory removed his coat and followed me back into the kitchen, pulled out a stool and sat at the counter. He pulled out his notebook and pen again.

'You saw her at the auction on Saturday,' Mallory said. 'Did you see her after that?'

'No. Just her car that was parked outside Eric's scrapyard,'

I reminded him. 'That would have been around six. It was still there when Shawn and I drove to Dartmouth. Staci was a carer, maybe she heard that Olive had moved onto the estate and went to check on her in her new home. Staci was wearing nurse scrubs.'

'It's possible,' said Mallory. 'Only Nightingale Care Agency uses an app which was on Staci's phone. She's legally required to record all her visits, the time she spent with each client and what they ate, as well as any medical issues that needed to be flagged up. They are very strict about logging home visits for obvious reasons. Since Staci would only get paid for the work she does, we can assume – not that I like to assume anything – that she didn't see Olive.' Our eyes met again. 'So what was she doing in Eric's scrapyard?'

'Perhaps the reason she was wearing the nursing scrubs was because she was working as a masseuse that afternoon.'

'You mean she was giving Eric Pugsley a massage?' Mallory asked.

I squashed the image of Eric in a towel lying face down on a massage table being manipulated by Staci's 'strong' fingers.

'And where was Trevor in all this?' Mallory asked.

'Out fishing with a friend,' I said. 'He told me he didn't return until midnight.'

Mallory shifted on the stool and yawned. 'Speaking of late nights. Excuse me.' He looked at his notes. 'So we have Staci outside Eric's scrapyard. Who else could have seen her car there?'

I was reluctant to say it, but I knew I had to. 'My mother might have seen her.'

Mallory raised a quizzical eyebrow. I noticed he had a habit of leaving an unspoken question in the air that compelled an answer.

'The entrance to my mother's Carriage House is opposite the gate to Eric's scrapyard,' I said. 'But my mother had never met Staci—'

'As far as you know.' A flash of amusement crossed Mallory's face. 'Shawn did warn me that Iris's name seems to come up in most investigations.'

'That's because Shawn never liked my mother,' I retorted.

Mallory seemed startled by my tone. I hadn't meant to sound sharp. At least I wouldn't have to deal with that anymore, I thought bitterly. 'And besides,' I went on, 'as I mentioned before, Mum had a meeting with Ruby and Gladys early evening on Saturday in her kitchen. I left when they arrived.'

'Ruby and Gladys?' Mallory cocked his head.

'Ruby Pritchard is the vicar's mother. Gladys Knight is the retired nurse,' I said. 'They were meeting about church matters.'

'And how long would that meeting have gone on for?' Mallory's pencil was poised.

'You would have to ask her that,' I said.

Mallory thought for a moment. 'You mentioned that Gladys had been a nurse?'

'A matron,' I corrected myself.

'Is it possible she might have known Staci Trotter?' Mallory mused. 'Even though Staci worked for a private care agency?'

'Maybe,' I said. 'Gladys hasn't lived in the village for very long. She worked in Derriford hospital in Plymouth.'

'Ah yes, I know it,' said Mallory.

Mallory continued to scribble in his notepad. 'Clive had mentioned that it had been a retired nurse who had spotted his father's serious heart condition. It sounds like Gladys saved his life.'

'Yes, that's what I heard, too.'

'Look, Kat,' Mallory began. 'You're an outsider. I'm an outsider. It's of no surprise to me that the local community closes ranks when something like this is happening. Although . . .' He frowned. 'In this case, Staci Trotter wasn't a local. She lived in Newton Abbot.'

'Just the mistress of a local,' I pointed out. 'Trevor was pretty cut up about her death.'

'Tell me more about the Banks family.' Mallory turned to a fresh page. 'What do you know about them – other than George Banks having been a war hero.'

'According to my mother – who as you know is the Honeychurch historian, the Banks family have worked on the estate for decades. The men were primarily gardeners and the women worked in the Hall. George and Olive had lived together in Ivy Cottage since the 1940s until George died and the cottage became uninhabitable.'

'How come?' Mallory asked.

'George had left the bath running. He fell asleep in it and drowned. The room flooded and brought the ceiling down but from what I've heard, the cottage should have been demolished years ago. It was in a terrible state.'

'You've seen it?'

I felt my face grow hot. 'No. Um. Oh dear, I'm repeating gossip, aren't I?'

Mallory grinned. 'No smoke without fire.' He thought for a moment. 'And you said that Paula was working at the Hall. What about Trevor?'

I explained that Trevor and Paula had been living in Vergers Cottage. 'According to Bethany, Trevor wanted to get Paula out and move Staci in. Danny felt it reflected badly on the church.' I felt my lips purse with disapproval as I thought of Danny and his secret girlfriend. 'Trevor had also financed Staci's training as a masseuse and bought her the pink Fiat. According to Bethany – maybe you should talk to Bethany, she knows more than I do—'

'I will, but go on,' Mallory said. 'I can't stand the suspense.'

'Well, according to Bethany, Paula had hoped to lease the old tearoom in Rose Cottage from Rupert – Lord Honeychurch – to open a café there but Trevor used their savings to help Staci get her masseuse licence. He also used the money to pay for his father's funeral.'

'Interesting,' Mallory mused. 'I wonder how Paula felt about that.'

'So you *are* treating Staci's death as suspicious,' I said, just to be sure.

Mallory didn't answer.

'She was out on Saturday night with Delia,' I reminded him. 'I saw her leave the cottage.'

'And that meant Paula and Delia would have driven past

the pink Fiat outside Eric's scrapyard, wouldn't it?' Mallory said.

'True,' I agreed. 'But I don't know if Paula *knew* about the new car.'

'All circumstantial, I'm afraid, with no evidence. Although . . .' Mallory got to his feet and paused. 'Have you heard of Occam's razor?' Seeing my blank look, he added, 'It's a principle of theory construction or evaluation that when faced with many possible explanations, the simpler one is usually the answer.'

Mallory pulled on his coat. 'One thing I am learning is that everyone in Little Dipperton is connected to the mothership.'

'The mothership?'

'Honeychurch Hall,' he said.

'Ha, yes. The mothership!' I grinned. 'And tonight, the village will be out in force for the showing of George Banks's favourite war film – that is, if it can actually be played.'

Mallory raised an eyebrow.

'It's a VHS cassette and apparently it's jammed in the video machine.'

'Do people still use those?' Mallory said. 'What's the name of the movie?'

'I have no idea,' I said. 'But donations are encouraged. For the restoration of the church clock, of course.'

'And everyone will be there,' Mallory said, half to himself. 'Will that include your good Samaritan, I wonder?'

'Peter? I don't know,' I said. 'But he is staying at the Hare and Hounds, which is where the movie is going to be shown.'

Mallory left. My valuation client came and went. She had brought me a beautiful Jumeau doll with a bisque face that had cracked and been badly repaired. Luckily, I was able to refer her to the hugely gifted Frances May who runs the Dolls Hospital in nearby Dartington.

I spent the rest of the afternoon downloading the photographs from the disastrous clock tower visit from my mobile onto my laptop, and from there onto a thumb drive for Danny and one for Peter. It took a lot longer than expected and involved a lot of cropping, editing and resizing the images.

My thoughts drifted to Paula. She had the motive to get Staci out of the way – especially if she had found out that Staci was pregnant – even if it turned out to be a lie. Since Mallory had claimed Staci had been poisoned, it would be easy enough for Paula to slip something into one of her picnic puffs. But where this theory fell short was Paula's opportunity for doing so. I had seen Paula leave with Delia to go to the pub. It would be easy enough for Mallory to check she had an alibi. I didn't even know if Paula and Staci had ever met unless she had bumped into her at Ivy Cottage. But I was jumping ahead. Mallory had said Staci had been poisoned but hadn't confirmed if it was deliberate. Yet.

It was around three forty-five when I heard a car pull up outside and a door slam.

A sharp knock was followed by a familiar, 'Kat! It's your mother and we need you!'

Chapter Seventeen

Mum stood in my showroom dressed as if she was going to church. A smart navy coat, leather gloves and black pumps. She was wearing a new lipstick – a flattering coral. It suited her colouring.

'Don't tell me,' I said. 'Danny's outside.'

My mother grinned. 'Yes. And Ruby and Peter, too.'

I was impressed. 'You managed to get Ruby to come out?'

'She doesn't know where we're really going yet,' Mum said sheepishly. 'Danny tricked her into thinking we were off for an afternoon drive on Dartmoor.'

'Danny said that?' *Manipulative, as well as deceptive*, I thought. I'd have to tell my mother about his girlfriend sooner rather than later. 'And where are you really going?'

'Hopefully, to see this chapel,' Mum said. 'Peter is adamant, and Danny is all gung-ho.'

'But . . . Edith made it clear that she didn't want anyone going to the chapel,' I said. 'You heard her. It's dangerous.'

'Edith's not in,' Mum said. 'We called ahead and spoke to Paula. We're meeting Lady Lavinia for tea so that's a start.'

My heart sank. 'I'd rather not come, if you don't mind.'

'We do mind,' Mum said. 'Please. Just for moral support.'

I stifled a groan. 'Fine. But I'm taking my own car so I can escape if I must.' I pointed to my mother's shoes. 'I don't think those are suitable. If you do get to see the chapel, it'll be muddy.'

'Oh.' Mum's face fell. 'I wanted to keep Ruby company with her choice of footwear.'

I raised an eyebrow.

'Danny told her that we weren't going to get out of the car,' Mum said. 'We were just going to look at Haytor, grab an ice cream from Mr Whippy – he's always up there in the afternoons – and then drive back in time for tonight's film at the pub.'

'So, he lied again.' Another black mark against the self-righteous Danny.

Mum looked taken aback by my tone. 'It's a white lie. He just wants her to get more involved with the community.'

I hesitated. Should I tell my mother now or wait until she was home and where she could throw a few chairs around without being arrested. 'I do need to talk to you afterwards. It's important.'

The car horn sounded, making her jump. 'What with that and the new doorbell, I swear I'll be needing Gladys to check my pulse.'

We went outside. I waved to Ruby who was sitting in the back seat of Peter's Skoda. Danny was riding shotgun. Mum made a comment on the muddy state of my car and climbed into the back with Ruby.

I followed them up the long drive to the Hall, admiring the flowering camelias and azaleas in a riot of pinks, scarlets and purples. In another month the rhododendrons would be in full bloom. I parked in the turning circle in front of the Hall.

I rarely used this entrance, so I was surprised to see how neat and tidy it was. There were no weeds sprouting through the gravel, and the flower beds were filled with spring daffodils, narcissi, tulips and grape hyacinths. Even the water sculpture in the centre was bubbling happily away. All thanks to Delia's excellent house and garden management skills.

The Hall looked imposing with its Palladian grand entrance and sash windows. When I first came here, the shutters were closed, and the house had a feeling of abandonment and neglect. I wasn't a fan of Delia's, but she had definitely turned the house around. There were even rumours in the village that they might think about opening it to the public on a regular basis.

Danny and Peter marched up the wide stone steps and rang the bell pull. There seemed to be some disagreement going on in the back of the Skoda between my mother and Ruby. Mum was holding the rear car door open, but Ruby was just sitting there. My mother waved me over.

'What's the matter?' I asked.

'Ruby wants to stay in the car.' Mum rolled her eyes.

Danny came over. He looked annoyed. 'What's the hold-up?'

'She doesn't want to come,' Mum said.

Danny and my mother changed places. He leaned in. 'Mother,' he said, 'now don't be silly. It's important that you join us and it's very rude of you to refuse an invitation from her ladyship.'

Ruby's jaw was set in a stubborn line. 'You told me we were going to the moors.'

'Yes, I did,' Danny admitted. 'But I didn't say when.'

Yet *another* lie! I was rapidly going off Danny.

'We're not going to the moors?' Mum feigned shock. 'Oh no! Ruby, you can't let me go in on my own. Please, dear.'

Now Peter joined us with Paula in tow. Paula was dressed in uniform and looked very official. She seemed distracted and worried and then, to my astonishment, suggested that my mother, Ruby and *I* should all stay in the car!

'Very well,' Danny said wearily. 'But what do I tell Lady Lavinia?'

'Lady Lavinia?' Ruby repeated. 'Why didn't you say it was Lady Lavinia?'

And to everyone's surprise, Ruby got out of the car and headed for the front door, cane tapping briskly over the gravel.

'Fancy that,' Mum declared. 'Ruby must have been afraid to meet the dowager countess.'

Paula caught Ruby up. She seemed nervous and told us to wait in the galleried reception area with its black and white marble floor, and hurried away.

I hadn't been in this part of the house since Delia had taken over and I was impressed at just how spotlessly clean it was. The huge crystal chandelier that hung suspended between the two domed-glass atriums was positively dazzling and the full-bodied suits of armour that were arranged randomly throughout the hall were burnished to within an inch of their lives. Small gold nameplates identified the family portraits that lined the walls and, although a few empty spaces implied that paintings had been sold, it still felt very grand. On the right, below each oil painting stood a highly polished seventeenth-century Dutch walnut marquetry side chair inlaid with flowers, foliage, parrots and urns. Interspersed between the chairs were flourishing aspidistras set on Victorian torchières.

On top of a gorgeous walnut circular table was a spectacular flower arrangement. Mum nudged me and said that Delia had taken a flower-arranging class.

Ruby gave a cry of delight. Standing by the magnificent fireplace was Florian, the stuffed, rearing polar bear dressed in a purple satin waistcoat. At the bear's feet stood a placard stating that he had been brought back from the Arctic by Gerald James Honeychurch 1840-1910, the Polar explorer. It was a sure sign that the plans to open the Hall to the public were well underway. The placard also said 'Do Not Touch' but it didn't stop Ruby.

She moved surprisingly fast with her cane and, to our astonishment, threw her arms – cane and all – around Florian's torso.

'Mother!' Danny exclaimed. 'What on earth—?'

'Don't touch the exhibit!' Paula shrieked as she hurried to Ruby's side.

'What? You think he'll bite?' Ruby sounded defiant and muttered something that sounded like, 'I've been longing to do that.'

'Her ladyship is waiting in the drawing room,' said Paula. 'Follow me.'

This too, had been transformed by Delia's magic duster. The elaborate cornices and decorative strapwork somehow seemed enhanced – possibly they had been dulled by years of grime – and even though the red silk wallpaper and tapestry hangings were faded, it only added to the richness of the room. Damask curtains fell gracefully from the four casement windows that overlooked the park. A copper Gibraltar gong sat in the corner. Daffodils and powerfully scented narcissi graced many of the little side tables that were dotted around the room. A lively fire crackled in the grate. Ruby went straight to the tiger-skin rug and poked her cane into its open mouth and giggled.

'What's wrong with Ruby?' Mum whispered, but before we could think any more about her strange behaviour, Lavinia swept into the room.

She was dressed in her usual dirty jodhpurs and a moth-eaten brown wool sweater. As always, her hair was clamped under a slumber net. There were greetings all round but Lavinia seemed flustered that there were five of us and not two.

As we waited for tea to arrive, Danny bombarded Lavinia with questions about the various antiques and *objets d'art* that graced the room. Although Lavinia answered quite happily, it was hard to follow exactly what she was saying although I did hear a lot of 'Inja' and 'Affca.'

At last Paula wheeled in the tea trolley. Along with a china pot of tea and matching sugar bowl and milk jug – Spode – there were only two cups and saucers. I spied a freshly baked fruitcake.

Delia followed closely behind, all smiles until she saw Ruby, Mum and me seated on the Chesterfield. Her eyes zeroed in on the lack of cups and saucers. She turned to Paula and the look she gave her was enough to freeze hell. Paula scuttled away.

'I'm sorry milady,' Delia said in an obsequious voice. 'Paula mentioned just two gentlemen were calling but she is still learning. Were you aware there were more?'

Lavinia mumbled something that sounded like it wasn't a problem. She also seemed intimidated by Delia's newfound power.

Paula returned with more cups and saucers. Delia supervised the pouring of the tea and the passing around of the fruit cake.

'Paula has made the cake, milady,' Delia said.

Lavinia mumbled something incoherent again, possibly 'oh *sooo*-per.'

'Is that gluten free?' Peter asked and when Paula looked blank, he added, 'I don't think I should risk it. No, thank you.'

Danny launched into the reason we were there. Delia left the room, leaving Paula standing to attention next to a rather fine eighteenth-century French tulipwood and parquetry display cabinet housing Edith's cherished porcelain snuff box collection.

'You want to see the chapel?' Lavinia seemed surprised.

Ruby uttered a small cry and then started stirring her teacup furiously. But when she lifted it to her mouth, I noticed that her hands were trembling.

I leaned over and asked her if she was feeling all right.

Ruby just nodded and attempted to put the teacup down. I took it from her and set it on the coffee table but noted that she kept hold of her plate of fruit cake.

Lavinia seemed bewildered. 'Isn't this about the village fete?'

Peter explained for the umpteenth time that he was doing a census on the number of disused chapels in the country.

'You don't need to come with us,' Peter said to Lavinia. 'Iris knows where the chapel is.'

'Vaguely,' Mum said. 'It's in the woods beyond the ha-ha. A quarter of a mile past the ornamental lake.'

'We just need permission to cross the Honeychurch grounds, nothing more,' said Peter.

'The thing is . . .' Lavinia seemed nervous. 'Edith said—'

'Obviously that would be a quicker route, but I've been looking. There is another way.' Peter produced a folded map and made a big deal of opening it and, like all ordnance survey maps, it exploded in size. He stood up and sat next to Lavinia with the map taking up most of the sofa. 'I've marked it up in yellow. Access to the chapel is a public right of way along this track here,' he traced the track with his finger, 'that is entered from that lane there. There's a cottage nearby—'

'Ivy Cottage, milady,' Mum said helpfully.

'With a footpath that goes through these woods here,' Peter jabbed at the map. 'And the chapel is there. Of course, it's much quicker to get to the chapel by cutting through the grounds but as I said – oh!'

Edith swept into the drawing room and stopped in surprise.

'Edith!' Lavinia leapt guiltily to her feet. The map fell to the floor. 'Tea in pot.'

Danny and Peter sprang to their feet, too. Ruby dropped her empty plate. With lightning speed Paula leapt forward to pick it up and darted back to her post.

Only Mum and I remained relatively calm.

Dressed in her side-saddle habit and boots, Edith looked decidedly put out and it was clear that she had not been told of our visit. I felt Ruby shift beside me. She pulled her hair forward over her scarred cheek.

Edith gave a dismissive gesture and the men sat down, but she remained standing.

'Paula,' Lavinia shouted. 'Tea. Edith.'

Paula darted forward again but Edith waved her away with a curt 'no, thank you.' She was annoyed and made no attempt at hiding it.

I waited for Lavinia to say something about why everyone was here, but Lavinia seemed paralysed. Even my mother didn't speak, and I knew why. Edith had made it very clear that the chapel was out of bounds and the two men were deliberately going behind her back.

Things were going to get ugly.

Danny cleared his throat and promptly threw Lavinia under the bus by adding, 'And if you would like to join us, Edith, you're more than welcome.'

Edith's eyes practically bugged out and I heard an intake of breath from my mother.

Danny looked keenly around the room, unaware of the two giant faux pas he had just made. Firstly, by addressing Edith and Lavinia so casually and secondly, by not just blatantly ignoring Edith's clear refusal but inviting her along to boot!

Lavinia looked miserable.

I stole a glance at Paula, who seemed to be enjoying the show. No doubt this little scene would be all over the village in the morning.

Edith pulled herself up to her full height. 'As I have already told you, that won't be possible.'

'It's for the church,' Peter said. 'Can I ask why?'

'Because it's dangerous,' Edith replied. 'If you're just doing a census, take it from me. It's a ruin and that's why it's fallen into disuse.'

Peter's expression hardened. 'I'd still like to look at it.'

'The answer is no,' Edith declared. 'And if you are considering using the public right of way, you are wasting your time. The chapel is on Honeychurch land and you would be trespassing.'

Peter and Danny both turned to my mother as if expecting her to intervene.

'And there's no point looking at Iris,' said Edith. 'The answer is still no.'

Mum seemed to find something fascinating about her shoes.

Danny gave a heavy sigh and stood up, defeated. 'Well. We tried. Sorry, Peter. We'll just have to focus on my clock.'

But I could tell from the grim expression of determination on Peter's face that he wasn't going to let this go. He started folding up the map with impressive skill. He'd obviously done it before.

'Thank you for the tea,' he said. 'But there is one more thing, milady. Do you happen to know anyone called Fudge?'

Edith stared at Peter. 'Fudge. *Fudge?* Are you talking about a pet? A rabbit, perhaps, or a hamster? Certainly not a horse. Paula will see you out.'

We had been dismissed. Lavinia made a bolt for the door but then the most extraordinary thing happened when Ruby got to her feet.

Edith hurried towards her and put a hand on Ruby's arm. 'Wait!'

Ruby froze.

'I know you.' Edith came closer and then, to my astonishment, she pushed Ruby's hair gently aside and, what was even more astonishing, Ruby let her do it.

We all watched mesmerised as Edith traced the scar on Ruby's cheek.

'It *is* you! Oh, little Ruby.' Edith seemed overcome with emotion. 'Where did you go? What on earth happened that night?'

Chapter Eighteen

Danny wasn't the only one who was shocked that Ruby had indeed been to Honeychurch Hall before and had never mentioned it – even when she knew that Little Dipperton would become their new home. I suddenly remembered Ruby's bizarre behaviour when she ran to embrace the stuffed polar bear and then stuck the tip of her cane into the mouth of the tiger-skin rug.

We all took our seats again.

It was Edith who told us that Ruby had been evacuated to Honeychurch Hall during the war. Mum seemed spellbound by this turn of events and Peter was transfixed. It sounded like Ruby had run away and no one had ever seen her again.

'I still remember the day you arrived,' Edith said. 'I was only fourteen. What were you? Eight? Nine? You arrived with a little boy—'

'Raymond, milady,' said Ruby. 'His parents came and got him, though. Just a month later.'

Mum took Ruby's hand and gave it a comforting squeeze.

'Your name was written on a luggage label that was pinned to your coat and you each carried a gas mask.' Edith's voice was gentle. 'Well meaning, but so cruel to separate children from their parents.'

'Unless they were dead,' Ruby whispered. 'Like mine were.'

'It was the bombing, milady,' Mum put in. 'During the first three days of the war, over six hundred and seventy thousand unaccompanied schoolchildren were moved to the country.'

Paula brought in a fresh pot of tea and seemed equally intrigued by this astonishing revelation, especially when it transpired that Ruby had stayed for a very short time with Olive and George in Ivy Cottage.

'Have you seen Olive yet?' Edith said, then added to herself, 'No. Perhaps not. You weren't at the funeral service or at the plaque-laying ceremony.'

'Mother doesn't like crowds,' Danny said, shooting a worried look at Ruby. 'Perhaps we should go.'

I glanced at Ruby's pale face. I could tell she was desperately uncomfortable.

'I'm so sorry about what happened,' Edith said quietly. 'I should have stayed behind but when my parents were killed . . .' A flash of pain crossed Edith's features. 'Yes, I should have taken better care of you.'

'What year was this, Ruby?' Peter said.

Ruby didn't answer. I studied her pinched face and in her eyes I saw something unexpected. It was panic.

'The vicar is right,' Edith cut in. 'You are looking tired,

dear. Perhaps you would like to come to tea one afternoon? You can tell me what you have been doing all these years.'

Ruby needed no encouragement to leave. She was up on her feet and heading for the door in no time at all.

Danny bounded ahead and took his mother's arm, calling a goodbye over his shoulder. Peter, Mum and I followed, leaving Edith watching motionless with an expression on her face that was impossible to read and when I said I'd see her tomorrow afternoon for our weekly ride, she didn't appear to hear me.

Mum pulled me aside in the galleried reception hall. 'We must talk!' She called out to Danny. 'We'll see you all later at the pub this evening. I'm going back with Kat.'

Moments later Mum and I were speeding down the drive. 'I don't believe it.' She was incredulous. 'Why on earth didn't Ruby say she'd been here before! Even her own son had no idea.'

'Perhaps that's why she avoids people in the village,' I suggested. 'Maybe she didn't have a very happy experience.'

'I'd love to be a fly on the wall when they get back to Vergers Cottage,' Mum declared. 'And did you see Edith's face? She looked very upset. What on earth happened? Ran away? Why would Ruby run away?'

'I wonder how old everyone was at that time,' I mused.

'Edith said she was fourteen,' said Mum. 'Olive must have been what, twenty, maybe a bit older than that and George was older than her. I'm trying to remember his date of birth on the plaque.'

'Did you notice how interested Peter was in all of it?' I said. 'And why does he keep asking about this person called Fudge?'

Mum shrugged. 'All well before my time, dear. But I do agree. As I have said before, there's just something off about him. I may do a bit of sleuthing.'

'So he's not a fish in your pond anymore?' I teased.

'No, my focus is on Danny now,' Mum said. 'I've got to beat Miss Pips to the post.'

I hated to burst Mum's bubble, but it had to be done before she made a fool of herself.

'Ah, we might want to talk about that,' I said quickly. 'Quick snifter before the pub? We've got time.'

Mum regarded me with suspicion. 'That's unusual for you to suggest it.' She suddenly reached across and gently gave my arm a squeeze. 'How thoughtless of me. Shawn is bound to be there this evening.'

I drove into the carriageway and cut the engine but didn't move.

'Why do I have that feeling that whatever it is, isn't going to be pleasant,' said Mum.

'Because you're right, it isn't.' I took a deep breath. 'Danny is already seeing someone.'

Mum roared with laughter. 'Oh, good grief, if you mean Gladys,' she scoffed. 'You couldn't be more wrong.'

'It's not Gladys,' I said. 'It's a woman in Newton Abbot.'

It felt as if all the air had left my car. I glanced at my mother, who looked as if she was about to be sick.

I was worried. 'Are you okay?'

'How do you know?' she said.

'Because when I went to Luxton's this morning, I had to park in a residential street. I saw his motorbike.'

'How do you know it was his?' Mum exclaimed.

'Apart from the fact it's very distinctive,' I said. 'I recognised his number plate. PRZ HM. And I saw him leaving this woman's house. I also saw Gladys this morning and she told me that Danny had been gone all night.'

'All night,' Mum whispered. 'I don't believe you.'

'Why would I lie?' I said, exasperated.

'No. That can't be right.' Mum's eyes watered. I thought for an awful moment that she might cry.

Now it was my turn to reach over and give her a comforting squeeze. 'I'm so sorry.' To be honest, I hadn't expected her to be this upset and felt terrible. Maybe I should have just kept out of things and let her find it out for herself. 'And it's obvious that Gladys doesn't know either,' I went on. 'Which must be of some consolation.'

'But . . .' Mum wiped away a tear. 'What about all his preaching and sermons about no sex before marriage and the Ten Commandments?'

I shrugged. 'Maybe that's why he wanted to move to Devon in the first place. Maybe he'd known this mystery woman before. You should ask your new best friend Ruby.'

'I will,' Mum said. 'But how could Danny have encouraged me like that! What a selfish thing to do! Unless . . .' She frowned, then brightened. 'Perhaps he was visiting someone in the parish.'

'Newton Abbot is not his parish,' I said. 'And besides, I saw her standing at the front door in a dressing gown. She looked angry and he seemed upset. I think they must have had an argument.'

'An argument!' Mum brightened again. 'So even if there was something to it, there might not be anymore.'

'I think you're missing the point,' I said.

'No. I'm not. Oh, what does it matter?' Mum slumped forward. 'I'm too old for all this nonsense. And anyway, at least I won't have to ride in that awful sidecar.'

'I'm sorry,' I said again. 'Are we going to just sit here, or shall we go inside and have a drink?'

We adjourned to the kitchen.

'You pour the drinks and give me a large one,' Mum said. 'I just need to do something.' And she left the room.

I did as I was told. Shortly afterwards, Mum, looking defiant, returned holding two framed samplers and put them on the kitchen table. Then, she removed the 'Cleanliness is Next to Godliness' sampler from the oak dresser. 'These are going to the charity shop first thing in the morning.'

'What? You're giving up all your good deeds?' I exclaimed. 'What about the church circular? The flower rota?'

'Gladys can knock herself out.' Mum picked up her glass and drained it. 'I don't think I'll bother going tonight.'

'You have to,' I said. 'I gave you moral support and tonight it's my turn. Shawn will be there.'

Mum pulled a face. 'All right but I'm only going just for you. What were you doing in Newton Abbot anyway?'

So I told her the whole sorry tale about taking Trevor back to Luxton's to hunt for a missing dagger.

Mum didn't seem to be listening. 'I can't believe Danny cheated on me. He led me on and all the time, he had someone else.'

I rolled my eyes. 'No, if anyone cheated on anyone, it was Staci. She cheated on Trevor and her long-term partner Brock.' And I filled Mum in on that conversation too in the hope that it would distract her from her own misery.

It worked.

Mum's jaw dropped. 'And you say this Staci masseuse person wasn't pregnant after all?'

'Not only that,' I said. 'Mallory believes she might have been poisoned! He wouldn't commit to saying if it was deliberate – they are still running tests.'

'I bet it was deliberate,' Mum said. 'And I bet I know who did it. Paula.'

'Not unless she can clone herself,' I said. 'Paula was with Delia on Saturday night at the pub. The timing doesn't work.'

'It might if it was a slow-acting poison like . . .' She frowned. 'Anti-freeze.'

'No, Mallory said it was something to do with alkaloids.'

'Aha! Plants!' Mum was triumphant. 'Told you. Paula must have done it. She's always foraging about in fields and rivers.' She thought for a moment. 'And Mallory told you all this?'

'He was very generous with his information,' I said.

Mum seemed impressed. 'Man B certainly makes a refreshing change from Man A.'

'Speaking of Man A,' I said. 'We should drink up and go. Don't forget to bring our tickets.'

'I wonder what the film is,' Mum mused. 'Something cheerful like *Saving Private Ryan*? Or maybe *Fury*. I loved Brad Pitt and his tank in *Fury*.'

'Alas no,' I said. 'It's some old black and white film. One of George's favourites, apparently. Maybe we can sneak out when the lights go dim.'

Chapter Nineteen

As usual, there was no room to park outside the pub. Danny's motorbike and sidecar were inexplicably parked on a dangerous bend.

'What's he parked there for?' Mum said with a sneer. 'I bet he plans on making a quick getaway to Newton Abbot.'

I didn't comment.

Much against my better judgement, I parked in the only spot in front of Gladys's Peugeot opposite Vergers Cottage. 'And if she blocks me in,' I said to Mum, 'I will scream.'

The Hare and Hounds was packed. We headed to the function room where Gladys – dressed as if she was going to a ball in a long black dress – was waiting for us at the door. She looked worried. She was also sweating. Beads of perspiration were gathering on her forehead and when she touched my arm, her hand felt clammy.

'Iris! Thank heavens you're here,' she exclaimed. 'It's a disaster! Danny's been asking for you.'

'Oh?' Mum sounded bored. 'Why?'

An hour ago, my mother would have elbowed everyone out of her way to get to Danny but not anymore.

'He thought he'd fixed the machine but when he put the cassette in again, there was click and a whirr,' said Gladys. 'Those magic fingers of his just couldn't get the cassette out again. He wants to screen something else and needs your opinion.'

'Does he now? My opinion?' Mum drawled. 'Lucky me.'

'I suggested *The Passion of the Christ* to get us in the mood for Lent,' Gladys went on. 'But he said no, it must be a war film. It's what Olive . . . ' She swayed slightly on her feet and reached out to steady herself on the wall. 'Goodness, I feel a little dizzy.'

I regarded her with concern. 'It is stuffy in here. Perhaps you should sit down. Mum and I will go and help Danny.'

Gladys mumbled a thank you and said something about going outside for some fresh air.

'Iris! There you are!' Danny prowled towards us. 'I need your advice.'

'Gladys told me that you've broken the video machine,' Mum said bluntly. 'Something about your fat fingers snapping the tape.'

Gladys hadn't said any such thing!

Danny seemed hurt. He reddened. 'I've brought my laptop and I can get onto Netflix. We need to pick another movie. Come this way.' He took her arm and steered her deftly through the throng and into the function room. I trailed after them, unable to stop looking to see if Shawn was already there. He was.

The function room had been transformed into a screening room with improvised arena-styled seating. Benches had been brought in from the beer garden – unfortunately some with green mildew – and whatever chairs were to hand.

The screen itself was the rear, white-painted wall – well, as white as it was possible to be in a function room that had not been decorated since smoking was made illegal. Danny had set his laptop and projector on a small side table.

People were taking their seats and there was an air of excited expectation with plenty of them trying to guess which film it might be. Olive was in the front row with Paula, Trevor, Clive and Janet. Everyone looked smart.

Danny, Mum and I huddled around his laptop.

'How about *Dad's Army*?' Mum suggested. 'It's got Catherine Zeta-Jones. Everyone loves her.'

'Olive doesn't want contemporary,' said Danny. 'She wants an old black and white war film.'

'How about *The Longest Day*?' I said. 'That's a classic. Loads of stars like Clint Eastwood and Richard Burton.' I gestured to the gathered viewers. 'So many of them would remember those actors and I bet you can find it on Netflix.'

Peter Becker, immaculately turned out as always in a navy blazer with a cravat, beige flannel trousers and navy loafers, came over to join us. 'Do you need some help?'

'I think we're okay, thank you,' said Danny with a slight edge to his voice. As a vicar, you'd think he would forgive and forget about the clock tower incident, but he was human after all.

Peter hovered. 'I thought perhaps the Honeychurch family would be here.'

'Delia Evans, who is head of house, is representing the family.' Danny gestured to Delia, who was dressed in a pinstripe suit and pearls, making small talk to some of the villagers.

'Rupert is buying the first round for everyone,' said Danny.

'You mean Lord Rupert,' Mum put in. 'That's his correct title, Danny.'

'And where is Ruby this evening?' Peter chimed in.

'At home,' said Danny. 'As you know, she doesn't like crowds.'

'Perhaps I could have a quick chat with her tomorrow?' Peter asked.

Danny eyed him with suspicion. 'What for?'

But before Peter could answer, Trevor appeared. 'What's the problem? Why hasn't the film started yet?'

Danny filled them in about the broken video player. 'Kat suggested *The Longest Day*. I can screen that from my laptop.'

Trevor nodded approval.

'What was the name of the original film that you wanted to show?' Peter asked Trevor.

'Maybe it *was The Longest Day*.' Trevor frowned. 'Day something.'

'Do you mean, *Went the Day Well?*' Peter asked.

'Yeah maybe,' said Trevor. 'Why?'

Peter grunted. 'Of course it would be.'

Trevor stuck out his jaw and took a menacing step towards Peter. 'Exactly what's that supposed to mean?'

Peter seemed surprised by Trevor's reaction and so was I. He raised his hands in surrender. 'Nothing. I'll go and take my seat. I bought a ticket.'

'We should find our seats, too,' Mum said to me.

'I've saved you a seat, Iris.' Danny pointed to a hardback chair next to the wall close to the projector.

'I'm sure Gladys will be happy to take it,' Mum retorted and left.

Danny looked after my mother with some bewilderment, and then at me. I shrugged a sorry.

But when Mum and I found our seats were numbered, I realised I was sitting on Shawn's right. His grandmother was on his left.

Mum lowered her voice. 'Do you want me to sit between you?'

'I'm okay. Honestly.'

Shawn jumped up politely when I made my way to take my place. He was wearing yet another tie that I had bought him. This one had been for Christmas. It was one hundred per cent silk and embroidered with 1960s-era railway engines in bright yellow and pale blue against a scarlet background.

Shawn saw I'd noticed and gave a hopeful smile. It only made me feel sad. And then he asked after my day, to which I answered, 'fine'. It felt awkward and fake.

Finally, everything was ready to go. Danny gestured for Olive to come to the front. Trevor materialised from the sidelines to help his mother with her walker. A cordless microphone was thrust into Olive's hand.

Olive spoke with surprising confidence. There wasn't a single quiver in her voice as she boasted about her husband's derring-do in the time of the Great Threat – as she named it – of a German invasion along the coastline.

'Unfortunately, the vicar has got the film my husband wanted to show this evening stuck in the video player,' Olive went on. There were heckles and catcalls. I felt sorry for Danny but only for a split second. 'But the message then was the same as it is in today's world.' Olive took a dramatic pause. 'We must always be vigilant and aware that strangers are not always what they seem.'

There were a few murmurs of surprise at this last comment. Mum gave me a nudge and whispered. 'Do you think she's talking about call-me-Danny or Peter the Pathetic?'

Danny sprang to his feet, took the microphone and initiated the applause with evangelical enthusiasm. 'Thank you, Olive. That was wonderful. So, without further ado, I give you *The Longest Day*. Lights, Gladys.'

The lights stayed on.

'Gladys?' Danny scanned the function room, as did everyone else, for his acolyte. There was no sign of Gladys.

Danny searched the audience and found my mother. 'Iris, the lights please.'

'I can't get out,' Mum said loudly.

'I'll do it!' Paula shouted and got up from the front row. She flipped the light switch and we were plunged into darkness.

The image from Danny's projector was a little blurry on the back wall and the sound would have played better with independent speakers, but it was just about watchable.

Three hours later, the lights went back on to starts of surprise and a lot of yawning.

'More like the longest night,' Mum muttered. 'What happened? I fell asleep.'

'The usual,' I said, having done the same.

There was a mass exodus to the bar. Shawn and Peggy Cropper went out by the fire exit, meaning I didn't speak to him again. I caught a glimpse of Mallory, who must have sneaked in during the film and was talking to Peter Becker beneath the arch to the snug.

'I'll get the drinks, you find us a table,' Mum said.

I spied Willow, home from uni, who often worked for me at Dartmouth Antique Emporium and was now helping her Aunt Doreen take around platters of canapés bearing flags with names like wild mushroom and garlic tart and chanterelle and watercress beignet.

I had brought the thumb drives containing the photos of the clock tower in my tote bag. Now seemed as good a time as any to hand them over. I made a beeline for Danny, who was sitting next to Olive engaged in a very serious conversation that I couldn't hear. When I hovered over them, the two abruptly stopped talking.

Peter Becker joined us and for the umpteenth time mentioned he was doing a census on all the disused chapels in the country. He handed Olive yet another business card.

'I hear that you and your late husband, my condolences by the way,' said Peter, 'lived at Ivy Cottage during the war.'

'We lived at Ivy Cottage right up until my husband died,' said Olive with a hint of pride. 'I'm hoping that the repairs to the cottage won't take too long so I can get home again.'

Home? Didn't Olive know that the cottage was going to be pulled down? But before I could mention it, Peter had plunged on. 'You must have been there when the chapel was hit by a stray bomb. Do you recall when it was?'

A flicker of something I couldn't understand crossed Olive's face. 'What was your name again, dear?'

'Peter Becker.'

Olive frowned. 'Now, let me see. George would have been on night patrol in the village. I'd usually sleep at the Hall when he wasn't home in case we had an air raid.' She closed her eyes, as if trying to remember. Peter looked on hopefully and then Olive's eyes snapped open. 'No, it's gone. I can't remember exactly when the chapel was bombed but if I do, I'll let you know. Why? Is it important?'

'Yes. For the census.' Peter thought for a moment. 'Does the name Fudge mean anything to you?'

'Fudge? Fudge. You mean like sweeties?' Olive shook her head slowly. 'No. Should it?'

Peter smiled. 'I just wondered. If you do remember, please call me.'

'When are you leaving?' Olive asked.

'Tomorrow evening,' said Peter.

'Tomorrow!' I exclaimed. 'Then I must give you this!' I delved into my tote bag for the two thumb drives of photographs. I gave one to Danny and the other to Peter. 'As promised,' I said. 'Photographs of St Mary's clock.'

'The clock?' said Olive. 'Goodness. Whatever for? I thought you were interested in the chapel.'

'We're going to restore the clock,' Danny declared. 'And Peter's going to help us, aren't you, Peter?'

Peter didn't look so sure.

'That's why we've been having all these fundraisers, Olive,' Danny went on. 'It's going to be digitised! We'll pull the old mechanism out and install a new one. No more climbing all those steps to wind it up. I believe you used to do that, didn't you?'

'No,' said Olive. 'I don't know who told you that. I've never been up in the tower. I ... I don't have a head for heights.'

'Join the club,' mumbled Peter.

'*Really?*' Danny seemed surprised. 'When your husband came to visit me he told me everyone in the village thought you were so brave to volunteer to wind up the clock.'

'His mind was gone,' Olive said. 'I don't know why he thought it was me. Where is Trevor? I'm getting tired now.'

'Let me go and find him for you.' Danny left just as Mum returned with two glasses of red wine and passed one to me. 'Sorry, I got waylaid by Delia. Cheers!'

'Not Gladys?' I asked.

'Haven't seen her all evening,' said Mum. 'What have I missed?'

'I was just talking to Olive about the chapel and if she remembered when it was bombed.' Peter clearly wasn't going to let anything go. 'You're the historian, Iris. Wouldn't it have been documented somewhere?'

'I'll do some sleuthing.' Iris said. 'Perhaps you should ask Ruby.'

'I did,' said Peter. 'She doesn't remember.'

'Isn't it a small world?' Mum turned to Olive. 'Fancy Ruby being evacuated to Little Dipperton during the war. Have you seen her yet, Olive?'

Olive looked blank. 'Evacuated? Who?'

'Ruby was evacuated from London to escape the bombings,' Mum said. 'I'm surprised Paula didn't mention it to you after we went up to the Hall this afternoon.'

A pink flush began to spread across Olive's cheeks. 'I don't know what you're talking about. I don't remember any children from London. Who told you that?'

'The dowager countess recognised Ruby,' Mum said. 'Apparently Ruby ran away. Her ladyship was quite shocked to see her again.'

'No. She's mistaken.' Olive shook her head vehemently. 'Put it down to old age.'

Danny returned with Trevor. 'Paula's got the car outside, Ma, but we've got to wait for Delia. She promised her a lift. Do you want to wait here or—'

'I'll wait in the car.' Olive stood up and grabbed her walker and left without saying goodbye to anyone – not even to the vicar.

Mum looked uncomfortable. 'Was it something I said?'

'Iris, do you fancy a nightcap?' Danny asked.

'No, thank you,' Mum said primly. 'I came with Kat, and I'll go home with Kat.'

Danny recoiled. In fact, his reactions to her barbed

comments were making me wonder if I had imagined him in Newton Abbot. Surely there couldn't be more than one Harley-Davidson and sidecar with the number plate PRZ HM?

Mum took my arm and we left, cutting through the graveyard to get back to my car.

'I don't believe it!' I wailed as I looked at Gladys's yellow Peugeot. Yet *again*, she had re-parked on the diagonal, blocking our exit. 'What is wrong with her?'

'She must have done it when the film was on,' Mum said.

'Or before,' I pointed out. 'I didn't see her during the evening at all.'

Mum offered her hand. 'Give me your car keys. I might be able to squeeze in. I've lost a bit of weight recently. That's what love does, or should I say, did. I suppose the pounds will pile back on now that whatever we had is over.'

I crossed the lane and hammered on the door of Blackberry Cottage. There was no answer, but all the lights were on. I knew Gladys was home.

'Gladys!' I yelled out. 'You need to move your car.'

I stepped back into the lane and looked up at the upstairs window. There didn't seem to be any movement. No curtain twitching. Nothing.

'She's home,' I heard a voice behind me say.

It was Ruby and she was dressed for bed in a tartan high-neck flannel nightdress and fluffy slippers.

'I saw her come home earlier than expected,' said Ruby. 'She moved her car, and then went inside.'

I was beginning to get concerned. Gladys hadn't looked very well earlier. For her to miss such a big event, and the opportunity to be close to Danny, was out of character. 'Do you think she's okay?'

'Go and find out.' Ruby pointed to a terracotta pot full of cheerful yellow pansies. 'She keeps her key under there.'

'Gladys might just be asleep but—' I felt a surge of annoyance. 'I still need to move her car.'

'Blocked you in again, has she?' Ruby gave a little laugh and lowered her voice. 'Danny's taken to parking his motorbike down the road. He got tired of having to knock on her door. I told her she's wasting her time with him, but she won't listen.'

I had wondered why Danny had been parked on that dangerous corner and now I knew.

The key was just where Ruby had said it was. I opened the door and called for Gladys again.

Like all the cottages in the village, the front door opened directly into the sitting room. It had a beamed low ceiling with a lot of good quality furniture. I remembered that Gladys's husband had left her heavily in debt. According to village gossip, she'd had to sell the family home to pay it off and that was why she was renting.

The fire in the grate had gone out but the TV was still on, broadcasting a reality cooking show. When I spied the four-top mahogany table pushed up against the wall, I couldn't believe what I was seeing.

The French bulldog was there along with the bears that I had dropped off that morning next to a stack of Krystalle Storm paperbacks. I moved closer and stopped in astonishment. Each toy had a price tag pinned to its ear and my mother's novels had stickers on the covers saying £10 per copy!

I was shocked and disappointed. Who does that? First, the toys were supposed to be a donation for sick children. And my mother's books? Weren't they going back into the community shop after Lent?

'Gladys!' I shouted out again and checked the kitchen, flipping the light switch. I noticed a bottle of Tums on the countertop along with a brochure for Viking Cruises.

A strange sense of unease began to seep through my body. I moved to the corner of the living room and opened the latch door to the staircase that led to the two rooms above.

The stench hit me straight away. It was the unmistakable acrid smell of vomit that made my stomach roil.

The bathroom door was ajar. The first thing I saw were Gladys's feet. She was lying outstretched on her back. The expression on her face was something I would never forget. Her mouth was stretched in a terrifying grimace, her eyes stared without seeing.

Gladys was dead.

Chapter Twenty

It took just five minutes for the Cruickshank twins to sprint across the graveyard from the pub. Although not technically on duty, they always carried a first response first aid kit wherever they went.

I waited outside, shaken and very upset, refusing Ruby's offer of hot sweet tea just as my Golf crawled into view with my mother at the wheel.

I opened the passenger door but before I could say a word she cut me off. 'Get in! Hurry!'

I suppose I was on autopilot because I got in.

We pulled away. I started to shake uncontrollably.

'What's the matter now?' Mum seemed agitated.

'Gladys has been poisoned.' I tried to forget the image of Gladys's agonised expression but failed.

'Poisoned!' Mum exclaimed. 'I thought she looked a bit peaky.'

'No, Mum,' I whispered. 'She's dead. The Cruickshank twins are with her but we need to go back.'

'Um. No. Most definitely not.' Mum hit the accelerator and we sped away.

'Sometimes, I just don't understand you.' I felt terrible. 'I know you didn't like Gladys but – oh Mum, it was awful.' I replayed the horrific scene and added that I had seen Mum's Krystalle Storm books there for sale as well as the French bulldog and my bears. 'She was selling them!'

But my mother didn't seem remotely interested. In fact, she didn't even comment. She just drove in silence and even when we stopped inside the carriageway, she didn't get out of the car.

'Didn't you hear anything I said at all?' I was puzzled. 'We're here, by the way.'

Still, my mother didn't move and then, finally, she turned to me. 'Oh, Kat, I've done something really naughty.'

My heart turned right over.

'No,' I whispered. 'Please tell me you didn't have anything to do with Gladys's death.'

'Of course I didn't!' Mum seemed insulted. 'But . . . it doesn't look good.'

And then, as we sat in my car, I listened with growing disbelief at one of the most stupid things my mother had ever done in her life.

'What do you mean *Vaseline*?' I was aghast. 'Why couldn't you have written a note and stuck it under the windscreen wipers like any normal person?'

'Because Vaseline was the only thing I had in my handbag,' said Mum. 'But I've just been thinking. Rain is forecast for tonight. It will wash off.'

I groaned. 'It won't. Vaseline can't be washed off with water.'

'Of course it can,' Mum faltered. 'Can't it?'

'No, Mother. You need white vinegar and hot water. We'll have to go back.' I clapped my hand over my forehead. 'But we can't! The police will be there by now. Oh no!'

Mum looked stricken. 'We have to . . . we have to . . . because . . .'

And then it hit me. 'What exactly did you write on Gladys's windscreen?'

My mother mumbled something incoherent.

'Excuse me?'

She gave a heavy sigh. 'All I wrote was "Idiot. You'll be sorry." That's all.'

'You'll be sorry? Oh, Mum.' I shook my head in dismay. 'That's just great, isn't it? Brilliant. And there were just two cars parked there – mine and Gladys's. Ruby knows I needed Gladys to move her car because she saw me.'

'Ruby won't say anything,' Mum said. 'She's my new friend. And besides, what is there to say?'

'I thought it was too good to be true,' I muttered.

'And what's that supposed to mean?' Mum demanded.

'You!' I exclaimed. 'You just can't help yourself, can you?' I was upset. It was a combination of so many things. Staci Trotter, Brock Leavey lying in wait for me, Shawn and me breaking up and now finding Gladys's body.

'I'm sorry,' Mum said in a small voice. 'We'll just go back and wipe it off. You can park the car at the pub. I can cut through the graveyard.'

'We don't really have a choice, do we?'

'Stay here, I'll get the supplies.' Mum slipped out of the car. I got into the driver's seat. As I waited, I thought of Staci and Gladys both being poisoned. I could see a motive for having Staci out of the way, but not Gladys. Perhaps Paula's foraging skills left a lot to be desired. But surely, if she'd baked a dodgy batch, wouldn't all the revellers be dropping like flies?

My mother seemed to be taking for ever but when I checked my watch, it had only been five minutes. I was about to go inside and find out what on earth she was doing when she reappeared dressed from head to toe in black. She carried a bottle of white vinegar and a pink Thermos emblazoned with what looked like one of her heroes from a Krystalle Storm book cover.

I threw open the passenger door. 'Why are you dressed as if you are going to rob a bank?'

'I found one of Alfred's balaclavas,' Mum said. 'He used to use them when he was on the job in the old days.' She pulled it over her head and turned to me, her eyes wide. 'What do you think?'

Despite the seriousness of the situation, I had to giggle.

'We'll be fine,' Mum said cheerfully. 'It'll be an adventure!'

Unfortunately, our good humour was short-lived. As we sped down the service drive another car approached, forcing us to stop in a turnout so it could pass.

It was a maroon Ford Escort. The car stopped and the window opened. To my dismay I stared into the face of Paula at the wheel and Trevor beside her. Olive and Delia were in the back.

'Don't stop,' Mum said desperately. 'Just let them pass.'

But Paula's car didn't move so we couldn't move either.

I opened my window.

'Did you hear what happened to Gladys?' Paula said.

Mum leaned over me – thankfully she had removed her balaclava. 'Yes, we're going back to see if there is anything we can do.'

'She's dead,' Paula said. 'Heart attack.'

'A heart attack,' Mum echoed. 'Fancy that.'

'We spoke to the twins,' Paula went on. 'And they said the call for help came from Kat. Where did you find her, Kat?'

'In the bathroom,' I said.

Mum leaned over me again. 'Kat's very experienced at finding bodies. It happens to her a lot. We must get back. Bye!' She hit my electric window button, cutting off whatever else Paula had been about to say. They drove on by and we continued our journey.

'Why would they say Gladys had a heart attack?' Mum mused.

'I have no idea,' I said. 'All I know is that I hope I never have to see something like that again. Can we change the subject?'

We drove the rest of the way to Little Dipperton in silence.

Ten minutes later, we were back in the village. Danny's motorbike and sidecar were still parked on the dangerous corner. A few lights were still on in the pub. I was able to take a space out front and partially hidden under a bank of overhanging trees. It gave me a good view of Peter's Skoda and the lychgate to the churchyard.

'I'll wait here,' I said. 'Take your mobile. I'll text you if it looks like anyone is coming. Hopefully Danny is tucked up in bed and poor Gladys has been taken to the morgue.'

Mum darted across the street, slipped through the lychgate, and was swallowed into the night.

I watched the bar slowly empty out. A few stragglers set off on foot. The last two remaining cars drove away.

I began to get anxious. Mum seemed to be taking a very long time. And then Peter Becker emerged from the Residents Only side door on the far left-hand side. He went straight to his Skoda and got in. I checked my watch. It was nearly eleven thirty. He started the engine and drove away. Where on earth would he be going at this time of night?

Mere seconds later, Mum yanked open the door and slid into the driver's seat. 'Gosh. I've got an adrenaline rush from doing that. I can't imagine why Alfred would have given up such a thrill!'

I started the car straight away. 'Did anyone see you?'

'I was delayed by a couple of teenage lovebirds in the graveyard,' Mum said. 'I think one was Willow.'

'No police? Ambulance?' I asked.

'Yes and no,' Mum said. 'No ambulance, no Mallory. But a young policeman was standing in front of Gladys's front door. He'll be there all night, poor boy.'

'How do you know?' I demanded.

'Because I saw Danny go outside with a Thermos of what I presume was hot soup for him.'

'Thermos!' I exclaimed. 'Where's yours?'

'Blast!' Mum exclaimed. 'I must have left it on the wall.'

'Oh Mum!' I groaned. And, as a police car passed us with lights flashing, I added, 'We can't go back now.'

It was as we left Little Dipperton behind that we came upon the Skoda. It was driving at a snail's pace, braking every few moments.

I immediately slowed down and cut the lights.

'What are you doing?' Mum said. 'We need to get home as quickly as possible.'

'That's Peter,' I said and told Mum that I had seen him sneak out of the pub.

And then the Skoda turned into a gap between two banks of trees.

'Where on earth is he going?' Mum sounded bemused.

I gasped. 'He must be looking for the access road to Ivy Cottage. And that's not it.'

'How do you know?'

'Because I ride this way all the time,' I said. 'That's just a farm track that ends in a gate. You can't go any further. Oh dear.'

'Why oh dear?'

'It's been raining. Not only will he get his car stuck, but he'll also find it difficult to reverse out!'

'In that case it looks like he's going to spend the night in his car,' Mum said. 'Well, he's more of an idiot than I thought.'

'Why is Peter so desperate to see the chapel, Mum?' It was something that had begun to niggle at me. 'Why does it matter when the bell tower was bombed?'

'I have no idea,' said Mum.

We didn't speak again until I pulled into the carriageway. Mum gave me a peck on the cheek and said, 'Perhaps Olive made a good point. Remember what she said? We must always be vigilant and aware that strangers are not always what they seem.'

'Amen to that,' I said, and bid Mum good night.

Chapter Twenty-one

The following morning dawned unusually sunny. I got up early and headed straight for the car wash in Totnes. I was desperate to talk to Mallory in the hope that he had an update on Gladys – and, for that matter, on Staci. I'd spent a restless night where Gladys's face haunted my dreams and the word 'vigilant' echoed in my head.

As I drove through Little Dipperton, I slowed down as I passed Church Lane. A police car was parked outside Blackberry Cottage. I didn't stop. I thought of the defaced windscreen on the yellow Peugeot and the forgotten Thermos and suspected that it was only a matter of time before both would be traced back to my mother.

I continued out of the village but as I drew closer to the entrance to that farm track, curiosity got the better of me. I had to know if Peter's car had been stuck there all night or not.

I donned wellies and started up the rutted track on foot, picking my way through deep puddles and slick mud. I could see that the Skoda's wheels had done their best to ride the furrows and grooves but there were numerous slide and skid marks that snaked ahead of me. In several places, the hedge had obvious indentations and torn branches, evidence of a bumper getting caught.

I rounded a corner and there was Peter's car. Not only that, Peter was there too. He was also wearing wellies and piling random large stones and pieces of slate under the wheels of his car.

I turned away quickly, but promptly lost my footing and, with a cry, fell heavily into the mud.

'Kat!' Peter made his way towards me. 'Are you all right?'

'Fine,' I muttered as I accepted his hand and allowed myself to be pulled to my feet.

'Thank God it's you,' he said. 'I'm so embarrassed.' I took in his appearance. He looked like he hadn't slept all night.

'Your coat is filthy!' he said with dismay.

Fortunately, I was wearing my go-to tattered Barbour. 'It's old, don't worry.'

It suddenly occurred to Peter that I was there. He frowned. 'What are you doing here?'

I hesitated before deciding that honesty was best. 'When Mum and I drove home last night from the pub, we saw you turn up here.'

'I thought it was the access road to Ivy Cottage,' he said ruefully. 'And by the time I realised it wasn't, it was too late.'

'You seem pretty determined to see this chapel,' I said.

'The trust insists on photographs.' He gestured to the Skoda. 'I don't know how I'm going to get this car out.'

'Eric is your man.' I'd slipped my mobile into my pocket, which was just as well. 'I'll send him a text. He's always pulling cars out of ditches or streams.'

'I will pay him,' said Peter.

I smiled. 'And he'll expect it!'

Eric replied to my text. 'Apparently he already knows you're stuck.'

Peter seemed shocked. 'How?'

'There are no secrets in this village,' I said. 'Are you going to stay and wait here? My car is on the road, but I can drop you back to the pub if you like.'

'I'll wait here, but thank you.' Peter regarded me with amusement. 'Don't you think it extraordinary?'

'Extraordinary?'

'You say that there are no secrets in this village and yet all the questions I ask about the chapel are met with silence.' He turned to me. 'Why? Why is that, Kat?'

He seemed so earnest I wasn't sure how to answer. 'I don't know,' I shrugged. 'I'm still very much an outsider here. You're leaving this evening, aren't you?'

He nodded. 'I'm going home.'

'And where is that?' I asked.

'Bournemouth,' he said.

'Bournemouth is a nice place,' I smiled again. 'I have a friend who lives in Southbourne. What about you?'

'I live near the cathedral,' he said. 'Thank you for all your help – ah! I think I can hear something.'

I could too. It was a tractor.

Eric's red Massey Ferguson, equipped with heavy chains

and a drawbar, came into view. He had reversed all the way from the lane. 'I'll leave you both to it.'

It was only when I got back to my car that I thought of something important – Bournemouth didn't have a cathedral. What's more, why would Peter have hired a rental car? Bournemouth couldn't be more than a hundred or so miles from here. Wouldn't Peter have used his own car to drive around the countryside?

Curious, I dug out Peter's business card from my tote bag. There was no address, no mobile phone number or office number either. Just an email.

Just like Mum, I'd also felt there was something off about Peter Becker. Since his arrival there had been two deaths but I couldn't see a connection. Was that just a coincidence?

But something Peter had said stayed with me. Why *was* the dowager countess so reluctant to let him see the chapel? And who was this mysterious person called Fudge?

Happily, the car wash in Totnes was open. For once, I managed to line up my wheels within the metal runners and tap in the code without being stuck in the middle of the tunnel, which happened to me more times than I cared to count.

Afterwards, I checked my tyre pressure and then used the outdoor vacuum machine.

But it was when I moved the driver's seat forward to hoover underneath that I found it.

Trapped in the folds of my collapsible umbrella was an unusual folding knife with metal clips on each side of a smooth wooden hilt. As I picked it up, I must have touched something because the blade slid free.

It was a straight, single-edged blade with a semi-spear point measuring around four inches in length. I must have touched something else too because a tapered steel spike popped out of the other end. I'd never seen a knife like it before. Fascinated, I took my loupe out of my tote bag to take a closer look at the maker's stamp on the blade. It showed a seated king sitting on the letters SMF, above the word Solingen.

I was puzzled. Surely this couldn't be the mysterious dagger that Trevor had been making such a fuss about. How could he have mistaken a dagger for what seemed like an elaborate penknife? I remembered something else. Trevor said he had never seen the dagger.

How on earth had this ended up under the driver's seat in my car?

And then I guessed.

It must have been when I had to brake suddenly on Saturday afternoon. The wooden crate had its lid tightly secured but the box of bears was open and had tumbled into the footwell.

My mind began to race. Mallory had shown me the flurry of texts going back and forth between Brock and Staci offering me money for the bears. Staci must have believed that this knife was the dagger in question and – although it seemed unbelievable I couldn't think of any other answer – she had somehow hidden the knife in the bear box. I also guessed when she must have done it – the moment the smoke alarm went off. What if Brock Leavey had had something to do with that? So Brock *had* been waiting for me outside

Bridge Cottage. He *had* wanted me to stop because he knew I had this knife.

Trevor had mentioned that George often showed Staci his Home Guard equipment. Staci must have been told that this knife was valuable. She'd passed the information on to her partner who had then contacted Curtis Mainwaring.

I stared at the maker's stamp again. Solingen. Was this a *German* knife? How could it have ended up in George Banks's Home Guard memorabilia?

Unless it had been stolen.

A man tapped on my window, breaking into my thoughts. 'Are you going to sit there all day, luv?'

'Sorry, no. I've finished.' I hadn't finished at all, but I needed to make some phone calls as quickly as possible. I slipped the knife into my tote bag, aware that my hands were trembling.

I left the service station and pulled into the first layby I could find to gather my thoughts.

I called my ex-fiancé. If anyone could give me some pointers, it would be David. He answered on the first ring and sounded pleased to hear my voice.

'How is Policeman Plod?' he teased.

'Very well,' I lied. 'And how is Fifi?'

David laughed. 'Fiona. Fine. But I know you are only calling because you want something.' Hearing him laugh filled me with nostalgia. *Careful*, *Kat*, I thought to myself. Rose-tinted spectacles are dangerous things.

Swiftly I brought him up to date as to what had transpired in the saleroom, the abrupt withdrawal of the lot and the

CCTV footage at Bridge Cottage implying that Brock Leavey might have been lying in wait for me.

'Do you think the knife could have been stolen?' I asked.

'Send me some photos,' said David. 'And I'll call you back. Don't go anywhere.'

I sent him a flurry of photographs with the knife in various positions – blade in, blade out, spike in, spike out and a close-up of the maker's stamp.

Twelve minutes later – I checked – David called me back.

'Okay,' he began. 'This is very interesting. First, it's not stolen. Or rather it hasn't been reported as stolen. It's also not particularly valuable. A few hundred pounds at most unless the owner was someone very important.'

I was baffled. 'Then why was I almost mugged to get it?'

'I can't help you with that,' said David. 'What you have is a *Flieger-Kappmesser* or Luftwaffe gravity knife.'

'Luftwaffe!' I squeaked. I was right. It was German.

'These gravity knives were issued to *Fallschirmjäger* – German paratroopers. The blade opens by the force of inertia or gravity. It was designed to allow a paratrooper, who already had one hand fully occupied trying to gather his billowing parachute, to cut the shroud lines and get free. The marlinspike could be used for untangling the cords. As you can imagine, a knife like this would be critical for an injured or trapped parachutist if he were tangled in a tree.'

I stared at the knife in my hand. 'So what you're saying is that this knife isn't particularly rare.'

'All paratroopers had gravity knives, but if you had a Luftwaffe air force issued combat knife, a ceremonial dagger with an interesting history or a highly sought after Leupold dagger, well, that would be a different story,' said David. 'Those are very scarce and would be something that would have appealed to Curtis Mainwaring.'

'What I want to know is how this gravity knife got into George Banks's collection of Home Guard memorabilia,' I said.

'Perhaps your man saw action in Europe?' David suggested. 'Collected it as a souvenir?'

'No,' I said. 'George Banks couldn't have done. Even though he was young, he had a serious disability.'

'You're certain?'

'A hundred per cent,' I said.

'I've got to run into a meeting,' David said. 'But if you find out anything else, let me know. I always enjoy solving a puzzle.'

He rang off.

David's answer had only thrown up more questions. Of course, I would return the gravity knife to Olive, but first I wanted to see Michael Luxton. I had to know how this had ended up in the bottom of a box of bears. I also wanted to know how it ended up in the catalogue described as a dagger.

I was ushered into Michael's office and got straight to the point. 'I think this is the knife that was missing from Lot 49.' I showed him. 'It wasn't a dagger.'

Michael's eyes lit up. 'Good heavens! It's a Luftwaffe *Fallschirmjäger-Messer*, sometimes called a *Flieger-Kappmesser*. A gravity knife.'

I told Michael how I had found it under my car seat and

how I thought it got into my box of bears when the smoke alarm went off. 'It's just a theory, but is there any way we can check?'

'Yes.' Michael nodded. 'There is. Come with me. In fact, I was going to call you. I've been making my own enquiries into the missing dagger – or should I say, gravity knife. You'll find the CCTV footage is very revealing.'

I followed him to a small room that was barely larger than a cupboard. A bank of screens broadcast various cameras that were positioned throughout the salerooms.

Although there was a stool in front of a narrow table with a computer keyboard, it was empty. 'We're understaffed. Often the cameras are used as a deterrent. As you can imagine, with all the activity and temptation of little things that can be slipped into a pocket, this is the best security we have.' He paused. 'But I can assure you we have the latest technology.'

With impressive speed, Michael easily located the relevant footage. 'There!' he exclaimed. 'There is your thief!'

I was right. It *was* Staci who took the knife from Lot 49, and she'd timed it perfectly. The smoke alarm went off and the porters ushered everyone outside. Staci ducked under a trestle table and waited for the right moment. She grabbed the knife from the wooden crate, darted over to the table on the opposite side of the room and put it at the bottom of my box of bears before ducking back under the trestle table again.

'We'll need to have a word with that young lady,' said Michael. 'We can't have that sort of thing going on.'

'That won't be possible,' I said and told him that Staci had died in a car accident. 'But she had an accomplice called Brock Leavey. I think he was responsible for triggering the smoke alarm. Do you know where the smoke originated from?'

'I can certainly find out.' Michael went through a series of keyboard actions before he sat back. 'Ah. Here we are. It was in the toilets. Is this her accomplice, do you think?'

Having not met Brock, it was hard to say but he was wearing motorcycle leathers.

'All we have to go on is tampering with a smoke alarm,' Michael said. 'How infuriating. Nothing was ultimately stolen, so really there is nothing more we can do here.'

I knew he was right and perhaps I should have been gratified that the mystery had been solved. But I wasn't. David had said the knife was of little value. Why go to all that trouble?

'You had mentioned you had some early online bids,' I said. 'Was Curtis Mainwaring one of them?'

'Old Curtis?' Michael seemed surprised. 'He's only interested in high-end Nazi treasures. Although the gravity knife is collectible, it's easily acquired. Let's go back to my office. Do you have time for a coffee?'

Michael's office was chaotic. Catalogues, boxes of assorted objects – some with lot stickers, others needing repair – jostled with a beautiful partners desk and a small Chesterfield. Bookshelves ranged along one wall, crammed with books on a variety of topics from glassware to metalwork. A Nespresso machine sat on top of a side table with a mini-fridge underneath.

We took the sofa with our coffees. Michael explained in great detail where the knife would have been carried and how it worked.

'The *Fallschirmjäger*'s trousers would have had a small pocket fastened with plastic press studs on the right thigh. The blade is weighted and deployed like so.' Michael demonstrated with a sharp sudden movement of one hand. The blade slid out and he locked it in place by flicking the thumb catch. 'A work of genius,' he enthused. 'It's not a fighting knife because the shape of the blade is relatively blunt. Although this marlinspike could do a bit of damage.'

I had a thought. 'With the blade out and locked in place, I suppose it could have been mistaken for a dagger.'

'Could have been but shouldn't have been. I'll be speaking to whoever listed this in the catalogue.' Michael pointed to the stamp on the blade. 'As you see, the manufacturer's logo is of a seated king. The abbreviation SMF stands for *Solinger Metallwaffenfabrik*. The town of Solingen, where the knife was made, has a centuries-old tradition of blade manufacturing, and still makes knives today.'

He set his empty coffee cup down on the floor and headed to the bookshelf, pulling out a slim paperback that he then handed to me. 'Here, this is a very interesting book. You'll find a lot more information in this.'

I looked at the title – *German Combat Knives 1939-1945* by Christian Méry – and leafed through dozens of photographs of different knives and daggers, all with distinguishing marks and purposes. Some had histories of their owners. I could see now that this gravity knife really wasn't that important at all.

'The bigger question is this, Kat,' Michael mused. 'There were no German soldiers in Devon during the Second World War. If it came from a *Fallschirmjäger*, then perhaps his plane was shot down. As you know, Plymouth saw a lot of enemy action. It was practically flattened during the war.'

'I thought of that,' I said. 'But other than a rumour about a fighter plane going down on Dartmoor no one has ever found the wreckage.'

'A fighter plane would have been a Focke-Wulf or a Messerschmitt. Your paratrooper would have been in a Junker, a transport plane for carrying troops.' Michael thought for a moment. 'Perhaps it was a treasure found by an American and given to your Home Guard man.'

'An American?' I was baffled.

'Operation Tiger, dear,' Michael said. 'April 1944 at Slapton Sands. The run-up to D-Day when the Allied Forces used that stretch of beach for a dress-rehearsal for the Normandy landings. If you've been to Slapton Sands, you would have seen the American Sherman tank that was brought up from the sea in 1984. I believe that was the year it was recovered.'

'Oh gosh, yes.' How could anyone in Devon not have heard about Operation Tiger! Kept a secret for decades by both the American and British military and governments, the exercise had been a disaster from the beginning. A string of avoidable blunders resulted in hundreds of troops being killed by friendly fire before it became a real battle as German E-boats, alerted by heavy radio traffic, attacked. Hundreds of American servicemen lost their lives.

'My parents lived close to Slapton at a neighbouring village called Strete,' Michael went on. 'Everyone, and I mean, everyone – villagers, farmers, all their livestock – was moved miles inland, away from the beach. It was top secret. Absolutely no one knew what was happening, not until decades later.'

'So it was unlikely that George would have known about it,' I said.

'Ah, there is one more possibility,' Michael said suddenly. 'There was a detention camp in Paignton.'

This was news to me. 'Seriously?'

Michael grinned. 'Not many people knew that in the first few weeks of the Second World War the British government requisitioned two holiday camps to intern enemy aliens – that is, German and Austrian men who were living in the country at the time. It hardly seems fair, but the Americans did that to the Japanese citizens who lived on the west coast of California, too.'

I vaguely remembered this from when I was at school.

'It was as if a curtain came down for those who were living quite happily here before 1939,' Michael continued. 'And then when war was declared, those law-abiding folks who had called England their home were suddenly the enemy.'

'And you say these camps were in Devon?'

'Warner's holiday camp in Seaton and Dixon's at Kings Ash in Paignton – I believe that later became Pontins,' Michael went on. 'There was a third but that was in Essex. I'm told that the Dixon's internment camp was quite luxurious. My great aunt worked there in the kitchens. It's very sad. A lot of them had just been living happy lives.'

'So it is possible that if a German paratrooper *was* captured, for example, he could have been taken to one of these camps and perhaps George met him there?'

'Possible, yes,' said Michael. 'But then it begs the question, if he had bailed out, was your paratrooper acting alone? Where were the others?'

I would talk to Olive and see what she knew. Thanking Michael, I left and he too asked to be kept informed.

I'd no sooner returned to my car when my phone rang. It was Mum.

'Kat,' she said. 'Um. Where are you?'

When I told her that I was just leaving Newton Abbot she said, 'You need to come back right away. I'm afraid . . . Mallory is here. He knows about the Vaseline.'

Chapter Twenty-two

Mallory and my mother were seated at the kitchen table. There was no inviting mug of coffee or open packet of chocolate digestives. This was an official visit.

Mallory looked calm and professional, but my mother seemed flustered. I pulled out a chair and sat down.

'I told him everything,' Mum said quickly. 'I didn't mean what I wrote on the windscreen. Gladys was just awful at parking.'

Mallory just listened.

'And anyway, who told you? Was it Ruby?' Mum demanded.

Mallory didn't answer. His expression was hard to read. He brought out his notebook. 'I wanted Kat to be here because I'm afraid what I'm about to tell you might come as a shock.' He paused before saying, 'Gladys was blackmailing someone in the village.'

'What?' Mum and I chorused. 'Who?'

Mallory neatly evaded the question. 'We found a large sum of cash in an envelope in a kitchen drawer. We know

that her husband had left her heavily in debt. She had retired
and the only money she got was from her pension.'

'To be honest, I'm not surprised she'd stoop so low,' Mum
said. 'She eavesdrops all the time on Danny's tête-à-têtes.'

Mallory looked blank.

'If you go into the church, you'll see she's set up a little
eavesdropping station,' Mum went on. 'It's behind a red
velvet curtain in a nook. You do know about Danny's open-
door policy, I assume?'

When Mallory didn't answer this direct question either,
my mother told him all about Danny's someone-to-talk-to-
in-confidence service. 'When I've been doing the flowers,
I've caught Gladys more than once with her ear pressed to
the vestry wall.'

Mallory wrote something down. 'And you say there is an
appointment book?'

'That's right,' Mum said. 'You'll see everyone who has
confided in him since he moved here.'

'And how long have you been volunteering at the church?'
Mallory asked.

'The vicar only moved here three weeks ago,' Mum said
defensively. 'I've been volunteering for two weeks and five
days.'

'As long as that?' Mallory's voice held a tinge of sarcasm
which Mum didn't seem to notice.

'When you say, a large sum of cash,' I said suddenly. 'Why
couldn't it belong to Gladys in the first place?'

'It could,' Mallory admitted. 'But she only had a small
amount of money in her bank account.'

'Perhaps she'd drawn all her savings out for a holiday,' Mum suggested. 'Gladys mentioned she wanted to go on a Viking cruise up the Rhine.'

'Perhaps.' Mallory turned to me. 'In Blackberry Cottage we found a French bulldog and some teddy bears, all with price tags, that I believe were the items you were donating to the children's ward. Were you aware that Gladys was selling them on eBay?'

Mum gasped. 'I don't believe it!'

'Yes, I knew they were mine,' I said, adding, 'but no, I didn't know she was selling them online.'

'She was also selling Krystalle Storm romance novels,' Mallory said. 'Bethany told me that Gladys had taken them from the community shop.'

'But wasn't it just temporary?' I said. 'Until after Lent?'

Mallory didn't answer, *again*! He sat back in his chair and looked my mother straight in the eye. 'That must have been very annoying having those books removed like that, don't you think so, Iris?'

Mum shrugged. 'Gladys was always trying to ingratiate herself with Danny with her holier than thou behaviour.'

'So it didn't bother you that they were no longer for sale or that Gladys was selling them privately, too?'

Mum shrugged again. 'Why should it?'

A peculiar feeling began to grow in the pit of my stomach. I looked at Mallory, who was watching my mother with an expression I had never seen before. It was the face of a policeman who had caught someone in a lie.

There was a moment when no one spoke and then, Mallory cocked his head. 'Was she blackmailing you?'

'Me?' Mum gasped. 'No. Why would Gladys be black-mailing me?'

Mallory gave a heavy sigh. 'I know who you really are, Iris. I think it's time you came clean.'

Mum went very still. 'I'm not sure what you mean, officer.'

I looked down at my clenched hands. I'd dug my nails into the flesh.

'Iris,' Mallory began. 'Or should I say Krystalle Storm? That's quite a secret you've been keeping for a very long time.'

All the colour drained out of Mum's face. 'I . . . I . . . don't know what you are talking about.'

Mallory tut-tutted. 'Do you really want to do this? Do you want me to show you proof, because I do have it.'

Mum shot me an agonised look. I didn't know what to do.

Mallory delved into his voluminous raincoat pocket and produced the pink Thermos in a ziploc bag. 'I believe this is yours. It was behind the wall in the graveyard. And to answer your question, no it wasn't Ruby or the vicar who alerted me to the culprit who vandalised the deceased's car.' He set the pink Thermos down. 'It was this.'

Mum opened her mouth to protest but no words came out.

Mallory picked the pink Thermos up and turned it slowly around, making a point of studying the image. Yes, the man depicted had long hair but the likeness was unmistakable. It was Mallory.

'I'm very flattered, of course,' he said. 'Unfortunately, in my job, long hair is out of the question. I also have a little more hair on my chest. But I do have a six-pack.'

His eyes met mine and in them I saw a twinkle of mischief.

Mallory tipped the Thermos upside down and pointed to the Krystalle Storm logo on the base.

'You see,' he began. 'My mother is a huge fan of Krystalle Storm's novels. She's in a nursing home in Torquay and her birthday is coming up. When I found this Thermos I thought this is just the sort of thing she would like. She loves impressing the other residents.' He paused. I got the feeling that he was thoroughly enjoying himself.

'So I called the publisher,' Mallory went on. 'I was told that the Thermos was going to be released in the summer as a promotional gimmick along with Krystalle Storm's new book, which I believe is called *The Rogue*.' He paused again. 'The publisher— Sorry, I should be precise, the head of marketing, told me that there was only one prototype and that the author had it.'

There was nothing my mother could say and she knew it. At last this nightmare of a secret was over.

But it wasn't.

'I called your bank in Jersey,' Mallory continued.

And there was *still* no comment from my mother.

Mallory gave a heavy sigh. 'Do you want me to invite your stepbrother and ask him about his little side trips across the Channel?' His voice was quiet, but hard.

'No!' Mum exclaimed. 'I mean, please. No. Don't – there's

no need to involve Alfred. Anything that he did, he did because I asked him to.'

'And Gladys?' Mallory said. 'Did you get fed up with giving her money? Did you ask Alfred to get rid of her? We know of his – how shall I say it? – *history* with the law.'

'No! No, of course I didn't!' Mum was panicking. 'Gladys never mentioned Krystalle Storm to me. You must believe me. Kat – you believe me, don't you?'

I desperately wanted to believe my mother, but she had lied so much it was hard to know when she was telling the truth.

'Gladys could have destroyed you,' Mallory's voice was cold.

'Could?' Mum seized on the word. '*Could?* You won't say anything? Oh, please, officer. I don't mind about myself but not Alfred. He's an old man.'

And Mum started to cry.

I couldn't look at either of them. I heard the chair scrape across the kitchen floor and his footsteps cross the room. A box of Kleenex was dropped onto the table. Mum snatched a handful and began to cry even harder. I had never heard her cry like that before. They were real tears.

I jumped up and threw my arm around her shoulders.

'I don't mind about myself,' she hiccupped. 'But not Alfred.' She gently pushed me away and straightened her shoulders. 'Should I get a solicitor?'

'If you really want to,' Mallory's tone had softened. 'But for now, perhaps Kat could make us some coffee?'

I headed for the kettle. The interview was far from over.

I felt sick at what else was going to come out. I needed to gather my thoughts and the obvious fall-out. Shawn said that Mallory did everything by the book. Surely he wouldn't arrest my mother for being Krystalle Storm. The only crime my mother had committed was defrauding the British government by not declaring her earnings. Tax evasion was not his department. There was something else going on. There had to be.

No one spoke as I made the coffee and hunted for a packet of chocolate digestives.

I set everything down on the table.

Mallory smiled. 'Now that we've got that out of the way, Iris,' he said. 'Tell me what you know about Staci Trotter.'

'I never even met her!' Mum wailed. 'What's she got to do with Gladys?'

'I have reason to believe that whoever poisoned Gladys poisoned Staci Trotter, too.' Seeing my horrified expression he nodded. 'Yes. Both were deliberate.'

Chapter Twenty-three

'We got the report back from the lab this morning.' Mallory's expression was grim. 'Staci was poisoned with coniine.'

I had never heard the name before. 'What on earth is that?'

'Coniine is otherwise known as hemlock water dropwort,' said Mallory. 'Or dead man's fingers.'

'A plant,' I said. 'And where would you find that?'

'It grows everywhere around here,' Mum put in. 'In the hedgerows, down by the river.' She gave a snort. 'Paula must have put it in her pastries by accident.'

'Exactly,' I nodded. 'It was an accident. It must have been.'

'I wish it was as simple as that,' said Mallory. 'If Paula had accidentally used hemlock in her picnic puffs I would have thought the entire village would have been wiped out. Hemlock water dropwort can be easily mistaken for chervil or parsley.'

'Paula has every motive to want Staci dead,' Mum pointed out.

'But not Gladys,' I said.

'What I didn't tell Kat was that when we recovered Staci's body from the wreckage,' said Mallory, 'she wore an expression that is described as a sardonic grin.'

'Oh!' I whispered. Clive had said that Staci looked as if she were laughing and then I thought of Gladys and her expression. Was that what I'd seen too?

'Yes, Kat,' Mallory said as if reading my mind. 'It was. I'm not sure if you are familiar with the term. It comes from the grisly practice in eighth-century Sardinia of disposing of criminals – and enemies – by poisoning them.'

'I'd never do anything like that,' Mum mumbled. 'Ever.'

'The poison acts by constricting the muscles and causing death by asphyxia with a rictus-like death grin.' Mallory looked grave. 'There is a sense of numbness that starts at the feet and slowly works its way up to the heart. The poison paralyses the organs. It was the same poison that Socrates elected to take.'

'What a horrible way to die,' I was appalled. 'Is there a cure if you catch it early enough?'

'It would depend on how quickly you got treatment and how much you had consumed.' Mallory said. 'You'd need to keep the airways clear and get the victim on a ventilator as quickly as possible but there is no antidote.'

'But how long does it take for the poison to take effect?' I asked. 'Mum and I saw Gladys at the Hare and Hounds.'

'She did look peaky,' Mum reminded me. 'She told us that she was feeling dizzy and she went out for some fresh air and didn't come back.'

'The food wasn't laid out until after the film,' I said. 'So Gladys couldn't have eaten anything there.'

'But she could have eaten something beforehand,' said Mallory. 'To answer your question, the poison can take effect within thirty minutes.'

'But what about Staci?' I asked.

There was a ping of an incoming text. Mallory brought out his phone, sent off a reply and put it back. He closed his notebook and stood up. 'I need to leave.'

Mum jumped to her feet. 'That's it? That's all? Am I a suspect?'

'Let's just say you are on our list,' he said.

'And what about . . . what about HMRC?' Mum was tense. 'Should I get a solicitor?'

'That's your call, not mine.' He pointed to the pink Thermos. 'And for the record. I would never wear a medallion.'

'I'll see you out,' I said and we left Mum in the kitchen.

We reached the carriageway. I wasn't sure what I was going to say to him. There was so much spinning in my head.

'I spoke to Brock Leavey,' he said. 'Naturally he was upset about Staci's death but when I told him he would be prosecuted for an attempted assault on you and tampering with a smoke alarm, he was surprisingly forthcoming. He's got a record and doesn't fancy going back inside again.'

'Go on,' I said.

'It turns out that this missing dagger was extremely valuable,' Mallory went on. 'George Banks had told Staci that it was a ceremonial dagger that had belonged to one of Hitler's left-hand men – a man called Erich Hartmann—'

'But . . . wait . . .'

'Hartmann was one of the most successful fighter pilots in the history of aerial warfare,' Mallory continued. 'I spoke to Curtis Mainwaring who reeled off mindboggling facts about this pilot. Let me see, that he had completed 1,400 missions in his Messerschmitt and shot down 352 allied planes, among other things. Brock confirmed that he had planned to sell the dagger privately to Curtis. They were going to go behind Trevor's back. They had always planned to steal the dagger in the saleroom during the auction by creating a diversion with the smoke alarm. It had all been planned. Even down to Staci buying your box of bears. Neither were very bright. I'm not sure how they thought they would get away with it. Aren't lots meticulously checked when sold?' He paused, waiting for me to comment, but I didn't because something didn't make sense. 'I suppose Lot 49 being withdrawn worked in their favour,' Mallory went on. 'What do you think?'

'It can't be true about Erich Hartmann,' I said slowly. 'Because I found this and it isn't a ceremonial dagger at all.' I delved in my tote bag and produced the gravity knife. 'Here it is. Look.'

'What?' Mallory was shocked. 'Why on earth didn't you say so?'

'I didn't have a chance!'

Mallory took the gravity knife from me and for the first time, he seemed unsure of himself. 'What is this?'

I told him everything: my conversations with David and Michael, the smoke alarm going off and the revealing footage of Staci taking the knife out of lot 49 and hiding it in my box of bears, confirming what he had just told me.

'So you see, it can't have belonged to this famous German pilot,' I went on. 'This kind of knife is specifically issued to paratroopers.'

Mallory fiddled with the thumb lock and side switches – eyes widening when the marlinspike popped out of the top.

'What else did Curtis Mainwaring say?' I asked.

'He was wary,' Mallory admitted. 'He was interested but he wouldn't meet Brock until he'd got the provenance.'

I shared Michael's theories that perhaps the knife came from one of the German civilians that had been interned at one of the camps. 'Or even an American soldier who was at Slapton for the D-Day rehearsals—'

'Operation Tiger,' Mallory nodded. 'It was top secret unless George had some kind of clearance, which was unlikely. Have you spoken to Olive Banks yet?'

'No,' I said. 'I'm going to return this to her after I leave here. Maybe the answer is simple.' I shrugged. 'Maybe George Banks just bought it online.'

'Let me know what she says,' Mallory said. 'I'm sorry. I've got to go.'

I returned to the kitchen, dreading to see what kind of state my mother was in. I found her on the phone. She was nodding vehemently and all I heard was, 'Yes, yes. And you're certain?'

When she put the phone down, her expression was triumphant.

'For someone who is about to go to prison for tax evasion,' I said. 'You're looking remarkably cheerful.'

'That was the Churches Conservation Trust,' Mum said. 'I called them earlier to find out about Peter Becker.'

'Oh, that.' In all the excitement I had forgotten about him.

'Well. He's a fraud,' Mum crowed. 'No one has ever heard of him or the Chapel Restoration Trust of Great Britain. And I bet Gladys knew that too and, if so, I wouldn't be surprised if it was *him* that she was blackmailing. And maybe he had something to do with her death. She left the function room before the film started and he only slipped in much later. He had the opportunity!'

'Mum,' I said patiently. 'Peter Becker only arrived on Saturday and Gladys died last night. That's very little time to hunt for hemlock water dropwort, let alone concoct something in his bedroom.'

'Regardless, Peter Becker is not who he says he is.' She was fired up. 'I'm going to see Danny and tell him right this minute. And you know what, Katherine?'

'What?'

'I'm fed up with all these cheats and liars! Fed up with the lot of them! Fed up with getting the blame for something I did not do – apart from swindling the government . . . but that's not the point! If I must answer for what I did, then so will everyone else. And that's final.'

'I think I'd better come with you to see the vicar,' I said wearily. 'I'll drive.'

But as we sped to Little Dipperton I was struck by the obvious and nearly stopped the car.

'I think we're missing the point here, Mum,' I said. 'If Peter Becker isn't who he says he is, what on earth is he doing in Little Dipperton and why is he so obsessed with the chapel?'

Chapter Twenty-four

Ruby answered the door.

'We've got some important information for the vicar,' Mum declared.

'He's busy,' Ruby said quickly.

'It can't wait.' Mum swept past, nearly knocking Ruby off her feet.

Ruby grabbed the door jamb. 'He's busy! Iris!' she shouted after my mother's retreating back. 'He's busy!'

I gave Ruby an apologetic shrug and followed my mother into the kitchen where I could hear bullets fired and explosions. Danny was hunched over his laptop on the kitchen table. The volume was turned up so loudly that he didn't hear us come in but when he realised we were standing there, he flipped the laptop shut and leapt to his feet.

I spied a library book on the table and caught a glimpse of the author. It was Graham Greene.

'Peter Becker is a fraud!' Mum blurted out. 'There is no such thing as the Chapel Restoration Trust of Great Britain.'

Danny went very still. 'Are you certain?'

'Very. Research is my forte,' Mum said. 'I googled Companies House and the government website and called the Churches Conservation Trust which oversees all the church trusts in the country. No one has ever heard of him. He's an imposter!'

Danny ran his hand through his hair. A stray lock fell across one eye. 'Well. I just don't know what to say.'

'So why is he pretending to be something he isn't?' Mum demanded.

'I don't know.' Danny caught Ruby's eye and made a quick nod to the dresser where an old video machine with mounds of broken tape spewing from the slot sat next to some scraps of a blue-grey fabric. Ruby snatched the fabric up and shoved it into a top drawer.

'Iris says that Peter Becker is a fraud, Mother,' Danny said quickly. 'What do you think?'

Ruby didn't answer.

'It certainly explains why he knows nothing about clocks!' Mum went on. 'And why he didn't have a head for heights in the clock tower!'

'Yes, you might be right,' said Danny, but he didn't seem as concerned as I would have expected.

'We've just spoken to Mallory,' Mum rushed on. 'We all know that Gladys was poisoned.'

'Poisoned?' Danny looked up sharply and shot a worried look at Ruby, who averted her eyes. 'I thought . . . but we were told Gladys had a heart attack.'

'Well, she didn't,' Mum declared. 'She was poisoned by hemlock water dropwort. What do you think about that?'

Danny and Ruby exchanged worried looks again. 'What do the police say?'

'They're on top of it.' Mum's eyes narrowed. 'You don't seem surprised.'

'We are surprised!' Danny said quickly again. 'Why? Surely it couldn't have been deliberate. Why would anyone want to poison Gladys?'

I thought my mother was going to self-destruct. 'Because Gladys used to eavesdrop on all your private conversations in the vestry, Danny,' Mum exclaimed. 'She was blackmailing someone in the village.'

'Well, it wasn't me,' Danny said. 'Or Mother, I can assure you of that.'

'What if it was Peter Becker she was blackmailing?' Mum said. 'What did he know that he didn't want anyone else to know but Gladys did know.' Mum looked sheepish. 'Well, I know what I'm trying say.'

'Iris, dear,' Danny said smoothly. 'Why don't we let the police do their job? And with regards to Peter, I believe he's leaving this evening so really, there's no harm done.'

'No harm done!' Mum exploded. 'He's an imposter!'

Danny didn't comment.

'Don't you care about Peter Becker?' Mum demanded. 'Why do you think he is lying? Why is he so interested in the chapel? He tried to find it last night in the dark, you know, but ended stuck up a farm track instead. Eric had to tow him out this morning.'

I caught Danny glance at Ruby, who had turned white. She reached for a kitchen chair and sat down heavily.

'I think we're all getting a little emotional.' I was confused by the bizarre scene in the kitchen. Danny's distraction, Ruby's obvious distress and my mother's embarrassing outburst. 'Perhaps we could all do with a cup of tea?'

'What's going on?' Mum's voice was shrill. 'Why is everyone lying?' She looked directly at Danny who had the grace to blush. 'Especially you.'

'There's nothing going on, Iris,' Danny crooned. 'You sound very upset. This isn't like you at all but if you'd like to get things off your chest, I can fit you in this afternoon at two thirty and we can talk about it then, but right now, I must go. I have an appointment and I'm going to be late.'

Mum didn't move. She just stood there, arms akimbo, wearing a mutinous expression. 'In Newton Abbot?'

Danny went pale. 'Excuse me?'

'Oh God,' I mumbled and looked down at my shoes.

'An appointment with your lady friend.' Mum gave a snort of disdain. 'All that talk in the pulpit about sex before marriage when it's obvious that you are having an affair with a married woman!' I had never seen my mother so angry. 'Kat saw you leave her house early yesterday morning. Gladys said you'd been out all night . . . wait!' Mum gasped. 'It's you! Gladys knew about your affair! It was you she was blackmailing! Oh God!'

'Stop it!' Danny boomed. 'Stop it this minute. Enough!'

Mum's mouth snapped shut and even I froze.

'It's his wife,' Ruby blurted out.

Mum gasped. 'What? Who?'

'Oh no,' I mumbled.

'Danny's wife lives in Newton Abbot,' said Ruby.

There was an ugly silence and then, 'But I thought you were a widower,' Mum said. 'I mean, it's like a shrine in here.' She gestured to the many framed collages of Danny and, presumably, his very-much-alive wife, hanging on the wall. 'You mean . . . Caroline's not dead? But,' she sputtered, 'you told me you had lost her!'

Mum pulled out a chair and sank down. I followed suit. Danny sat down too.

'I'll put the kettle on,' said Ruby and she did just that.

'But I fear I have lost her,' Danny said in a very small voice. 'We're having a temporary separation, but I desperately want her back.'

Mum glowered at Ruby. 'Why didn't you tell me?'

Ruby shrugged. 'Because it's not my secret to tell. But believe me, the last thing I wanted to do was to move down here of all places. I do not have happy memories of Little Dipperton or the Honeychurch Hall estate. Why else do you think I keep myself to myself?'

'And I didn't know Mother had been here before,' Danny said. 'If I had, I wouldn't have accepted the position.'

Ruby gave a snort. 'If you think that, you're deceiving yourself, son. You've always been obsessed with Caroline.'

'I'm sorry, Mother,' Danny seemed contrite. 'I didn't know how awful it must have been here for you.'

'It was,' Ruby said. 'Oh – I didn't mind living at the Hall. Her ladyship was in her teens. She was lovely. Treated me like a little sister. No, it was when I had to go and live with *her* that it all went horribly wrong.'

'You mean Olive?' I ventured.

Ruby pulled back her hair and pointed to the scar on her face. 'You see this? She did this. She held my face down on the hotplate.'

'Mother—' Danny's tone made it clear he did not want Ruby to continue.

'She did *what*?' Mum was horrified. 'What kind of monster does that to a child?'

'Mother,' Danny began again. 'Sometimes our memories play tricks on us. I don't really think—'

'You can think what you like,' Ruby said coldly. 'I know what happened.'

'Is that why you ran away?' I asked.

Ruby nodded. 'I couldn't handle any more of her and him neither and they didn't like me. I wasn't allowed to eat with them. I had to eat in my room. Always watery soup on a tray. They locked me in my bedroom every night but I was able to get out of the window.'

Danny caught my eye as if to imply that his mother was exaggerating. I had to admit I knew all about mothers exaggerating.

'Perhaps you should confront Olive,' Mum suggested. 'I would if I was you. I'll come with you.'

'Don't be silly,' Danny said quickly. 'It's all in the past. Let sleeping dogs lie.'

'Never. She's evil. Wicked.' Ruby's voice was full of hatred. 'I thought she would be dead by now, but she's not.'

I had a brief flash of Olive and Ruby as young women.

'And I keep telling you that there was a war on, Mother,'

Danny reminded her. 'Sometimes people are dealing with their own problems and don't mean to hurt others.' He stole a sideways glance at my mother, who looked let down. It briefly crossed my mind that perhaps he had genuinely liked her. Maybe he was confused about his feelings for his wife. I remembered how distraught he was when he left Caroline's house that morning and felt a little kinder towards him. After all, if he was still married, he wasn't exactly a hypocrite. If anything, he was doing his best to save his marriage.

'I didn't want to hurt you, Iris,' said Danny. 'And I'm sorry.'

'Well, you did,' Mum said quietly. 'Very much.'

'Caroline didn't want me to become a priest,' Danny went on. 'I was offered a headship at a private school in northern England but I had always wanted to become a vicar. I did my training and I thought Caroline was happy with my decision but she wasn't. She didn't want to be a vicar's wife.' He gave a wry smile. 'All those parish council meetings and flower rotas. It's not everyone's cup of tea and—'

'Caroline had an affair,' Ruby said bluntly.

Pain etched on Danny's face. 'It was with one of the younger teachers at the last school where I taught maths and science. We had a trial separation and she moved down to Newton Abbot to be close to her sister.' Danny reached out and gave Mum's hand a squeeze. 'If I wasn't still in love with my wife . . .'

'No!' Mum shot back. 'Don't go there. Because you are in love with your wife.' She thought for a moment. 'And do you think you'll get back together?'

'I just don't know,' said Danny. 'I'm hoping the renovations at the vicarage will tempt her. She's always been fond of lovely things.'

So that was that.

There was a horribly uncomfortable silence. I struggled for something to say but couldn't think of a single thing.

Mum pushed her unfinished tea aside. 'Well. This has been a very enlightening conversation.'

'How are we getting on with the church circular?' said Danny, now all business.

'I'm afraid you'll have to find someone else to do it,' Mum said. 'I'm very busy writing my books! Krystalle Storm awaits! Come along, Kat. Aren't you supposed to be riding with Edith this afternoon?'

And with 'Krystalle Storm? What books?' coming from Danny, I followed Mum outside to my car.

I started the engine in shock. 'You told him you were writing your books. You mentioned Krystalle Storm! Are you out of your mind?'

'No. Quite sane,' Mum said bitterly. 'I'll have plenty of time to write when I'm in prison. Just take me home.'

Chapter Twenty-five

I dropped Mum off at the entrance to the carriageway. It was clear she wanted to be left alone but Danny's revelations, and Ruby's too, had thrown up even more questions.

Two cases of poison, Danny's confession that he was still married, Ruby's accusations of Olive's cruelty, to say nothing of Mallory knowing who my mother really was and the fall-out that came from that. And what had Danny been watching on his laptop? It sounded like a war film. I'd noticed the broken cassette player so perhaps he'd located a copy of George's favourite film online. And what did Ruby shove in that drawer when we both walked in?'

If this was all connected to Staci and Gladys, I wasn't sure how.

Mallory liked to say that people were killed for four things. They saw something, they heard something, they had something or they knew something.

I replayed the sequence of events. George Banks told Staci he had a valuable dagger that had belonged to a famous

Luftwaffe fighter pilot. Trevor must have known about that
even if he hadn't seen it. Staci told her partner Brock who
offered it to Curtis Mainwaring. Olive – for whatever
reason – changed her mind about selling her husband's
memorabilia and the lot was withdrawn. Under the guise of
the smoke alarm, Staci took the knife – presumably she'd
seen it in George's possession with the blade out, believing
it *was* a dagger – and put it in the box of bears that she
thought she'd bought.

Brock freaked out when he realised Staci had not bought
the bears after all. He knew where I lived and planned on
waylaying me at Bridge Cottage to get the knife back but
then Peter Becker – whoever he really was – appeared on
the scene.

And then Staci was poisoned, then two days later, so was
Gladys. I kept circling back to Paula being responsible –
accidentally or not.

My ride with Edith was set for three p.m. I would have
time to drop the knife back to Olive on my way home to
change into jodhpurs and grab my riding hat. Hopefully
Olive would shed some light on the mystery. I just hoped that
I would catch Olive on her own.

Unfortunately she wasn't. Trevor was there. He answered
the door, wearing heavy boots, an outdoor coat and carrying
work gloves, clearly on his way out. Eric emerged from the
cottage next door and waved a greeting.

'Ready, Trev?' he said. 'We've got to make a stop at the
scrapyard to pick up some equipment.'

Trevor grunted an assent.

'Good news, Trevor,' I said. 'I found that missing er . . . *dagger*.'

Trevor's eyes went wide. 'You did? Where is it? Let me see it!'

I kept my arm clamped over my tote bag.

'Who is it?' came the shrill cry from beyond.

'It's Kat, Mrs Banks,' I cried. 'I've got something for you.'

'Come on!' Eric shouted to Trevor. 'His lordship wants the fence repaired today.'

'Excuse me.' I smiled and swept past Trevor and into the cottage.

I found Olive seated at the kitchen table knitting a scarf in a hideous shade of mustard on giant needles. Her walker was close to hand.

There was the distinct smell of fried food. A dirty frying pan was on the top of the hotplate. Plates streaked with dried egg and tomato ketchup were still on the draining board. Three circular packages wrapped in aluminium foil bearing the labels chervil, goat and chanterelle were on the counter-top. A pot of tea sat on the table.

Olive saw me looking. 'Working her to the bone, that Delia Evans is. Poor kid. She puts in a long day at the Hall and comes back and is up all hours filling her orders for that new farm shop on the Dartmouth road. Then she's off at dawn delivering them before she starts her day. I told her, you can't keep this up for much longer, Paula.'

Paula. Maybe she had made an error of judgement and mixed her cow parsley up with her hemlock water dropwort. The two looked very similar with their umbels of white flowers. It was obvious that Olive was clueless about the possibility that her daughter-in-law could have had a hand in both Staci's and Gladys's deaths.

I glanced over to the windowsill. The leafy plants and bunches of weeds now took on a more sinister air but hemlock wasn't one of them.

'Paula told me about the retired nurse dying like that,' Olive went on. 'The police are saying it was a heart attack but I heard she ate a bad mushroom.'

'Oh?' This was a new rumour. 'What else are the police saying about Gladys?'

'Paula's worried that she'll get the blame but there were plenty of witnesses at the pub last night who claimed Gladys was poorly before the event.'

'Yes, I didn't think she looked very well.'

'Poisoned herself, more like.' Olive tut-tutted. 'It's fashionable these days to forage and eat weeds. I don't know what this world is coming to. Give me a white loaf of bread and a fry-up and I'm happy. There are a few baked beans in that can if you wanted to heat them up with some toast. You've just missed Trevor, otherwise he would have done it for you.'

'I saw him leave with Eric,' I said. 'It sounds like he's working at the Hall, too.'

'Gardening and odd jobs.' Olive made a grunting noise. 'He and Trevor go way back. I told Trevor he should rent that caravan out long term. This cottage is too small for the three of us. I don't know how long I'll be staying here.'

I remembered when I first came to the Hall seeing a

battered caravan that Eric used as an office. And then it hit me. 'Has Trevor been staying at the caravan?'

'That's right,' said Olive. 'All that secrecy and Paula takes him back anyway.'

My stomach flipped over. Staci's car had been parked outside the entrance to Eric's scrapyard late on Saturday afternoon because she had been visiting Trevor, not Eric, but Trevor had been out fishing that day and in the Sprat and Mackerel afterwards. Had Staci eaten something in Eric's caravan? But no, Paula didn't know Trevor was there and besides, Paula was out with Delia all evening.

'Make a fresh pot of tea, why don't you?' said Olive.

'I'm riding with the dowager countess this afternoon,' I said. 'Otherwise I would have said yes.'

'Perhaps you can ask her when my cottage will be ready for me to move back in,' said Olive. 'I was born in that cottage, you know. Now, did I hear you say that you had something for me?'

I took the gravity knife out of my tote bag and set it on the table. I didn't mention the word dagger. I just wanted to gauge her reaction.

Olive broke into a smile of obvious relief. 'Good heavens! Clever you!' She didn't touch it. 'Well I never. I suppose they had it at Luxton's all the time.'

This was the question I had been dreading and one I had decided not to answer. The explanation was too complicated and would mean I'd have to elaborate on Trevor's love triangle.

'I'm curious,' I said. 'Do you know much about this knife?'

'I know it's German, if that's what you mean.' Olive's eyes met mine. Steady and unflinching. 'Why do you ask?'

'You're right. It is.' I said. 'What else do you know about it?'

'Not much,' Olive said. 'Thank you for bringing it back, dear.' She still made no attempt to touch it. The knife just sat on the table in front of her.

'There weren't any German soldiers in the area during the war,' I said and then had an idea. 'If you want to sell it, the buyer always likes to know the provenance – the chain of title.'

Olive didn't speak for a moment and then, 'George was a great collector of military items. He may have even bought it himself on the computer.'

'You mean, like eBay?' I suggested.

Olive shrugged. 'I don't know what it's called. That's Paula. She's very good at computers. She might have done it. You can ask her.'

I took a deep breath. 'Trevor was under the impression that it was a valuable military dagger that had belonged to a famous fighter pilot.'

Olive roared with laughter. 'Trevor's so gullible! And that's typical of my George. Always exaggerating to make himself sound important. The stories he used to tell that young Staci, too.'

I had this sudden urge to leave. I didn't like being in the kitchen. It was claustrophobic, especially with the plants on the windowsill that seemed to be draining what light there was in this dingy backroom. I felt I had stumbled onto a movie set from *The Day of the Triffids*.

'Well,' I said. 'I'd better let you get on with your knitting. What are you making?'

'A scarf.' Olive picked up the giant needles and fiddled with the wool. 'You know, I do remember Ruby after all. She was such a funny little thing. Very troubled. She's another one prone to exaggerating!'

My stomach made that weird lurch it always did when something felt wrong. This was a different story to the one that Olive had mentioned the night before at the pub, when she became defensive and insisted she couldn't remember any children being evacuated to Honeychurch Hall during the war. Olive must have sensed my discomfort because she laughed again.

'Ah, I thought as much.' She gave a heavy sigh. 'I suppose Ruby told you that I held her face to the hotplate?'

This was awkward. I didn't know whether to be honest or not.

Olive plunged on. 'Ruby was a troublemaker. A thief. Did she tell you why she ran away?'

I shook my head.

'Because she stole our ration books and what small amount of cash I had in my purse,' Olive said. 'A nasty piece of work.'

'Oh,' was all I could say.

'I'd forgotten all about her until you mentioned it yesterday,' Olive went on. 'Wanted to forget, I should say. George and I just didn't know what to do with her.'

'Oh.' I said again.

'We had to lock her in her bedroom, you know,' Olive

went on. 'Ruby used to creep out after curfew. With George being in the Home Guard, it proved very awkward for him. She was always getting caught. She was a right little madam.'

I could tell that Olive was getting upset. Her face had gone very red. She looked me straight in the eye. 'Why did Ruby come back here? She ran away. She should have stayed away.'

'I don't think she expected to come back to Little Dipperton,' I said. 'It was the vicar who accepted the position here. Ruby never told him she'd been evacuated during the war.'

'Well, she wouldn't have told him, would she!' Olive declared. 'Too ashamed, I would say.'

I hovered awkwardly by the kitchen door. 'I'm sorry, I really have to go.'

'There is just one thing.' Olive thought for a moment. 'The clock man. The man staying at the Hare and Hounds.'

'Peter Becker.' I hesitated, unsure if I should say something about the fact that we had found out that he was a fraud.

'He didn't seem to know much about clocks, did he?' There was a malicious gleam in her eye. 'Or have a head for heights. It's all over the village, you know. Will he be staying here long?'

'I think he's going home tonight,' I said, wondering where Peter's real home was. It certainly wasn't Bournemouth.

Promising that I would call around again and next time stop for a cup of tea, I made my escape.

Chapter Twenty-six

As I sped back to Jane's Cottage, I couldn't stop thinking about what Olive had said about Ruby. I wasn't sure who to believe.

As I crested the hill my heart flipped over.

Shawn's car was parked outside my front door. He leapt out as I drew alongside, looking slightly nervous. I hadn't expected to see him, especially on a weekday, but then I remembered he had taken some time off supposedly for us to have spent quality time together. So much for that.

I fiddled with the ignition for a few seconds to gather my composure. My mind was racing. What did Shawn want? Why was he here?

Shawn opened my car door with his usual gallantry. 'I thought I would see how you are.'

'Why?' I said cautiously.

Shawn seemed hurt. 'Because I heard about Gladys and I know you were the one who found her,' he said. 'I wanted to see if you were all right. I still care about you.'

'I'm fine,' I said, but I knew I wasn't and so did Shawn. 'It was horrible. Awful. The expression on her face . . . I'll never forget it as long as I live.'

'Let's go inside,' he said gently and took my tote bag and my arm and led me to the front door. I let him take my house keys, open the front door and usher me inside.

Shawn tried to pull me into his arms but I stepped back.

'Don't,' I said.

He muttered an apology of sorts which sounded like 'force of habit.' I ignored it.

'Mallory has told me that both Staci and Gladys were poisoned with hemlock water dropwort,' he said.

We were back on safe ground. 'Yes. But as I'm sure you're going to say, it's not your case.'

'You're right. It's not.' Shawn agreed. 'But I just wanted to remind you that this information is not public knowledge yet. He wants to stick with the heart attack story for now—'

'There's also a bad mushroom rumour doing the rounds—'

'Oh.' Shawn faltered. 'Well regardless, Mallory told me that you and Iris know the truth but I just wanted to make sure that you didn't broadcast the truth. Iris can be very indiscreet.'

I didn't answer, mainly because it was true.

Shawn seemed to take my silence as a sign that I understood. 'He mentioned you found a dagger—'

'It's a gravity knife,' I corrected him. 'Not a dagger.'

'I'd love to see it.'

'I already gave it back to Olive,' I said.

'And what did she say about it?' said Shawn.

'That George bought it online, but I don't believe that for a moment.' I regarded Shawn with suspicion. 'You know something about this, I can tell. And of course,' I added bitterly, 'you're not going to tell me, are you?'

Shawn seemed stung by my tone. 'The only things I couldn't tell you about before were those of an ongoing investigation. That's all.'

'Okay. So what do you know?'

'It's not a fact, it's just a rumour.' Shawn gave a wry smile. 'Yes, a village gossip rumour.'

I didn't return the smile.

'The rumour was that a German fighter plane was hit by anti-aircraft fire on a return bombing raid from Plymouth. Fighters would accompany bombers when flying so far from base. The plane came down somewhere on Dartmoor.'

'And the wreckage?'

'It was never found,' Shawn said. 'Nor any trace of any aircrew. As I said, it was just a rumour.'

I thought for a moment. 'But what if the rumour was true? Maybe the pilot bailed out? What if a member of the Home Guard or the Auxiliary Patrol found him?'

'Now that would be something for George Banks to boast about, but nothing was ever reported.' Shawn thought for a moment. 'Besides, if any German aircrew had been captured, they would have been handed over to the authorities.'

I had a sudden thought. 'No. That wouldn't be right. Michael Luxton specifically identified the gravity knife as standard issue for a paratrooper.'

'And that's why I think the downed plane is an urban legend,' Shawn smiled and in that smile was a sign of desperation. I knew he wanted to stay friends. I could tell but it was far too soon for anything like that. 'I wouldn't mind a coffee.'

'I have to go,' I said. 'I'm riding with Edith and I dare not be late. I need to change my clothes.'

Shawn stood there, his hands hanging limply by his side. 'Right. Yes. Of course.'

And I turned and went upstairs.

I heard the front door close and his car start and drive away.

I forced myself not to think of Shawn. Instead I focused on the rumour about the downed fighter plane.

As Mallory liked to say, there was no smoke without fire.

I'd have Edith to myself this afternoon and I would ask her what she knew. I also wanted to ask her more about Ruby. She'd seemed so relieved to see Ruby that her reaction didn't fit with Olive's obvious dislike and accusations of theft and bad behaviour.

Yes, I would ask Edith outright.

Chapter Twenty-seven

It wasn't until we had reached Gibbet Cross, the northern boundary of the vast estate, that I had a chance to talk to Edith at all.

She had been unusually quiet when we set off on our respective mounts – Tinkerbell, Edith's beloved chestnut mare, and Duchess, 'my' dapple-grey mare. Tinkerbell seemed to have picked up on Edith's mood and, for once, led the way at a gentle walk with none of her usual shying and dancing at creepy shapes and bogeymen along the way.

It was one of those grey afternoons with a biting wind. The old saying 'If March comes in like a lion, it will go out like a lamb' never seemed truer – at least the lion part. I pulled my hacking jacket closer and wished I'd worn another layer of clothing underneath. Whenever I rode out with Edith, who looked immaculate in her habit, I always made sure to look smart, too.

Edith drew rein in front of what remained of the old gallows – an upright post on a grassy knoll. Four beaten-mud tracks went off in different directions. The panoramic view was breathtakingly beautiful but today it felt unfriendly and bleak.

Edith pulled out her hip flask, lifted her veil and took a sip of cherry brandy, then offered it to me. I took a hefty swig and returned it.

'The years pass so quickly,' Edith said suddenly. 'I used to ride Briar Patch up here in the war. Beautiful mare. I've always preferred mares to geldings.'

'Is she buried in the equine cemetery?' I asked as I thought of the many horses resting on the gentle slopes that over-looked the River Dart, each grave bearing an epitaph that captured the horse's nature. 'What was Briar Patch like?'

'Prickly. The name suited her.' Edith smiled. 'And she was bullet-proof. Never flinched when the planes flew over in the war.'

'Ah, yes, I heard that they did.' I had decided to be ultra-careful about how I broached the subject of the war and was surprised that she had brought the topic up first.

'I was the youngest member of the Dartmoor Patrol,' said Edith in a wistful voice. 'We would ride out at dawn and at dusk to patrol the skies.'

'And you liaised with the Home Guard?' I asked casually.

Edith nodded. 'We would sometimes meet in the kitchen at the Hall. Most of the men in the village had enlisted but those that were left behind took their role very seriously.'

'George Banks being one of them,' I said.

Edith chuckled. 'Yes. George. I always thought he had a

Napoleon complex. He was a little man but quite a character. Devoted to Olive.'

I was beginning to see George and Olive Banks in a completely different light – younger, in love, filled with ideology and passion for keeping their corner of England safe.

'The Home Guard were kept very busy,' Edith went on. 'We were on the flight path for the aircrew stationed at the wartime airfields – thirteen airfields, no less. We'd watch our planes limping back home from France and Germany. That's why Plymouth was such a target for the Luftwaffe, but the bombing was nothing compared to London.'

It was the perfect opening to ask about Ruby. 'It seems unbelievable that little kids were sent away to live with strangers.'

'It was a different time,' said Edith.

'What was Ruby like?' I said.

Edith hesitated. I couldn't see her expression beneath the old-fashioned veil.

'Shy. Quiet. Nervous,' she said.

'When did she arrive?' I said. 'Mum told me that the first evacuees were sent out in 1939 even before war was officially declared.'

'I can't really remember,' Edith said. 'You'd have to ask her. I think she was evacuated more than once. She kept running back to London. She found it hard to believe that her parents had been killed. It was all very sad.'

'But it sounds like she liked living at the Hall to begin with,' I ventured.

'Yes,' said Edith. 'She helped in the house and, of course, we had a victory garden. George – as head gardener

– oversaw that. He and Olive seemed very fond of Ruby. That's why I thought she would like to live with them when I left. She begged to stay at the Hall but she was far too young to be there alone. Most of the house had been shut down.'

I knew I had to ask. 'How did Ruby get that scar?'

'I don't really know,' said Edith. 'I heard that she'd tripped and fallen. When I came back to the Hall, Ruby had gone and no one knew where. Olive was extremely upset. I made enquiries but it was as if Ruby had vanished off the face of the earth.'

'It's little wonder that you were surprised to see her again,' I said.

Edith didn't answer. She seemed lost in thoughts of the past. 'All so long ago,' she whispered.

And I also knew I had to ask about the German paratrooper. I took a deep breath. 'I heard a rumour that a German fighter plane came down somewhere on Dartmoor.'

'If it did, we didn't know about it,' said Edith.

'Wouldn't there have been any wreckage?'

Edith shook her head. 'Nearly all of the wreckage was recovered by the RAF after the war, and even during the war scrap metal was needed for the war effort and was collected immediately.' She frowned. 'But there was talk once of a Messerschmitt flying a reconnaissance mission when it ran into difficulties.'

My heart began to beat a little faster. 'And?' I prompted.

'The pilot bailed out and was captured as a prisoner of war,' Edith declared.

I felt disappointed. 'And you're certain he was turned in to the authorities?'

'Absolutely,' Edith said. 'One hundred per cent. And of course George Banks would have loved to have been the man to do that. But no, nothing like that happened in Little Dipperton.'

'But you moved to London, didn't you?' I said. 'Perhaps something happened when you were away?'

Edith looked at me sharply. 'What do you mean?'

'This is a bit of a stretch,' I said and told Edith all about the gravity knife that had been found in George Banks's memorabilia. 'It's a paratrooper's knife which seems to suggest that . . . perhaps a German paratrooper had—'

'No!' Edith burst into laughter. 'Dropped behind enemy lines?' She shook her head as if finding the idea amusing but her laughter sounded fake. I stole a glance but again, couldn't see Edith's expression beneath the veil.

'Believe me, we would have all known about it,' Edith said. 'I'm sure you've already asked Olive how he came by it.'

'I did,' I said. 'She believes he got it on eBay.'

'Well, there's your answer,' Edith said.

'Speaking of Olive,' I said. 'She seems to think she'll be moving back to Ivy Cottage.'

'Oh dear,' said Edith. 'I'm afraid the cottage is going to be pulled down. It's beyond repair. We'll ride back that way and I'll show you what I mean.'

We fell back into single file and wove through thick trees, zig-zagging our way down to another pine forest that Harry called the Black Forest. It seemed an apt name given my conversation with Edith about the war. The top of the ruined bell tower peeped above the trees in the near distance.

We emerged into a clearing and, quite suddenly, I realised we were right beside Ivy Cottage. A faded picket fence, grey with age, was broken in places, the little gate dangling from just one hinge. Covered in thick ivy and with thatch that was green with mildew and mould, the old house looked derelict to me. The diamond-paned windows were thick with grime and barely visible under the unruly vines. To my left I saw an abandoned hen house with chicken wire and other detritus lying forlornly in a sea of weeds.

And to think that up until George died, Olive had lived here! I found it depressing.

Edith must have sensed my shock. 'It's frightful, isn't it? George and Olive refused to allow anyone inside. When we modernised the estate cottages – plumbing and heating and whatnot in the seventies, George and Olive said they didn't want it. In the end, we gave up asking.'

Suddenly, Tinkerbell jumped backwards, almost unseating Edith.

Peter Becker stepped out of the shadows and swiftly grasped Tinkerbell's bridle.

'Peter!' I was shocked.

'Easy, girl,' Peter crooned as he attempted to steady the mare but Edith was furious and, to my horror, made a swipe at him with her riding crop.

'Let go of my horse.' Tinkerbell sensed her panic and began to back up. Edith grabbed the pommel and clung on. My heart was in my mouth as she struggled to keep her balance on the saddle with her right knee clamped firmly over the queen, and her left under the leaping head.

Tinkerbell's eyes rolled and she snorted. Peter held on for dear life. 'Don't worry! I've got her!'

'Peter!' I screamed. 'Let go of the reins!'

And suddenly he did. He dropped them and seemed stunned by what had nearly happened. Edith nudged Tinkerbell a few yards away, whispering comforting words and stroking her chestnut shoulder. If Edith was shaken, she didn't show it.

But I was.

'What on earth were you thinking?' I shouted at him. 'Edith could have come off!'

'I was trying to help.' Peter ran his fingers through his hair. He seemed distraught. 'I'm sorry,' he said. 'Forgive me, please.'

I didn't know what to do. And then I was struck by how isolated Edith and I were, out in the far corner of the Honeychurch Hall estate. 'You must leave now, please.'

Edith sat on Tinkerbell, rigid and stiff. 'I think we should call the police. You are trespassing.'

But Peter just seemed to fall to pieces. 'I give up. Prosecute me. Do what you like. It doesn't matter.' He sank onto a fallen log and put his head in his hands.

I was alarmed and looked anxiously at Edith, whose expression under her black netting I still couldn't see. Peter's despair was tangible – and puzzling. 'Edith, why don't you go on home and I'll catch you up,' I said. 'I'll make sure Peter's all right.'

Edith didn't hesitate. She seemed desperate to get away. But Tinkerbell didn't want to leave her equine friend behind and Edith struggled to urge Tinkerbell on. Duchess was restless and whinnied once or twice but then put her head down to graze at the thick grass growing around the broken picket fence.

I dismounted and tied Duchess to the gatepost then sat down beside Peter.

'Why are you here?' I asked gently. 'I know you don't work for the trust and you certainly don't know anything about church clocks.'

When Peter's eyes met mine, I saw a deep sadness in them. 'My father came here during the war. He was German.'

And just like that, it all fell into place.

'He was a paratrooper, wasn't he?' I said.

Peter seemed shocked. 'Yes. But how did you know? I only found out myself two weeks ago.'

The gravity knife must have belonged to Peter's father. Not only had I given it back to Olive, she must have lied about how George had got it.

'Did your father's plane go down? Did he bail out?'

Peter shook his head. 'In 1944 my father – Klaus – came here on a mission. He never completed it. He never came back and no one ever heard from him again. My father was never arrested nor was he registered as a prisoner of war.'

I frowned. 'On a mission? You mean his plane wasn't hit or crashed?'

'No,' said Peter.

'But . . . there were no German soldiers in this area,' I said. 'Just the Americans training for the D-Day landings and even those were a dozen miles away and it was top secret. No one knew.'

'I know,' he said.

'Are you certain your father wasn't found by the Americans?' I suggested.

He shook his head again. 'You mean was he connected to Operation Tiger? No. Don't you see, that makes it even more important that he should have been captured alive. His knowledge and intelligence would have been of vital national security to your country.'

'What about your mother?'

'I'm here *because* of my mother!' Peter exclaimed. 'I can see how close you are to yours and I'm sure you would do the same if you were in my situation.'

I wasn't sure how to respond to that but his words rang true when I thought of all the things I had done to protect my mother.

'You see,' Peter went on. 'My mother was English and she lived in Little Dipperton.'

'Here!' I was astonished.

'She moved to Berlin, found she was pregnant with me, but Father was in intelligence and had one more mission to undertake. He came here and then vanished.'

I was stunned. 'So he did drop behind enemy lines.'

Peter nodded. 'My mother spent her entire life refusing to believe that he had abandoned us. She tried everything she could to find out what happened to him. She never got over him. Never moved on. I just wanted her to be happy.'

'I'm so sorry,' I said and I was. 'Is your mother still alive?'

Peter nodded. 'She was moved into a hospice a month ago. It was when I was clearing out her flat that I found her diaries and letters. Something happened!' Peter was growing emotional again. 'Something happened *here*. I know it! I know something happened at the chapel. It was where they always met.'

I was growing uncomfortable. I was certain now that Olive had to have known more than she was letting on and for some reason, she was lying about it.

'But why make up this story about the census?' I said. 'Why not be honest?'

At this he looked at me as if I was mad. 'I knew that finding the truth would be difficult,' Peter said. 'Among my mother's papers she spoke about her best friend. Her nickname was Fudge. I thought – hoped – that someone here would have known who that person was. Half of me had hoped she would still be alive.'

There was a rustle and the sound of twigs snapping in the undergrowth. Edith appeared on foot. She'd removed her hat and veil and must have tethered Tinkerbell somewhere close by.

Peter sprang to his feet.

'Edith!' I exclaimed, shocked at how tiny and frail she suddenly looked. And incredibly old.

'I'm Fudge,' said Edith. 'It's me.'

Chapter Twenty-eight

Peter gasped. 'You! It's you? You're Fudge! Oh, Edith. Tell me. You know what happened to my father? You must know!' He looked around for somewhere for her to sit, then shrugged off his coat and put it down on the log. 'Please. Please sit.'

So Edith sat. 'I wondered for all these years what had happened to Lottie,' Edith said, but there was no warmth in her voice.

'Lottie? Lottie who?' I asked.

'Pole,' Peter put in. 'My mother was Charlotte Pole.'

The name Pole rang a bell and then I knew where I'd heard it before. It was from Lavinia.

Edith's expression was grim. If she and Lottie had been such close friends, something must have happened to have changed that.

'Lottie met Klaus in Berlin before war broke out,' Edith began. 'They were desperately in love but . . .' Her lips pursed with disapproval. 'Lottie fell into a bad lot. Oswald Mosley. The Blackshirts. They had a very strong following in Devon.'

'That's right,' Peter nodded. 'My mother had always believed in the cause.'

'Lottie was blinded by her love for your father,' Edith said harshly. 'And because he was a true believer in Fascism, she adopted his ideology. She was a romantic. And a fool.'

Edith's tone shocked me. There was no wistful nostalgia here. Anger. Even hatred. It certainly explained why she hadn't kept in touch with her best friend and, up until now, had denied all knowledge of being the mysterious Fudge.

'And it was a long time ago,' Peter said quietly. 'I just want answers. Nothing more. Just for my mother. If you know something, surely you can let her find peace before she dies.'

My mind was grappling to make sense of this revelation. 'But if your father was on a mission,' I said. 'Surely he wasn't acting alone.'

'He wasn't,' Edith said bitterly. 'Lottie helped him.'

'But you said that Lottie went back to Berlin.'

'She did,' Peter nodded. 'She left him the night before, making her way back through their underground network.'

'Your mother was a traitor!' Edith burst out. 'Have you any idea how it feels to know that someone you trusted is willing to betray her friends, her country? Everyone!'

'My mother loved you, Edith,' Peter protested. 'Her diaries are full of remorse. She never meant to deceive you! Her one big regret was losing your friendship. You must believe me.'

'This mission,' I said. 'Do you know what it was?'

Peter straightened his shoulders and I saw a hint of pride. 'Father was a saboteur. There is a viaduct not too far from here—'

'The *Rattery* Viaduct.' I was gobsmacked. Built in the mid-nineteenth century, the railway viaduct was a miraculous feat of engineering. It was made from rock-faced granite with six bays of round arches and piers. It was also the main railway line from London to the southwest and would have been critical for troop manoeuvres and supplies. 'You mean,' I sputtered, 'he was supposed to blow up the viaduct!'

There had been no report of the viaduct being blown up – it would have been in all the history books. It must have failed. 'But . . . but . . . how would he have got the explosives?'

'They were dropped with him,' Peter said simply. 'I told you. My mother was his contact on the ground.'

Edith gave a snort of disgust. I suddenly remembered that Edith's parents had been killed. How could she have felt any affection for a traitor – and a traitor who she must have felt had betrayed her.

Peter began pacing up and down. 'What happened?' He spun around and jabbed an accusatory finger at Edith. 'I know you know! I know it!'

Edith was so pale now I wasn't even sure if she would make it back to the Hall on horseback.

'You know full well what happened,' Peter hissed. 'Did you find him? Did you kill my father, because someone sure as hell did!'

'I'm not answering any of these questions,' Edith stammered. 'You are mad. Quite mad. Go home, Peter. Leave the past where it belongs. Please. I beg of you.'

Peter stopped pacing. He looked so wretched that my heart went out to him. And, without another word, leaving his coat behind, he turned on his heel and left us. We heard the car drive away.

I was shaken and couldn't imagine that Edith had not been affected by this devastating confession. I didn't know what to say or do.

Finally, she seemed to pull herself together. 'Help me onto Tinkerbell.'

I retrieved both horses and managed to get Edith up into the saddle using the same log that she had been sitting on. I grabbed Peter's coat, not relishing the fact of having to return it to him later.

Edith rode on ahead.

Something had stopped me from mentioning the gravity knife to Peter and now I knew why. It would have only thrown up more questions. Ivy Cottage was a short walk to the chapel. Perhaps George Banks had discovered Peter's father after all. The question was, what happened when he did?

The secrecy on all sides suggested a cover-up. Edith's insistence she knew nothing, Olive claiming the knife was bought on eBay and Ruby suddenly running away.

It had to be connected but I wasn't going to be the one to do it. Even though this had happened decades ago, this was much too big for me.

I needed to tell Mallory everything.

Edith and I didn't speak again. By the time I'd untacked Duchess in her loose box and fed and watered her, Edith had returned to the Hall.

The moment I got back to my car, I reached for my mobile to call Mallory but it rang before I had even dialled.

It was my mother and she sounded excited. 'You'll never guess what's happened. Paula has been arrested!'

Chapter Twenty-nine

I found Mum in the kitchen surrounded by ledgers, a calculator, a yellow legal pad and pens and highlighters.

'What happened to Paula?' I exclaimed.

'Delia rang and said that Mallory had turned up to take her into custody,' Mum said. 'We were right. She's behind it all. Delia didn't give any details but she said that Paula was distraught and claiming she was innocent. Pity I'm not writing the church circular because I have the perfect headline.'

I raised an eyebrow.

'Pair of Parishioners Poisoned by Paula.'

Gesturing to the mounds of paperwork I asked, 'What's happening here?'

'What do you think?' Mum pulled a face. 'I'm trying to see how much I'll owe the tax man.'

'Millions?' I said lightly. 'Perhaps they'll do a payment plan.'

'Or I could sell my body. I don't want to talk about it.' She pushed all the papers and ledgers back into a cardboard box. 'Out of sight, out of mind.'

'I've got something to tell you that will take your mind off it,' I said.

'Does this require alcohol?' Mum said.

'Definitely.' I mixed two gin and tonics and returned to the table.

'You're pregnant.'

I rolled my eyes. 'Very funny. No. I'm not but I'll tell you who was.'

Mum listened open-mouthed as I told her all I knew about Lavinia's great-aunt Lottie and her love affair with Klaus Becker that had begun before the war and that Peter was their son. When I told her about Klaus's mission to blow up the Rattery Viaduct, Mum was shocked.

'Lottie Pole,' Mum mused. 'A Nazi sympathiser. There were a lot of them about in the west country, you know. The Blackshirts were rife in Exeter and Bovey Tracey.'

I waited for my mother to mention Wallis Simpson and the abdicated King, who everyone knew planned to be crowned King and Queen of England if Germany won the war. But Mum just wore a faraway look and seemed fixated on the back door.

I told her that Olive must know more than she was letting on. I kept the best bit to last; namely that Edith was the mysterious Fudge.

I waited for a cry of astonishment but my mother said nothing.

'Mum? Didn't you hear what I said?'

'*Abandoned*,' Mum declared. 'That's the title of my next book. Pregnant and abandoned by the man she never saw again. Fighting for a cause they desperately believed in. And yet,' she paused dramatically. 'Their love, although forbidden, was stronger than loyalty to their countries. But . . . it ends in tragedy. Yes! Forbidden love, star-crossed lovers, victims of a cruel world!'

'Well, I'm glad to hear that you can exploit their tragic love affair,' I said wryly.

'And yes, I did hear what you said about Edith,' Mum went on. 'There must have been a good reason why this was all kept so secret.'

'But what should I do about that gravity knife?' I said. 'It must belong to Peter's father. The coincidence is just too hard to ignore.'

'Yes, it must,' came a familiar voice and Peter Becker stood in the kitchen doorway.

I leapt to my feet. I felt nervous. Upset. Unsure of what to do next. How long had he been standing there? How much had he heard?

'We didn't hear the doorbell ring!' Mum said gaily.

'Because I didn't ring it,' he said. 'The door was unlocked.'

Mum glared at me then smiled at Peter. 'Come in and have a drink, do!'

Peter came towards me. I felt threatened and took a step back. He held out his hand. 'Show me the knife.'

'I don't have it,' I said.

Peter grabbed my shoulders. 'Show it to me.'

'I don't have it anymore,' I said. 'I really don't.'

'Kat returned it to Olive Banks,' Mum said quickly. 'You should ask her.'

Peter regarded me with such disappointment that I found myself protesting that I had only found the knife that morning and tried to explain how it had ended up under the front seat of my car.

Peter's eyes narrowed with suspicion. 'It was for sale? Why?'

'But then the lot was withdrawn. Olive changed her mind,' Mum said and then went on the attack. 'Why couldn't you tell us that you had nothing to do with chapels or churches or clocks? Why all the lies and secrecy?'

'Why?' Peter gave a bitter laugh. 'Because I believe my father was murdered and it was hushed up. That's why.'

There was a silence. I had been thinking along those very same lines and I knew that my mother had, too.

'The moment I see this knife I'll know if it belonged to him,' Peter went on. 'Father's initials would be on it somewhere.'

I didn't dare mention that I hadn't noticed any initials.

'Olive Banks lives at number two Honeychurch Cottages, I believe,' Peter continued. 'Bethany told me in the post office. Funny how a villager can't keep a secret but a village can.'

'It was all a long time ago,' Mum said, echoing Edith's words. 'It was a different time. Life moves on. People change.'

'Maybe for you,' Peter's anger surfaced again. 'But not for my mother. She couldn't move on and, in a way, neither could I. Such a waste. Clinging to the past. I just want to be able to give her some peace during the last weeks of her life. That's all.'

'I'll come with you to see Olive,' I said suddenly.

'I'm not sure that's a good idea, Kat,' Mum seemed dubious. 'Unless . . .' She thought for a moment. 'Perhaps you could pose as a collector, Peter? That way you could look at this knife – just to be sure it did or didn't belong to your father.'

We agreed but took separate cars.

As Peter followed me up the service road in his Skoda, I started to have serious reservations. How would Olive react? What would Trevor say if he was there? Had the village gossip-tree already spread the word that Peter Becker was an imposter?

There was only one way to find out.

Chapter Thirty

It was as if Olive had been expecting us. For a moment I wondered if my mother had called ahead and tipped her off.

Olive was – unnervingly – all smiles. 'Come on through,' she said and we trailed after her into the dark kitchen beyond. Olive sank onto a kitchen chair and gestured for us to take a seat, too. 'Would you like some tea?'

'No, thank you,' I said.

'No, thank you,' Peter echoed. 'I won't keep you long, Mrs Banks. I understand you have a Luftwaffe *Fallschirmjäger-Messer*, apologies for lapsing into German.' He gave a chilling smile. 'I mean, a paratrooper's gravity knife, that I would like to see.'

Olive turned ashen. All the colour drained out of her face. She hastily looked down at her hands.

But then she looked up and met Peter's piercing gaze with one of her own.

'You have been talking to Kat,' Olive said smoothly. 'Yes. My husband bought a knife online a few years ago. He was a great collector of military memorabilia. Kat, dear, it's in the wooden crate on the dining room table. Perhaps you could get it for this gentleman.'

Peter shot me a look of triumph.

I darted into the living room and took the lid off the wooden crate. The knife – with the blade out – lay on the top, as if it had been casually thrown in. I could see why it could have been mistaken for a dagger.

I returned to the kitchen and handed Peter the knife. He inspected the blade and wooden hilt but it seemed to me that he was having doubts.

'Do you have a magnifying glass?' he asked me.

'If you can tell me what you're looking for,' said Olive. 'Perhaps I can help? I know it was made in Germany.'

Peter nodded but kept turning the knife this way and that. I knew he was looking for his father's initials and I knew they weren't there.

'Here. Try this.' I produced my loupe from my tote bag. Peter lodged it in his eye socket and looked closely at the knife again before handing the loupe back to me. He was obviously disappointed. Whatever he had hoped the existence of this knife would prove had come to nothing and his father's death would remain a mystery.

'I'll buy it from you,' Peter said suddenly. 'I'll give you five thousand pounds.'

Olive's eyes bugged out. 'Five thousand pounds!'

The knife wasn't worth a thousand, let alone five, but it wasn't for me to say.

'I'll transfer it into a bank account of your choice but there is a condition.' Peter eyes were cold. 'You mentioned your husband bought it online. I would like to see a copy of the transaction.' He turned to me. 'Provenance. Isn't that right, Kat?'

I nodded.

'I wouldn't know where to begin.' Olive gave an apologetic smile. 'I'm sorry I can't help. Now if you'll excuse me—'

'My mother was Lottie Pole.' Peter's voice was icy. 'She left detailed diaries about meeting my father, Klaus Becker, at the chapel. You lived at Ivy Cottage. I know you saw something. What happened to him? That's all I want to know!'

And suddenly Olive started talking. 'You can't possibly understand what it was like in those days,' she began. 'We were all so frightened. England was losing the war. We were convinced that at any moment the Germans would invade. We knew something had to be happening on the south coast because people close to the beaches were being moved miles inland. We didn't know that the Americans were rehearsing for D-Day. We thought the Germans had arrived in Devon. After all, they'd occupied the Channel Islands for four years already!'

'Go on,' said Peter. 'I'm listening.'

'No one cares anymore about the sacrifices my generation made to keep our country safe.' Olive was becoming emotional. 'If my husband was still alive, he would still regard you as the enemy. There is nothing to tell. You are wasting your time.'

Peter's constant questions were beginning to take their toll on Olive. She was growing red in the face and was visibly distressed. I was getting concerned.

'What about Ruby Pritchard, the vicar's mother?' Peter persisted. 'She lived with you. I know she did. Maybe she saw something.'

'Ruby?' Olive said sharply. 'You don't want to believe anything she tells you. And she ran away. She wasn't here when that happened.'

'What happened?' Peter said sharply.

'I don't know,' Olive started rocking back and forth, making a strange keening sound. 'I don't know what you want me to say. I don't know anything!'

'We should go,' I said quickly and stood up. Peter snatched the knife off the table and put it in his pocket. Olive didn't try to stop him. The whole meeting had been a disaster.

And then Trevor flung open the kitchen door. He seemed distraught. 'I heard Paula's been arrested! She needs a solicitor. The police are coming and they'll search . . . oh!' Trevor saw us behind the door and his eyes widened. 'What the hell is going on here? Ma?'

Olive's face crumpled. She looked close to collapse. 'Ask them,' she whispered. 'They keep asking questions about the war. I don't know what they want me to say.'

He pointed a finger at me. 'Why can't you just leave my mother alone! She's not well. Just get out!'

Peter started to say something but I grabbed his arm and propelled him out of the kitchen and into the dark night. I was shaking.

Peter threw my arm aside. 'What's all this about Paula being arrested? Is that the housekeeper at the Hall? The woman who makes all those strange dishes with weeds and grass?'

In for a penny, in for a pound. 'She's been arrested on suspicion of poisoning two people in the village.'

Peter's jaw dropped. 'Poison? Are you . . . are you serious? What kind of village is this?'

It was a question I had been asking myself. It seemed that Little Dipperton suffered more murders than *Midsomer Murders* on the TV.

'Just because Olive Banks is old, doesn't mean she should get away with it.' Peter was angry now. 'My father was a highly trained soldier. He came here on a mission and vanished. Olive was right when she said some people don't forget. Well, my mother hasn't and I won't either. I will get to the bottom of this. Whatever it takes.'

Chapter Thirty-one

I drove on to Jane's Cottage feeling a mixture of guilt, annoyance and curiosity. I wasn't Peter's keeper and he had to do what he had to do and that would now be without me. But he was right, something bad had happened and someone was still covering it up, all these years later.

I kept replaying Peter's conversation with Olive. There was something she said that had stuck with me. The fear that the Germans had already invaded England.

What if the Home Guard – already on high alert and nervous – *had* found Peter's father at the chapel? Did they know that Lottie Pole – Lavinia's great-aunt – was involved in helping him? Edith certainly did.

And then there was Ruby.

As I reached for the phone I saw I had three missed calls from my mother. I rang her back.

'You told me you'd let me know how it went with Olive,' she said. 'I've been worried.'

'Not great.' As I brought my mother up to date, she was so shocked that she didn't speak for thirty seconds. I checked.

'I think I should go and sit with Ruby just in case Peter turns up,' Mum said. 'Perhaps – without wanting to sound like a clichéd German interrogator from *Hogan's Heroes* – he has ways of making people talk and when they don't . . .'

'Not funny, Mum,' I said. 'He's hardly going to hurt Ruby. She's old! And anyway, Danny will be there.'

'He won't,' Mum said coldly. 'If you recall, Danny spends his nights with his beloved Caroline. I don't like Ruby being all alone if Peter is on the rampage, especially now you tell me he took that knife.'

'She probably wouldn't even open the door to him. You know what Ruby is like.'

'True,' Mum declared. 'But I'm going to go over there.'

I was about to ring off when I remembered something.

'One more thing,' I said. 'What was the name of that book that Danny had on his kitchen table?'

'It was a collection of short stories by Graham Greene,' Mum said. 'Why?'

'It was a library book,' I said. 'Don't you think that's weird? Why would Danny have taken that specific book out of the library?'

'Maybe it was for Ruby?' Mum suggested.

'Maybe,' I admitted. 'And maybe you can ask her what she was hiding when we went around there yesterday. She grabbed some material off the countertop and shoved it into the dresser drawer. If you ask me, what with Danny snapping his laptop shut and her being very secretive, they were up to something.'

Mum gave a heavy sigh. 'I'll ask her.'

I ended the call, changed into sweatpants and sweatshirt, and poured myself a glass of wine. There was a bit of cheese in the fridge which I might have later. I wasn't hungry. Too much had happened today and I felt very unsettled.

For a brief moment, Shawn entered my mind, but then he was gone.

I opened my laptop. It took just seconds to pull up the name of Graham Greene's book, *The Last Word and Other Stories*. A further listing gave the short story 'The Lieutenant Died Last' a special mention and said that it had been made into a well-known war film called *Went The Day Well?* My stomach turned over.

Peter Becker had mentioned the title of that film when we were discussing what to screen last night. George Banks had bought the VHS cassette many years ago and it must have meant something to him – enough for George to want it screened in his honour; enough to have given the video player to Danny so that he could do so.

I searched my internet browser for *Went the Day Well?* and pulled up the synopsis.

The film was made in 1942 in black and white and directed by Alberto Cavalcanti and was regarded as unofficial propaganda for the war effort. I read, 'The film shows a southern English village taken over by German paratroopers, reflecting the greatest potential nightmare for the British public of the time. The film is notable for its unusually frank depiction of ruthless violence.'

I was able to find the film on YouTube. I was certain this

must have been what Danny had been watching when we interrupted him but, for some reason, he didn't want us to know. I googled for more information and discovered a rampant conspiracy theory during the war years, namely the infiltration of a so-called fifth column.

Olive had said they were frightened of a German invasion. I was convinced now that Peter's father must have been discovered by the Home Guard. Perhaps by George Banks himself.

Little wonder that there had been so much secrecy. But what had happened to Klaus Becker? He hadn't been imprisoned or questioned – which left only one alternative.

Peter was right. His father had been murdered.

Had Edith known? Was Olive covering for her dead husband? And where did Ruby fit in?

I reached for my mobile and automatically dialled Shawn's number but hung up before I got a ring tone. Habit! I tried Mallory but there was no answer. Of course, Paula had been arrested and that would take priority.

I checked my watch. It was almost ten thirty. Mum should be back from Ruby's by now and, since I hadn't heard from her, I assumed there had been nothing to worry about.

I changed back into my jeans and sweater, grabbed a coat and my car keys, and left.

I sped down the service road. As I reached the terrace of cottages, I slowed down to pass the white van and police car that were outside number two Honeychurch Cottages. The cottage was lit up – lights blazing from every window.

Delia waved me down. She was wearing a fluffy onesie that did nothing for her figure.

'You've heard about Paula.' Delia was expiring with excitement. 'They're in there now, going through everything. It's just like the telly. Men in white overalls with bags on their feet.'

There was no Ford Escort. 'Where are Trevor and Paula?'

'Gone to the police station in Dartmouth,' Delia said. 'That's what Trevor told me. I've never seen a man so upset. Protesting she's innocent and all that. Turns out that Gladys didn't have a heart attack. She was poisoned by Paula's cooking! I knew foraging was just a gimmick. I suppose that's manslaughter if it's an accident. Though frankly, if it is, why are the men in white coats here?'

I remembered Shawn's instructions to keep quiet so did just that.

Delia finally drew breath so I could speak. 'I thought Trevor had lost his driving licence.'

'He has, but Olive hasn't.' Delia rolled her eyes. 'You should have seen the palaver getting her into the driving seat but she was adamant that they should go! Well. I don't know what to do now. I'll have to hire a new housekeeper, I suppose.'

I drove away, leaving Delia hovering by the white van, a pale grey blob in the moonlight.

I pulled into the carriageway just as my mother emerged from the back door. She was wrapped up in a coat.

'Haven't you been to check on Ruby yet?' I exclaimed.

'I did,' Mum looked worried. 'She wouldn't answer the door so I came home. But now I'm going out again.'

'What's going on?'

'I just had a call from Danny,' she said. 'Ruby has disappeared.'

Chapter Thirty-two

We sped back to Little Dipperton as Mum told me that Danny had returned unexpectedly from Newton Abbot to find Ruby wasn't at home.

'Perhaps she just went for an evening stroll and Danny is overreacting?' I suggested hopefully.

'And bumped into Peter!' Mum gasped. 'Oh, Kat, what if he's kidnapped her?'

'Don't be silly,' I said briskly. 'And what would be the point of that?'

But even so, the sight of Peter's Skoda on the forecourt in front of the pub filled me with relief. 'You see! He's still here.'

'But he said he was driving home tonight, remember?' Mum's anxiety was contagious. 'And that was a rental car. Maybe he just left it there.'

'And what?' I said. 'Got a taxi? Don't be daft. He probably just changed his mind.'

'Exactly!' Mum exclaimed. 'To torture Ruby!'

'I'm not even going to bother to comment on that silly remark,' I said, but deep down I was concerned. Peter's mental state was very worrying and his last words to me left no doubt that he was determined to get to the bottom of it. Whatever it took.

We turned into Church Lane. There was no sign of Danny's motorbike and sidecar. I parked my Golf and we got out.

'Danny told me he was going out to look for her,' said Mum.

'She can't have gone far,' I pointed out. 'She can hardly walk!'

Mum suddenly seized my arm. 'Perhaps Peter was staking out the cottage from the graveyard. He saw my car parked outside Vergers Cottage, waited for me to leave, made his move and abducted her.'

'Or maybe she sneaked back home and is tucked up in bed,' I said.

We headed for Vergers Cottage. It was hard not to miss the crime scene tape barring entry to Blackberry Cottage next door. For a split second, I saw Gladys lying on the bathroom floor again; her face contorted in a sardonic grin.

Mum wrapped smartly on the door. There was no answer.

I knelt and peered through the letterbox. The cottage was in darkness. 'Let's check inside first.' I recovered the key from the flowerpot – with eyerolls from Mum about an open invitation for burglars – and went inside.

Mum turned on the sitting room lights. Ruby didn't answer our greetings. She certainly wasn't downstairs. I started to feel nauseous as I remembered the last time I went in search of a senior citizen. 'Will you go upstairs and check, Mum?'

'Oh.' Her face fell as she realised what I was implying. 'But surely . . . with Paula arrested . . .'

'Please, Mum.'

I saw the Graham Greene book that was still on the kitchen table along with the VHS cassette that Danny had wrenched from the broken machine. The tape had unravelled but on the front was the label: *Went The Day Well?* I was right.

When my mother returned – thankfully with the only bad news being that Ruby wasn't there and that Danny slept in the smaller bedroom and in a single bed – I told her I had just watched *Went The Day Well?* on YouTube.

'It's about an English village that is infiltrated by the fifth column – an undercover German unit pretending to be British soldiers.'

Mum's jaw dropped. 'And you think that Klaus Becker was trying to do just that?'

'Not exactly. He had a mission, remember,' I said. 'But George Banks might have thought so.'

'Wait a moment,' Mum marched to the kitchen dresser, opening and closing the drawers and rummaging around.

It made me jittery. 'What are you doing? What if Ruby comes back! Or Danny!'

'You were the one who told me to look. Oh God, Katherine.' Mum found what she was looking for. She dropped the scrap of blue-grey cloth onto the table as if it was a hot potato.

I picked it up and my heart skipped a beat. There was no denying the distinctive Luftwaffe breast eagle insignia. 'It looks like . . .'

Our eyes met in mutual horror.

'Part of a German uniform,' Mum whispered. 'I'm trying to remember the last time I watched *Where Eagles Dare*. There were plenty of German paratroopers in that.'

'But why is it here? Why would Ruby have it?' I said. 'Do you think . . . ?'

'No I don't,' Mum declared. 'Ruby was just a kid!'

'Is it possible that the uniform had belonged to Klaus Becker?' I stared at the broken cassette and the library book on the kitchen table. 'Danny knows.'

'I'm going to call him right now.' Mum pulled out her mobile and when Danny answered his, she blurted, 'We're in your kitchen and we've found part of a German uniform.'

I couldn't hear Danny's reply but it was short and sweet.

Mum disconnected the line. Her face was etched with worry.

'What did he say?'

'He didn't deny it.' She frowned, as if trying to make sense of something. 'Danny said we must find Ruby. He's worried about what she might do.'

'What *she* might do?' I was astonished. 'Like what?'

'I don't know,' Mum said.

'I'll go to the pub. Maybe she's there with Peter after all and they're having a lovely drink together. I've got his coat in my car! He took it off so Edith could sit on it.'

'That's as good an excuse as any, I suppose.'

'You check the church,' I said. 'Maybe Ruby has gone in there to . . . I don't know. Pray or something!'

Outside the cottage, we split up.

I hurried through the graveyard and entered the Hare and Hounds, which was unusually quiet, probably because everyone had been there the night before for the film. Doreen was behind the bar.

I cut to the chase. 'Have you seen Ruby tonight?'

Doreen's expression said it all. 'Here? Are you joking? We never see her. Why?'

'What about Peter? I saw his car outside. Wasn't he supposed to be leaving tonight?'

'You're not the only one asking for him,' Doreen said. 'Trevor was in here several hours ago.'

I'd thought that Trevor and Olive were dashing to the police station. I remembered how angry Trevor had been. Perhaps he'd come to pick a fight! Or get the knife that Peter had slipped into his pocket.

'Did Trevor and Peter meet up?' I asked.

'Trevor Banks is banned from this pub,' Doreen declared. 'It was only out of respect for his father that we allowed him in here at all. Trevor has always been nothing but trouble.'

'So, Trevor didn't see Peter tonight?' I had to know. 'What sort of mood was he in?'

'Mood? What do you mean, mood?' Doreen thought for a moment. 'Well, he was in a bit of a rush, to tell you the truth. He said he was off to the police station to see Paula. I assume you know she's been arrested. Ridiculous. Paula might have a temper on her but she's like a kitten. I've known her for decades. That's just not who she is. I told her this foraging lark would end badly.'

I wanted to get to the point, not gossip. 'But why did Trevor come here?'

'He dropped something off for Peter,' Doreen said. 'Stan took it upstairs.'

I needed to have peace of mind to know that Ruby wasn't in Peter's room. I brandished Peter's coat. 'And I need to drop this off upstairs too.'

'Be my guest,' said Doreen. 'He's in Rose. The bedroom at the end of the corridor.'

Thanking her, I headed for the stairs, noticing the faded red carpet and the musty smell that always seemed to accompany any ancient pub where people had been drinking for hundreds of years.

I tapped on Rose. 'Peter? It's Kat.'

There was no reply.

I tapped harder. 'It's Kat!'

And then I heard a strange, muffled cry. My stomach turned over. 'Peter!' I rattled the door handle. 'Are you okay?'

I tore back down the stairs and moments later I was back with Doreen and her master key. We burst into his room. Peter was lying flat on his back. His eyes were wide open but he wasn't moving.

'Can't feel my feet,' he whispered. 'Numb.'

I guessed straight away. 'He's been poisoned. Quickly Doreen, call an ambulance.'

I dropped beside him and reached for his pulse. It was racing. Desperate, I scanned the room and saw, on the top of a rolltop desk, an open foil package.

Peter followed my gaze. 'The picnic puff. Tried it but it's not gluten-free.'

Doreen returned bearing a tube with a balloon-shaped squeeze ball. 'Out of the way, dear.'

With astonishing expertise she dropped to her knees and without a moment's hesitation, thrust it down Peter's throat. He didn't try to fight it. He'd already lapsed into unconsciousness. Doreen began to pump air into his lungs. 'We need to keep the airways open. Try to stop him going into respiratory arrest. Stan's called for an ambulance.'

I stood helplessly by, amazed at this side of the jolly landlady of the Hare and Hounds that I had never seen before.

'We'll take it from here,' came the familiar voices of the Cruickshank twins as they entered the room.

I stepped out of the bedroom, severely shaken up. 'Will he survive?'

'I don't know, dear,' Doreen looked worried.

'You were incredible,' I said.

'Gladys wasn't the only person in the village with medical training, you know,' Doreen said with a smile. 'I just couldn't hack the stress of hospital life.'

I headed back to find Mum, feeling deeply troubled.

Trevor had delivered the poison-laced picnic puff to Peter. It had been deliberate and yet neither Trevor nor Paula – who was in custody anyway – had an axe to grind with Peter.

Which left Olive.

Chapter Thirty-three

A group of nosy villagers had gathered around the waiting ambulance. Word of the attempted poisoning had spread and, as to be expected, that the police had lied about Gladys's heart attack. Poor Staci's demise wasn't even mentioned – something that struck me as unusual. Both had been poisoned and yet I still couldn't figure out the connection.

'Danny says Ruby has taken Gladys's car,' Mum declared as I found her and Danny outside the pub car park.

'The yellow Peugeot?' I was shocked. 'But . . . I thought Ruby didn't drive.'

'She doesn't,' said Danny. 'But she can. Oh God . . .'

'But . . . where can she be going at this time of night?' I asked.

'I think . . .' Danny's voice was barely a whisper. 'I think she's gone to confront Olive.'

'Olive?' Mum and I chorused.

'About what?' I demanded.

'We may already be too late,' Danny was in full-on panic mode now. 'This is all my fault.'

'Well, you've got nothing to worry about there,' Mum said cheerfully. 'What are they going to do? Push each other over and hope someone breaks a hip?'

But Danny didn't laugh. 'You don't understand. We must find her. I've been looking everywhere! I don't know what to do.'

'I suppose you could ask Him,' Mum said gently.

'I'm going to text Mallory,' I said and did so. To my relief he called me back immediately.

'Have you seen Trevor?' Mallory dispensed with the pleasantries. 'Paula's been trying to reach her husband all evening and, to be honest, I'd quite like to go home.'

'But . . .' I stammered. 'Aren't Trevor and Olive at the police station with you?'

'They never showed up,' said Mallory. 'Why?'

When I brought him quickly up to date with the fact that Ruby had vanished and Danny believed she had gone to find Olive and, for some reason, it desperately concerned him, Mallory told us all to sit tight. He would leave Paula in custody and be with us within the half hour.

Doreen found us in the car park. 'I'm not sure if this is helpful,' she began. 'But one of my regulars just mentioned he saw Gladys's yellow car going out of the village on the top road. He thought he saw Ruby driving, which is why he thought it odd – what with Gladys being dead, you understand.'

'What else did he say?' Danny cut in.

'That the car turned off by the roadside hutch that used to sell eggs? I think it leads to—'

'Ivy Cottage,' I exclaimed. 'I'm sure of it. Thank you, Doreen. Mum, Danny, get in my car. I'll drive.'

'Well, we certainly can't all squeeze into Danny's sidecar,' Mum muttered.

The three of us raced back to the church car park and piled into my Golf. Danny rode shotgun and Mum was in the back. We sped out of the village.

Danny finally began to talk.

'George came to me to offload his conscience,' he said. 'He was suffering from dementia and a lot of what he said I took with a pinch of salt. He became obsessed with the war and how he saved Little Dipperton from a German invasion.'

'Which was why he wanted us to screen *Went the Day Well?*' I said.

'I didn't understand the significance of that film at first,' Danny went on. 'George was convinced that the Germans had infiltrated the village and that he was justified in not signing up for regular service.'

'*Justified*?' I was confused. 'Justified in what way?'

'He seemed riddled with guilt about something,' said Danny. 'It was the photographs that made me realise that everything George had said was true.'

'Photographs? What photographs?' Mum demanded.

'The photographs that Kat took.' Danny took a deep breath. 'The reason the clock stopped working in 1944,' Danny paused, as if he could hardly believe what he was about to say, 'was because a German uniform was stuffed into the workings.'

Mum and I were so stunned neither of us could speak.

'Most of it I can't reach. It's damp and rotten,' said Danny. 'I was only able to retrieve that scrap of fabric – a sleeve – that you saw in the cottage. When Mother realised what I'd found in the clock, she passed out.'

'So you're saying that Ruby was as shocked as you were at finding the uniform?' I said slowly.

Danny nodded.

'So who put the uniform into the clock?' Mum demanded. 'It had to be George Banks.'

'But how could he have done that with his gimpy foot?' I pointed out. 'Believe me. You can only ascend with your foot sideways on each step. He couldn't have done it.'

'I bet it was Olive!' Mum exclaimed. 'She lied when she said she'd never been up the tower. Do you think Ruby knew? Is that why she wants to confront Olive? But—' Mum shook her head. 'Why? Why now?'

'I don't know,' Danny said miserably.

Mum leaned forward and grabbed my shoulder. 'I think we're missing something far more important here. If all this was true, George and Olive Banks murdered Klaus Becker and if they did, what did they do with his body?'

'It's obvious,' I said. 'It must be in the grounds of the chapel. Perhaps that's why Edith . . . Oh God. Do you think Edith knows what happened and is covering it all up? You know how loyal she is to her people.'

Mum and I continued to make ourselves even more

frightened as we explored various theories but Danny had stopped talking. He sat tense and rigid in the front seat.

The roadside hutch that marked the entrance to the track loomed ahead in the moonlight. 'We're here.'

I stopped the car.

'Why are we stopping?' Mum demanded. 'You think we should go in on foot?'

'Don't we need a plan?' I said. 'Trevor is with them. You know he has a reputation for being violent.'

'Just drive,' Danny said suddenly. 'There's no time to lose.'

I eased into first gear and made the turn down the narrow lane. It was bumpy and full of potholes filled with water.

'Shouldn't you cut the lights?' Mum said.

'No,' Danny's voice held a note of panic. 'They need to know someone is coming.'

The chimney of Ivy Cottage came into view above the trees. I could see the silhouette of the old bell tower on a slight rise in the woods beyond. It reminded me of a film set and when I said so, Mum replied, 'Yes, a horror film.'

We passed the yellow Peugeot, parked next to the picket fence. Ruby wasn't inside.

And suddenly, someone dashed in front of my car.

I hit the brakes just as a hand slammed down hard on the bonnet. Mum screamed. Shocked, I looked over to find Trevor yanking my door open. His eyes were wide with terror.

'For God's sake,' he shouted. 'Hurry. Hurry.'

Danny was out in a flash. 'Where is she? Is Mother hurt?'

Trevor was close to hysterics. 'They're in the car.' He pointed wildly to the Ford Escort which was parked ahead in an open gateway.

'Thank God,' said Danny, almost collapsing with relief.

'No,' Trevor was sobbing. 'You don't understand. Ruby has a grenade.'

Chapter Thirty-four

For a moment no one moved, but then all three of us scrambled out of my Golf. Danny took off at a run towards the Ford Escort but Trevor – with astonishing speed – raced after him and brought the vicar down in a rugby tackle. 'You can't!' Trevor panted. 'It's too dangerous!'

Mum grabbed my arm, jabbering about being blown to pieces. The enormity of what could happen if the grenade went off seemed to hit us all at the same time.

Trevor brought Danny back to us, holding his arm tightly. Danny's man-bun had come loose and his grey hair cascaded onto his shoulders.

'Let me go and reason with her, I beg you,' Danny pleaded. 'She'll listen to me.'

'No!' Trevor kept hold of Danny's arm. 'I tried that already and when I did, Ruby held up the grenade and threatened to pull out the pin. I've called the police and they said the bomb squad will be here in twenty minutes.'

'We might all be dead by then!' Mum exclaimed.

Danny began to pray under his breath.

'Are you sure it was a grenade?' Mum asked Trevor.

'Why?' Trevor's voice was shrill. 'Do you think I would make something like that up?'

'Let's move back, away into the garden,' I suggested, so the four of us did, casting terrified glances over at the Ford Escort where there seemed to be no movement at all.

'You're a big man, Trevor,' Mum pointed out. 'Why couldn't you have overpowered her?'

'Well he didn't, did he?' Danny said. 'Tell us exactly what happened, Trevor, please.'

'Ruby got here before we did,' said Trevor. 'She just came up to the car all friendly like and told me to get into the back seat. Ma was driving. I got into the back just thinking they were going to have a chat about something, although Ma warned me that Ruby was crazy and made me promise to stay with her.'

'Go on,' Mum prompted.

'And then, Ruby just brings it out of her handbag,' said Trevor. 'As if she was offering Ma a piece of chocolate! I saw what it was straight away.' He swallowed hard. 'So I leapt out and ran.' Trevor was obviously traumatised. He began to tremble. 'I left her. I left my Ma. And if she dies it's my fault.'

Danny gave Trevor a pat on the shoulder. 'You did what you had to do.'

Trevor rounded on Danny. 'You knew Ruby was insane. You knew it!' If anyone was crazy, it was Trevor.

'But how did Ruby get the grenade in the first place?' Mum suddenly declared. 'Where did she get it from?'

My heart was thundering in my chest. 'Now isn't the time to ask why, Mum.'

'Of course it is,' she retorted. 'Is it a war relic?' And wouldn't the grenade have gone off by now if Ruby had really intended to do it? She's bluffing!'

'Does it matter?' Danny was distraught. 'I blame myself for—'

'Oh, get over yourself, Danny,' Mum shot back. 'Your mother is holding Trevor's mother to ransom for some reason. It's about the dead German, isn't it? It must be.'

'What dead German?' Trevor seemed confused.

'It wasn't a dagger in your father's memorabilia,' Mum said. 'It was a special knife that belonged to a German paratrooper who dropped behind enemy lines and who was murdered by *your* parents!'

Trevor reeled backwards in shock. 'I didn't know. Oh no. I didn't know!'

But he'd loosened his grip on Danny's arm. Danny broke ranks and ran towards the car crying, 'Mum! Don't do it!'

'Stay back!' screamed Ruby's voice from inside the Ford Escort. It was shrill and terrifying. Danny stopped in his tracks.

'Stay back,' came a loud, crackling voice accompanied by a lot of static.

We turned to see Mallory stride towards us on foot, holding a megaphone. No one had heard his car. He swiftly took charge. 'I need you all to move further back. Behind the hen house, please. Sir! Over here now.'

Danny slunk back to the fold. Mum joined him, stroking

his arm and whispering presumably comforting words. Trevor was transfixed, his eyes not leaving the Ford Escort.

Mallory pulled me aside. 'The bomb squad have got lost,' he said in a low voice. 'They can't find the location.'

And we waited. And the seconds ticked by with agonising slowness. The atmosphere was electric. Still, there was no movement from the Ford Escort. Just the silhouettes of the two women sitting in the front of the car lit by a shaft of moonlight. It was cold. I started to shiver.

And then suddenly, the passenger door opened.

Ruby got out very slowly. Staggering slightly, unsteady and unstable. She leaned on her cane with one hand and was clutching something in the other.

'She's still got the grenade!' Trevor shrieked.

Mallory took off across the uneven ground.

'No! Don't!' I screamed and instinctively went to stop him but Mum hauled me backwards.

'Don't be a fool,' she snapped, more in fear than anything else.

It's true what they say, that car crashes always happen in slow motion. It's supposedly a way the brain tries to protect you in times of great stress.

I felt my heart had stopped as I watched Mallory reach Ruby and snatch the grenade from her hand. He lifted it high above his head before delivering a powerful overarm throw, hurling the bomb towards the woods.

And then time speeded up.

Mallory pulled Ruby down to the ground, covering her body with his own. There was a thunderous ear-splitting boom and the night sky was awash in a bright light of fiery red and brilliant orange. A cluster of trees erupted into flames, spitting and splitting and filling the air with acrid smoke, illuminating the ruined bell tower in the woods.

We all fell backwards, knocked off our feet by the blasts which just kept on coming. One after the other, as if an entire factory of fireworks had been ignited by a match.

The wind was knocked out of me, my eardrums hummed but then, miraculously, the noise stopped, the smoke cleared and other than the distant crackle of burning trees, it was eerily quiet.

We began to move slowly, checking for broken limbs and getting to our feet. I sought comfort in Mum's welcoming arms.

And then a helicopter appeared overhead. A fire engine, a fleet of army vehicles and an ambulance burst into view. It felt surreal, noisy and chaotic, with firemen rolling out hoses to douse the flaming trees in water and army personnel realising that they'd missed the show. A young sergeant approached to ask who was in charge. Danny pointed to Mallory, who was still on the ground.

I was alarmed. 'He's injured!' I tore across the grass but as I drew closer, I saw that Mallory was taking care of Ruby who was lying on her back. He looked up. Our eyes met.

'Oh God,' I whispered. 'I thought you . . .' and promptly burst into tears.

Mum was right behind me, closely followed by Danny and Trevor.

'Is she all right?' Danny sounded desperate. 'Is Mother okay?'

'She's fine,' said Mallory, then scrambled to his feet to stop Trevor from opening the Ford Escort door. 'Sir, please stay where you are.'

Trevor tried to duck under Mallory's arm to reach the car. 'Ma! Is she—?'

'I'm afraid so,' said Mallory. 'The shock of expecting the grenade to go off must have given her a heart attack.'

Trevor sank onto Mallory's shoulders, devastated. Mallory gently led him away just as the Cruickshank twins arrived with the stretcher. The helicopter vanished. Vehicles were being moved but it would be a while before we could leave.

'Let's go inside Ivy Cottage,' Mum suggested. 'Olive has only been gone a couple of weeks. Perhaps we might find a few teabags.'

The front door to the cottage was locked but I managed to climb in through the kitchen window at the back.

The musk of rot and damp from the flooded bathroom hit my senses straight away. The bathroom had been above the kitchen and what remained of the ceiling lay on the quarry-tiled floor in mounds of plaster and rubble.

I opened the front door and let Danny, Ruby and my mother inside.

Mum picked her way through the debris to get to the kitchen cupboards and found a box of teabags and some Carnation powdered milk, a bag of sugar and some mugs. She put on the kettle. Thankfully, the power hadn't been disconnected yet. Together we found a tray and carried everything into the small front room where the others had assembled.

Olive's cardigan and possessions were still strewn about. It was as if she had left for the day and planned on coming home later.

Mallory arrived with Trevor in tow. 'The fire is contained,' said Mallory. 'The explosion turned out to be a cache of old ammunition from the war that had been buried in the grounds of the chapel.'

'Do you think they were the explosives intended for the Rattery Viaduct?' I whispered to Mum.

'And Edith said the chapel was dangerous,' Mum whispered back. 'Now we know why.'

But then Trevor turned on Ruby. His face was purple with rage. 'This is all your fault, you horrible old witch.'

'Steady on, sir,' Mallory said.

'She told us to come!' he exclaimed. 'Ma always said you were evil.'

Ruby returned his stare with one of her own. Hatred.

'She was the one who called my Ma,' Trevor raged. '*She* said it was time that they had a chat and to let bygones be bygones. She even made a joke about offering Olive the olive branch. Ma was nervous and that's why she wanted me to go with her.'

'But you said you were going to the police station to see Paula,' I reminded him.

'Ruby rang when we were on our way so we turned around,' said Trevor. 'What's that got to do with anything?'

Something didn't add up. 'But not before you stopped at the Hare and Hounds to deliver a picnic puff to Peter.'

'Who nearly died,' Mum put in. 'It was poisoned.'

Trevor was taken aback. 'I don't know what you're talking about. Ma just told me he was leaving and that Paula had made him a snack for the journey. I didn't even know what it was.'

Ruby uttered a cry of shock. Her face was white.

There was something bothering me. 'Why did you want to talk to Olive, Ruby?' I turned to Danny, who wouldn't meet my eye. 'You said your mother wanted to confront her. What was it about?' I turned back to Ruby. 'Why did you want to meet Olive here?'

Ruby didn't answer for a moment. It was as if she was struggling to find the right words.

'I killed that soldier,' she whispered. 'It wasn't Olive who did it. It was me.'

Chapter Thirty-five

There was a stunned silence. Even Trevor seemed frozen to the spot.

'Don't be silly,' Mum said briskly. 'You're in shock. You don't know what you're saying!'

Ruby appealed to Danny who gave a nod of encouragement. 'It's okay, Mother. Tell them everything.'

And it all came tumbling out.

'I didn't know he was German, you see,' Ruby said. 'He was wearing an American uniform.'

'What? How is that possible?' Mum sounded as bewildered as me.

'Olive told me to help our allies,' said Ruby. 'She told me that the American soldier was in love with an English girl.'

'That must have been Lottie Pole,' Mum declared.

'I knew they used to meet at the chapel,' Ruby went on. 'Sometimes I'd watch them together. I thought it so romantic. She brought him clothes. And one day I saw her bring a box of something. Later, I went and found out where she'd hidden it. It was a box of explosives.'

And I suspected they were the same ones that had just been detonated.

'Is that where you found the grenade?' Mum asked.

'Oh,' Ruby gave a harsh laugh. 'I stole that years ago and hid it in a crevice in the wall. I told George Banks that if he ever touched me again I would kill him. Of course Olive refused to believe me. She thought the sun shone out of his backside, she did.'

'Go on, Mother,' Danny said gently and gave her a squeeze of reassurance.

'So one day, Olive made the soldier a sandwich and told me to go and give it to him.' Ruby paused. Her defiant expression changing to guilt and horror at the memory. 'He was very friendly, very nice. He spoke in a funny accent but I just thought it was because he was American. I didn't know he was a German soldier. I didn't know!'

'We know you didn't, Mother,' said Danny. 'We know.'

'Olive made me do it.' Ruby started shaking. 'Just like she made Paula poison Staci and Gladys—'

'And Peter,' Mum put in.

Trevor remained rooted to the spot, his jaw slack.

'And then what happened?' said Danny.

'So I gave the soldier the sandwich,' Ruby whispered. 'We were sitting in the sunshine on a bit of stone wall near the bell tower. Olive told me to stay with him until she came to fetch me. I didn't know why. I was only nine and I was scared of her so I did what she said. After about half an hour, he started sweating and complaining that he couldn't feel his feet. And then Mr Banks came out of the woods with Olive. He was angry with her but Olive just laughed.' Ruby stopped talking to compose herself. 'As if she was proud of what she'd done. And then the soldier died.'

None of us spoke. Not even Trevor.

'And I ran away but Mr Banks ran after me and caught me and dragged me back,' Ruby rushed on. 'Olive held my face to the hotplate and told me that if I ever told anyone, she would find me and force the poison down my throat and bury me alive.'

Ruby just sat there with a look of such terror on her face that there was no doubt in my mind that she was telling the truth. It all finally seemed to make sense.

'And that's why the German uniform was hidden in the clock,' I said.

Ruby nodded. 'Olive forced me to hide it there.'

'And George Banks's obsession with that German war film,' Mum chimed in. 'George genuinely believed that he was saving the country from the elusive fifth column.'

'But he should have been turned over to the authorities,' Danny said. 'What on earth possessed Olive to kill him like that?'

Mum shrugged. 'Fear of the enemy? Cruelty?'

And then something Ruby had said hit me. 'You told us that George Banks ran after you the day Klaus Becker was murdered.'

'Yes,' she said. 'I ran and ran through the woods but he still caught me.'

'But . . . I thought he couldn't run,' I said. 'Wasn't that why he didn't sign up for active service?'

Danny looked uncomfortable and fiddled with his man-bun.

'You know something, Danny!' Mum exclaimed. 'What is it?'

'I . . . well . . . I can't,' said Danny. 'I'm betraying a confidence.'

'To hell – pardon my French – with confidences!' Mum fumed. 'What is it? It's important! And,' Mum struggled to find the right words, 'if it's connected to this fiasco, it will help your mother's defence. It doesn't matter about the circumstances.'

I put out a restraining hand. 'Mum. Don't.'

'It's true!' Mum said. 'You've already confessed you did it, Ruby. Olive is dead. It's your word against evidence!'

Danny seemed in an agonising dilemma. Ruby just sat there, mute.

'There was nothing wrong with George's feet,' Danny blurted out. 'He had all his toes. He lied and he felt bad about that. He really did.'

My mother started to giggle. Something she always did when she was highly nervous, but I was incredulous. 'I don't believe it! You mean . . . everyone has been lauding him as a great war hero when all the time he was a coward!'

'That's all well and good now,' Mum declared, still tittering. 'But without a body, no one can prove anything.'

'But there is.' Ruby pointed to her feet. 'Klaus Becker is buried in the cellar.'

Chapter Thirty-six

The sun came out for the grand opening of Paula's Field Pantry in the former tearoom in the village. Happily, the locals had not been put off by Paula's experimental cooking and eagerly devoured her foraging fare. As with any scandal that revolved around the Honeychurch Hall estate, the details and rumours of poisonings were played down with the focus being on the surprise discovery of a cache of Second World War ammunition that had to be detonated by the Army. That they arrived after the fact was neither here nor there.

It turned out that the cash found in Gladys's house was the exact amount she'd received from blackmailing Olive, money that had been earmarked for George Banks's funeral. So Trevor had unwittingly funded it.

Mum had been right when she'd said that Gladys had been eavesdropping on Danny's confidential consultations. A notebook in Gladys's bedroom revealed that she'd been threatening to go to the newspapers about exposing George Banks's full set of toes. Presumably, Olive was frightened that Gladys must have known about the German soldier too but, with all three dead, we would never really know.

It was only right that the money be returned to Trevor and now, with Trevor and Paula reconciled, it was the perfect time for them to make a fresh start.

Only Delia was disappointed. Now that Paula had opened her dream business, she no longer wanted – or needed – to work under Delia's thumb. Trevor and Paula moved into the flat above the tearoom, leaving number two Honeychurch Cottages empty and Delia one pair of hands short. Trevor would continue to work at the Hall in the grounds.

With Olive out of the picture, Ruby was happy to stay in Vergers Cottage, at least until a new verger could be found.

Work on the vicarage was going great guns and Danny got his wish when Caroline came to vet the new kitchen and bathroom and agreed to give their marriage another chance. To my relief, Mum didn't seem to mind and when she saw Caroline and her curves squashed into the sidecar of Danny's Harley-Davidson, she felt she'd had a lucky escape.

'It was the flies, Kat,' Mum remarked. 'Caroline's teeth were spattered with flies.'

The dowager countess had insisted that George Banks's plaque remain in the church. After all, he had been right about one thing – the fifth column did arrive, even if it was just one man.

Klaus Becker's body was exhumed and, given Mallory's connections with the powers that be, his autopsy was fast-tracked, proving that he had been poisoned with hemlock water dropwort. Although the body was badly decomposed, a photograph of Lottie with baby Peter in her arms was successfully recovered in what remained of the American uniform Klaus had been buried in.

Peter made a full recovery and was so grateful to have the answers he'd been seeking all his life that he and his ailing mother gave the church a generous donation to replace the old clock – where the rest of his father's German uniform was discovered – with a state-of-the-art digital version. No one would ever have to climb those hundred steps again.

As for the gravity knife, Peter was right when he said that his father always carved his initials somewhere. By removing the trefoil-shaped bolster the wooden handle could be opened and there, carved on the underside, were the initials KPB. Klaus Peter Becker.

Mum's books were back in the community shop. I knew that she had been on the phone to various solicitors about her 'options' as she called them, but she refused to discuss any of them with me. I was naturally worried about her future and it was all I could do to keep those fears to myself.

It seemed that all the mysteries were solved. Except for one. With Paula no longer a suspect and Olive the culprit, what had compelled Olive to poison Staci? There seemed to be no motive at all.

At that moment, Mallory entered the tearoom so I went to ask him.

I listened in shock as Mallory recounted his full conversation with Brock. 'Apart from the fact that Staci and Brock had stolen from her clients in the past, it turns out that when Staci found George in the bath the day he died, she noticed that he had all his toes. In the war, George would have been a young man of twenty-four and could easily have gone to the front. Instead, he headed up the Home Guard and enjoyed all the kudos of being famous.'

'Do you think Staci said something to Olive about George's foot?' I asked.

Mallory nodded. 'Brock told me that she did. Apparently, Staci thought it hilarious but Olive was upset. What does the younger generation know or care about a war that ended over seventy years ago but to Olive, George had always been a legend and she wanted to keep it that way.'

'Okay,' I said slowly. 'But when could Olive have poisoned Staci?'

'On the Saturday evening.' said Mallory. 'When we went back to Eric's caravan, we found a note in the grass with some tape on it. Presumably it had been stuck on the door of the caravan.'

'So Staci *did* go to Eric's caravan,' I exclaimed. 'And yet Trevor was out fishing and not back until later.'

'Staci had been waiting to see Trevor in Eric's caravan – the note implied she was apologising for their argument that morning. The note said she was going to call in on Olive since she was close by. It was not recorded on the Nightingale Care Agency app. Staci had made a spontaneous visit and she paid for her generosity with her life.'

The irony of it all is that if George hadn't bragged about a valuable dagger to a young woman who accepted what he said at face value, Klaus Becker's body would never have been discovered or his murder solved.

'There's one thing that's been bugging me,' I said to Mallory. 'Since Olive knew that George was confiding in the vicar, why had she never tried to poison Danny? She certainly tried to poison Peter.'

'She did,' said a voice. Ruby appeared beside us along with Edith, who was making a rare public appearance.

'I swore I would never eat any of Olive's food ever again,' said Ruby. 'If you want to look in my rubbish bin, be my guest. Paula would often drop by with a beignet or a picnic puff for Danny but I always got there first and threw them out.'

'Clever you.' Edith gave Ruby an affectionate smile. 'And I've just spoken to Lottie on the phone. Learning the truth about Klaus has given her a new lease of life. We've made our peace and, of course, she's family now.' Seeing Mallory's confusion, Edith added, 'By default. Lavinia's great-aunt was a Pole. She and Peter are distant cousins.'

'Ah, I see.' Mallory nodded and smiled.

Edith looked at Mallory and then at me. She seemed to find something amusing and gave Ruby a nudge. 'Come along,' she said. 'Let's leave Kat with Man B, shall we?'

And they wandered off, leaving me in shock. *Man B*?

'What was all that about?' Mallory asked.

I felt my face burn with embarrassment and of course, it begged the obvious question. Was it possible that it was Edith who penned the 'Dear Amanda' problem page?

I tried to gather my composure, searching desperately for

something to say. 'Edith wondered where your girlfriend was today.' *But not that, Kat!* I could have kicked myself!

'Did she now.' Mallory's eyes sparkled with mischief. 'What girlfriend?'

Now I was really flustered. 'Stella. Shawn and I saw you in Dartmouth. You sent over the champagne.'

'Ah, Stella.' Mallory seemed to be really enjoying my discomfort. 'I had a few loose ends to tie up. After all, I am a policeman.' He hesitated and then, 'I'm sorry things didn't work out between you and Shawn. He told me.'

'Oh,' I said, aware that my heart had begun to thunder in my chest.

There was an excruciating silence as our eyes met but neither of us looked away.

The new clock chimed the hour and the spell was broken.

'I've never been inside the clock tower,' Mallory said suddenly. 'Would you like to show me?' The horror must have shown on my face because he roared with laughter. I gave him a playful punch. He caught my hand and pulled me into his arms, murmuring, 'What a pity we don't have any mistletoe.'

'Do we need it?' I whispered.

And he kissed me.

Acknowledgements

Writing the acknowledgements is always something I look forward to, but at the same time dread. *Did I miss someone out?*

As the old saying goes, it takes a village to raise a child, and, in the same spirit, it takes a LOT of people to create the finished book, from the spark of an idea (and as writers, we are always asked where we find our ideas) to the excitement of release day.

The spark for *Dagger of Death at Honeychurch Hall* started with my lovely mum. I'd been longing to use her wartime experience as an evacuee in a story. In 1939, just before war was officially declared, she was one of thousands of children – some as young as five – who were evacuated from London to the countryside armed only with a change of underwear, a toothbrush, a comb and a gas mask. My mother was only nine and she was away for four years!

It's hard to imagine what life was like during those dark days. With cities, dockyards and airfields being bombed, the fear of a German invasion was very real. History focuses on

London, but other cities were flattened throughout the war. Devonport Dockyard in Plymouth, a critically important naval base, was such a place and still bears those scars today. In April 1944, Slapton Sands, a mere thirteen miles from where I live now, played a huge role in the lead up to the D-Day invasion that June. Slapton's three-mile beach was used for the dress rehearsal for the invasion of Omaha Beach in Normandy. Code-named Operation Tiger, the exercise was a disaster and ended in tragedy. Although I've touched on factual history, as far as I know the elusive fifth column has only been immortalised on film.

The challenge was dipping into the Second World War and making the timeframe fit the present (since the first Honeychurch Hall mystery was published in 2013, it would mean that the dowager countess would be in her mid-to-late nineties by now, but she isn't), so I hope I'm forgiven for slowing down time. If only we could do that in real life!

Speaking of time, a huge thank you to Bob Seymour of Berry Pomeroy – fondly known as 'Bob the Clock' – who explained the fascinating workings of church clocks. Unlike the dowager countess, Bob *is* in his mid-nineties and he can still climb the steps in any clock tower in England. And speaking of steps, I'm grateful to Matt White for taking me up to the roof of our local church. Everything I wrote about that one-hundred-step climb is true. So too is the description of the workings of St Andrew's Church clock, because I shamelessly copied it from the Harberton Church Community Fund pamphlet in the village. I couldn't improve on it, so I'd rather give them the credit.

The idea of using hemlock water dropwort was suggested by Bethan Phillips, who, along with her passion for genealogy, is a seasoned forager. It's been a real eye-opener to realise that what lurks in our hedgerows and streams is a mixture of delicious culinary fare and a treasure trove of poisons! Which leads me to thank my friend Andra St Ivanyi and Dr Linda Sterry for advising me which poisons are, and which are not, survivable. To be honest, death by amanita phalloides is so *passé*.

Since I always feature an antique or two, I wanted to thank Sue Davis, who gifted me a vintage French bulldog (who really is French) wearing a jaunty straw boater. I've been itching to put him in a book. Sue is married to my long-suffering boss, Mark, the Chairman and CEO of Davis Elen Advertising, who has been my biggest supporter over the past two decades. There are no adequate words to convey my deepest gratitude.

Thanks to Clare Smith, my friend and neighbour, for filling in the authentic parts of working at an auction house. And the Vaseline incident? Well, that's true – I won't name the culprit, but I do want to thank her. A prime example that fact is stranger than fiction!

My special heartfelt thanks to:

My incredible publishing team at Constable, with a special thank you to the amazing Publishing Director, Krystyna Green, who shares my love of dogs; to Editorial Manager, Rebecca Sheppard, for her efficient multi-tasking; and to copyeditor Colin Murray, whose sharp eye and attention to detail happily saved me from a gazillion grammatical errors.

Liane Payne for creating a map of the Honeychurch Hall estate. I couldn't be happier. Her vision is exactly as I had imagined it to be.

All my talented writer friends: Kate Carlisle, Carolyn Hart, Clare Langley-Hawthorne, Jenn McKinlay, Paige Shelton, Marty Wingate and Daryl Wood Gerber, with a special mention to Elizabeth Duncan for her suggestions and support. It's always comforting to have fellow scribes through thick and thin.

All my family and non-writer friends who humour my moods when I'm not writing (miserable) and when I am writing (more miserable), and who celebrate my little victories with enthusiasm and wine. I'm kidding about the misery, of course, but not the wine.

As always, my beautiful daughter Sarah, for listening to my ideas with good humour, and the canine gods for sending me my muses, the Hungarian Vizslas: Draco and Athena. With them, I can't hold back time, and now their golden rust-coloured noses are speckled with grey.

And finally, I speak for all my kindred spirits when I thank YOU, the reader. Without you, none of our stories would be given life. And please, let's not forget our wonderful libraries and independent bookstores that continue to survive and thrive. Long may they continue.